Payback
is a
Bitch

By

Douglas Ewan Cameron

Argus Enterprises International
New Jersey***North Carolina

A-Argus Better Book Publishers, LLC
For information:
A-Argus Better Book Publishers, LLC
9001 Ridge Hill Street
Kernersville, North Carolina 27285
www.a-argusbooks.com

ISBN: 978-0-6156606-7-7
ISBN: 0-6156606-7-3

Book Cover designed by Dubya

Printed in the United States of America

Acknowledgements

Special thanks to Gary Andrew Bokas, Esq., who once again gave me valuable insight into courtroom procedures.

Thanks to Rich Day and Glen Hemminger for introducing me to the fundamental aspects of investment banking and to several sources that I used in getting to know Stuart Andrews's vocation; Carole and Aaron Mall for listening to me read the preliminary version as we travelled to and from Mackinac Island; Mary von Zittwitz for proofreading a semifinal version; Jan and Dave Buchthal for their time during a winter cruise reading and critiquing the almost final version; and last, but never least, my wife Nancy Calhoun Cameron for reading and rereading this book in search for that last elusive error.

Patrick LaPlace (who in this book discovers the wreckage of Quentin's boat) is a real St. Barth's fisherman and it was on an excursion with him on March 2, 2009, that this story came to me.

Many of the supporting concepts and details I obtained from the World Wide Web, a source as valuable to me as it was to Stuart. I wish to thank Dubya for such a gorgeous cover.

Finally, as I will do in all my published works, I must acknowledge two writers who have influenced me. First (and only chronologically) is Mary Higgins Clark whom I heard speak at a Book and Author Luncheon (or dinner) sponsored by The Plain Dealer of Cleveland, Ohio. She said that many of her works got their genesis with the words "What if." And thus it was with this book as during a visit to St. Barth's on the Pacific Princess Alan Katz, Gregg Nelson, Chris Showler and I set out on a fishing excursion I had arranged. I did not know them prior to boarding the ship and seeking people to accompany me fishing. As we were heading out to fish the thought struck me, "What if these guys try to drown me and leave me for dead?" On that excursion all of us except Alan Katz caught a fish ¬– I hope this makes up for it.

The other writer is the late Philip R. Craig, author of the Martha's Vineyard based J.W. Jackson mysteries. My wife and I met he and his wife Shirley on a riverboat trip from Constanta, Romania to Amsterdam, Netherlands in 2005 and shared many a happy meal together including my wife's birthday dinner. He told me that in his writing, while he knew the story line, he often didn't know how it was going to come out and let the characters lead him. Often that is what I do, and I did in this book.

Dedication

To Alan Katz, Gregg Nelson, and Chris Showler who by accompanying me on a fishing expedition in St. Barth's unwittingly became the inspiration for this story.

PART I
SURVIVAL

CHAPTER 1

They were leaving. I didn't wave. They didn't wave. They didn't even look back! I guess you don't if you've just killed someone. Especially if that someone is your brother-in-law.

I got all this information as I momentarily crested a wave and chanced a quick look through half-opened eyes. Even opening my eyes just a slit and quickly closing them made my head throb.

I tried to relax and float but my clothes were getting heavy – especially my shoes. I mentally kicked myself for wearing sneakers and not boat shoes or sandals. But how was I to know that Howard was going to kill me – okay, make that "try to kill me?"

I felt the next wave carry me to its crest and snuck another peek. The boat was definitely moving away and I could hear the low rumble of its twin Yamaha 150s that suddenly turned into a roar, as Quentin must have pushed the throttles full bore. I just hoped that they wouldn't come round and try to run me over to be certain that the job was done. I didn't think Howard had it in him but maybe Keith did. I didn't know much about Keith – or Quentin for that matter.

Trying to relax, I thought about what had happened to get me into this predicament.

My wife Elise and I were on a Caribbean cruise and headed for Aruba for a week in the sun – a second honeymoon so to speak. Several weeks before, at the suggestion of my wife, I had used the web (a favorite tool of mine) to find a charter captain on St. Nantes. He had picked up Howard, Keith and me at the pier after we were dropped off from the first tender ashore from our ship, the Caribbean Isle, the flagship of Caribbean Cruise Line. Howard is my brother-in-law – rephrase that – my no-good brother-in-law. Keith is a guy to whom Howard had introduced me on the ship and I asked if he wanted to join my little excursion. He had immediately jumped on board – looking back on it, much too quickly.

We had headed out deep-sea fishing for mahi mahi and anything else that came along in Quentin's thirty-six foot boat. A fast run of forty-five minutes south through two to three-foot emerald blue swells had brought us into the area that Quentin had selected.

"Zere are a lot of fish here," he had said as he baited both lines and set them out and then got the boat slowly up to trolling speed.

We had been offered water, beer, or coke and all of us had selected beer – Heineken in 250 milliliter bottles bearing no regional brewery notation, which I had found strange. Quentin had expertly used his knife pulled from the sheaf in one of the rod holders to remove the caps. Even at 11:00 in the morning, the first draught was welcome. The three of us had touched bottles and wished each other "Taut Lines" and settled in to wait for the first strike that we had decided would be mine as I had organized the excursion.

The sun was high in an azure blue sky and infrequent seabirds crossed our vision as we questioned Quentin about the island and his life. He was a seventh generation island resident and had been fishing all his life, twenty years taking out charters for either inshore (barracuda and an occasional mahi mahi) or deep sea like today. I had chosen the latter, even knowing that its five-hour length would push the envelope getting us back for the last tender to the ship, but that was a chance we were all willing to take. We knew that the Caribbean Isle would not wait for us if we were late since it was not a ship-sponsored excursion. You pay your money and take your chance.

Suddenly the reel to my immediate left began to whine and the rod rattled heavily in its holder. Before any of the three of us could shout "Fish on!" Quentin had throttled back and was halfway to the rod holder. I stood up from my seat in the stern moving starboard to get out of his way, clutching the fighting belt and frantically searching for the snap buckle. "Don't put et on until we have a fish," he had said in his heavy French accent as he explained the technique, "et's bad luck!" Little did he know! Or, on second thought, maybe he did.

I settled back against the rod rack (no fighting chair on this boat) and Quentin brought the rod and snapped it into the holder. I gripped the rod above the reel with my left hand, moved my thumb against the line and starting winding, pushing the line to the right as I did so. Pulling the rod up and cranking it down to keep the line tight, thumb moving left or right guiding the line. Well, at least that is what I tried to do but the fish (mahi mahi, hopefully) had other ideas. The line went out and there was no way to stop it. Then I started reeling line and worked at it, pumping the rod and keeping the line going from side to side. I remember thinking that it would make more sense if these huge Penn reels had a line guide like my freshwater reels did.

The fish was huge and kept taking the line out, erasing what little progress I seemed to make. However, little by little the battle was won and at last, after what seemed like hours because of the adrenaline pumping through my veins but was actually mere minutes, Quentin told me to stop. That was an easy request to obey. Quentin wrapped the line around his hand and started pulling the fish up.

"Get over by the fish for a good picture," Keith had shouted as he had volunteered to be the cameraman on the first fish and I had given him my camera.

I moved a few feet toward the port side where Quentin was at work.

There was a flash of green ...

CHAPTER 2

And now I was in the water being turned over by the wave action. My thoughts were interrupted by the sound of a boat's engines. I let the wave turn me over while semi-automatically taking a deep breath and let myself sink below the water's surface. The engines' roar assaulted my ears. I remained motionless while my lungs started to ache.

I felt myself sinking but knew that it was best not to move. After what seemed like an eternity and with my lungs on fire, I knew that I had to get to the surface soon or die. Kicking and stroking I hoped that I hadn't turned over and that I was going in the right direction. My right arm broke the surface and I quit fighting as my head broached the wave and I gasped needed air. Then it was back below the waves again.

The engines were not as loud and seemed to be coming from a different direction but with my aching head I couldn't be certain. Had I been seen? Was the boat coming back? I had an instinctive feeling, this time definitely shouting at me, that I should not try to be seen. There had been no other boat in the area so it had to be Quentin's and being spotted by Howard or Keith would not be good. Being in the water was not an accident!

Again I waited as long as I could before surfacing and getting another gulp of needed air. It was harder this time, I seemed heavier, my legs harder to move but I reached the surface briefly and sank again. My feet felt leaden – my shoes were dragging me down. In what would have been slow motion on dry land, I tried unsuccessfully to remove my left sneaker with my right foot.

Then my navy training popped out of its hiding place in the recesses of my mind.

"It's the cannonball float, midshipman," Lieutenant Bruce was screaming at me from the side of the pool. *"Knees against the chest and wrap your arms around your legs."*

As I had all those years ago, I tried to comply. Bringing my knees to my chest in an excruciating agonizing movement, I was able to reach my left shoe with my right hand and remove it and the sock. Then I was choking on water and struggling for the surface.

I must have been living right – maybe King Neptune was looking after me or Davy Jones had no room in his locker that day – and air was just a stroke away. I rolled on to my back, gagging and sucking air and water into my lungs. Coughing, choking, not caring about the noise until suddenly, I realized that those were the only sounds I was hearing. I forced myself to relax and lay quietly in the water.

There wasn't a sound other than gentle noises of water lapping against me. As I listened, straining my ears to catch any sound, I once again started to sink beneath the waves. My shoe and clothes were dragging me to my death. Grabbing a quick breath, I once again cannonballed, and managed to contribute my right sneaker and sock into Davy Jones's keeping. With my shoes gone, it was time for my pants. I undid the belt buckle, unsnapped and unzipped, and then I found myself removing my pants and letting them go.

"No, midshipman," Lieutenant Bruce cried at me from the back of my mind, *"those pants make a floatation device."*

I grabbed frantically, thrashing my arms wildly and finding nothing but water. I broke surface, gulping in several breaths of air and did a surface dive that would have scored at most two points from one of the five judges and less than one from the rest. Using a breaststroke arm motion and scissor kicking as hard and fast as I could, I moved through the water in some direction finding … nothing.

With almost bursting lungs I quit and let water's nature take over. When I felt myself moving in a definite direction, I started swimming in that direction hoping that it was up, as it seemed to be lighter in that direction but it was difficult to tell with half-open eyes. Whatever direction it was, it was approximately the right one since my head soon broke surface just as my lungs were about to collapse.

As I gulped that wonderful air, I realized that there was strange weight on my left shoulder. I grasped with my right hand and discovered nylon fabric – my pants. I grasped them fiercely with both hands, turned on my back clutching them to my chest, and tried to float.

Floating didn't last very long and as I started to sink I starting kicking my legs to hold myself erect. Once I had managed to control that maneuver, I took a chance to look around. I was in a trough between waves and could really see nothing.

I waited until I started to crest a wave and then grabbed a quick look before I was taken down the other side. *"Water, water everywhere and not a drop to drink."* The quote from Coleridge's *The Rime of the Ancient Mariner* found its way to my thoughts' surface. There was no boat to be seen, at least where I had looked.

I needed to make a 360-degree search. I prepared myself and as I crested the next wave, I scissored my legs rapidly and used my arms to spin me around. My legs propelled me upward and my arms did spin me somewhat but how much I didn't know.

I repeated this process a number of times until I reasoned that I had at least completed a 360. Regardless I was pooped and needed to relax, which I could do because I was satisfied that there was no boat close to me.

"Get moving, midshipman, or you'll drown," Lieutenant *Bruce screamed at me.*

My energy was waning quickly not only because of my own efforts but because of the temperature of the water. I had no idea what it was but although warm on the surface, it was cold not too far below. The feel of the pants fabric reminded me of my project.

"Knot the legs as close to the end as you can," Lieutenant Bruce shouted. *"They need to hold as much air as possible."*

Mechanically, if such an effort exists after a twenty-four year hiatus, I made knots in the legs.

"Close the zipper and button the fly to make as much space as possible." The voice of Lieutenant Bruce, my freshman N.R.O.T.C. instructor, shouted in my ear. *He must have been right next to me.*

"*Okay, now what?*" I thought. I needed to get air into the pants to make them float but how?

"Try pulling them over your head like a scoop."

That is not as easy as it sounds especially when you are tired and my first effort totally sucked. I succeeded only in getting my head and face covered with heavy wet fabric that forced me under water. A second semi-Herculean effort (the first one was definitely not Herculean) brought the waistband of the pants smacking into the water in front of me.

Both legs had some air in them but not enough to keep me afloat.

"Now what?" I asked the Lieutenant.

"You need to get some more air inside," the Lieutenant answered. "Think."

As I tried to think, I found myself sinking below the waves and took a breath. Floating there as I tried to remember, I slowly let air escape from my mouth and through half-open eyes watched the bubbles floating upward.

That was it!

I pulled the pants toward me and expelled air inside the waistband. After an uncountable number of such efforts I found that the pants would support my weight. I put the belt end through the buckle and pulled it tight to close the hole. It wasn't totally closed but would cut down on the escaping air. Then I tried to crawl aboard and thankfully got a pant leg under each arm and relaxed.

CHAPTER 3

I was startled into wakefulness, or out of my reverie, by the feeling of something cold against my cheek. I was instantly alert and realized the float was sinking. I loosened the belt, enlarged the waist hole and repeated the process of inflating the float from below.

I wondered how long I had been asleep – well, dozing, daydreaming – and looked at my watch. It wasn't there and neither was my wedding ring, I realized. I checked the pockets of my shirt – it had quite a few as it was a guide shirt – and found nothing other than lint. There had been a small bottle of aloe, sunscreen, and some gum. I repeated the process on my cargo pants – umh, floatation device – and found them to be empty also.

Howard or Keith had been thorough in that. If my body was to be found there was no easy method of identification. I couldn't remember the last time I had been to a dentist and didn't even know what the name of my dentist is (or was) so identification that way would be difficult. My pants had only contained a small pill bottle (aspirin) and a small wallet. It was basically a money clip with two slots for credit card-type things and one pocket in which I kept a copy of the picture page from my wife's passport. She similarly carried a copy of mine.

I had a credit card (Visa as many Caribbean merchants don't take AMEX, but Visa, at least according to the commercials, is accepted everywhere.), bank ATM, and the ship's boarding pass. The Visa card was useless to anyone else as it had my picture on it, as did the ATM card. Those won't do anyone any good but they can't help identify me either. Comforting thought.

Having satisfied myself that I had nothing other than my basic clothing, I set about deciding how to continue my survival program. The sun was not directly overhead and I hadn't paid much attention to where it was before the incident. *Oww!* I unconsciously had checked my head to find a large knot that hurt to my touch. Since I was feeling pain I must be alive. That was one point for me. Make that two, as I had successfully created a flotation device despite its need for constant air replenishment.

As I crested a wave I took a quick look around or at least the 180 degrees I could see in front of me. There was nothing but water. I swam my way approximately 180 degrees around and waited for the next wave to lift me up. When I did I could make out something at 2:00 – low, dim, and gray on the horizon. Its size indicated that it was land of some sort and so I decided to set off for that. Fortunately the waves seemed to be going in that direction, or at least sixty degrees off, so they would be some help.

Kicking my legs slowly, I set off. I knew that my progress would be slow and quickly resolved not to keep peeking at my target. Rather I started counting leg strokes and thought that every one hundred I would rest and sneak a peek to be certain that I was on track. I was incredibly thirsty as the Caribbean sun is quite hot and my last drink (the Heineken) was probably several hours ago. I knew that drinking salt water – even a small quantity – was not a good idea and resolved not to do so.

It became quickly evident that one hundred strokes wasn't going to work. Even sans pants, it was hard work kicking and was an effort to which I wasn't accustomed. I worked in an office in front of a computer or on the phone twelve hours a day, often six or seven days a week and don't have time (or the inclination) to exercise. I would have to change that if – make that when – I got to dry land. Thus even making fifty strokes was an effort. So to conserve energy, I cut my goal to twenty-five and counted groups of four to get one hundred, resting briefly after each group: one – one; one – two; one – three, … one – twenty-five; rest; two – one …

After the first group of twenty-five fours, I could see no appreciable change in my goal. That hit me hard and sacked me for a moment – but just a moment. I was a financial advisor of sorts, planning stock and investment opportunities with retirement goals for my clients, so I was used to long-range planning with short-term way posts. I started thinking about my current effort in those terms: Reaching land (that particular land) was my long-term goal and the four-groups were my short-term goals.

I considered counting the four-groups but knew I couldn't keep track and quickly discarded that idea. I did mentally keep tabs and for the first, I don't know, let's say one hundred four-groups, I would do a quick three-sixty looking at my goal and searching for something that would let me change that long term goal for something more immediate – a boat for example – but spotted nothing.

After that first one hundred four-groups when I took aim at my target, I thought that it had moved. It seemed to me to be about eight minutes after the hour rather than ten minutes after the hour. Of course that didn't mean that I was getting close but it certainly meant that I was make progress in some way.

The back of my head and my lower arms felt warm and I knew it was from the sun. I would be lucky if I reached land before the part of me out of the water was well done. It would give any cannibals living on that island something to snack on while they waited for the rest of my body to cook.

I knew that thought wasn't good. I began to wonder if the island itself was a hallucination – optical illusion, whatever. Such hallucinations (at least in movies involving a desert) were always wavy and this one wasn't – it was solid. Maybe the waviness is just Hollywood's way to identify a hallucination.

Something brushed my foot and I kicked wildly and spun around half expecting to see a Great White poised to eat my foot but I saw nothing. I realized that I knew nothing about sharks in this part of the world (or any other part for that matter) Great Whites included. Daaaaa Dum, Daaaaa Dum ... the theme from *Jaws* started running through my head. Where in the world was Lieutenant Bruce when I needed him? He hadn't appeared since I successfully made this floatation device.

"Where the hell are you," I yelled, only it was not a yell but more of a screech through parched, salt encrusted cracked lips. Automatically, remembering too many demerits my first year in N.R.O.T.C., I added, "Sir." Although not physically in tone, I maintain a strict mental discipline that is the only thing that gets me through difficult times and will be the only thing to get me through this. I knew I had to keep my cool because getting mad would only use valuable energy. In college, I had a friend (for a while) who would keep things bottled up until, uncapped by some innocently related idea, his rage would burst forth no matter where we were and it would all spew out. He was in N.R.O.T.C. also but he was a contract member meaning that he didn't get his tuition paid. One day one of these rants occurred on the parade field when he was being dressed down by a senior and that cost him dearly. I was standing next to him at the time and resolved that our budding friendship was terminated. He was also released from the N.R.O.T.C. and didn't survive the first semester.

Maybe it was a barracuda, I thought and quickly dismissed it.

Barracudas only live in the shallow water so I would have to watch out for them as I neared land. Or is "barracudas only live in shallow water" like "piranha only live in the still water parts of the Amazon"? I would have to find out the answer to both of those questions if – strike that – when I made it.

One – one, Daaaaa Dum, one – two, Daaaaa Dum, one – three...

CHAPTER 4

Bet Mike Mullins is upset.

The thought came unbidden into my head in the middle of a third four. Why, I don't know. Mike had been a client of mine for five years and I thought we were doing well. Actually make that "I thought I was doing well." About the middle of summer 2008 when things began to tank, Mike panicked.

Like everyone else, I wasn't happy with the economy – even more so, because I make my living from charging for investing for these people and have done very well throughout the years. Rephrase that: "I have done extremely well" not only for my clients but for myself as well. I wasn't happy with the way things were headed. I had known things were going downhill but hadn't realized that the hill was so steep.

Mike didn't even ask me for my opinion. He simply pulled all his investments out from under me without even consulting me. They had been moved to Merrill-Lynch, that much I knew. I guess he thought that a big company could do better for him than a one-man operation could. Saying one-man isn't quite right since I had ten people working for me before I had to downsize like everyone else. Now it's a total of five – counting me.

I heard on CNN International this morning on our cabin's television before heading out on the fishing charter that Merrill-Lynch had announced its biggest loss ever – actually the biggest quarterly loss by a business ever. *Hope that Mike is happy!*

However, that was not my problem. Survival was my problem. *Now where was I? ... Four – one; four – two, ...*

The sun was much lower on the horizon now. It was late afternoon. I was guessing five-ish. *Time for cocktails.*

The ship would be preparing to leave now. Back on board, the time was 5:00. Last shuttle from the dock to ship was 4:30 and I won't be on it. The passenger roster will be at least one short this port – me.

I wondered what they would do. Obviously try to contact my cabin. What would Elise say? Would she be panicked because I hadn't returned from the fishing trip?

No, I guess she wouldn't, at least not without a really good story from Howard. But what would Howard say?

"Sorry, Elise, Stuart fell overboard clutching the pole. It was a big fish (maybe a shark) and it pulled him right down. He wouldn't let go of the pole and he just disappeared. We waited for a long time…"

Or, *"Stuart was sitting on the side and we hit a big wave and he fell off. We circled around as fast as we could but he went under. I dove in …"*

That last wouldn't wash because Howard didn't swim any better than I did and he basically didn't give a shit about me.

"We just sat and watched him go under …"

That last was true – almost. They probably did see me go under or lost track of me before they headed back. But they were not going to tell Elise that … or were they? What if she was in on it?

She had to be! Howard had nothing to gain. He didn't get any of my estate except what Elise shares with him. Damn! I knew things weren't the best between us; that's what working 24/7 does do a relationship. But she hadn't complained except to bitch (almost constantly) about my work schedule recently. She certainly had not complained about the new Benz I gave her two weeks ago.

But that may have been too late. This murder (make that "attempted murder" at least for now) had to have been in the works by then. *Damn! She has to be in on it. Howard doesn't have the brains and Keith … who the hell is Keith? Her lover?*

He was introduced to me by Howard who said that he met him in the Horizon Lounge during the Sail Away Party leaving Ft. Lauderdale. He had mentioned the fishing excursion to him and he asked if there was room for a third.

I was willing – a third person cuts down on the expenses and in this down-turned economy every nickel helps. So Keith had to be in on it from the start or nearly from the start. But why was he needed?

Probably in case the blow didn't really knock me out or if I sensed something wrong and started to fight or if Quentin put up a fight. That had to be it. Quentin wouldn't just stand there and watch someone be put overboard. He'd try to stop it and it might take two of them to stop him.

They must have won because otherwise Quentin would have brought the boat around and picked up the body – make that, picked me up. But he didn't so he must have been overpowered. What would they do with him? Dump him also? They couldn't let him live because he would blab to the authorities. How would they explain the disappearance of two people?

"Stuart was pulled over board by a Great White and Quentin jumped in after him. The Great White turned and took him in one gulp – cut him in half. His dying scream was terrible. Then the Great White looked around and said, 'Well, big boy, see anything we missed?'"

That's an old joke and wouldn't fly because sharks can't talk. Francis the Talking Mule could and Mr. Ed could. Flipper was a pretty good communicator, but a Great White talk…

Wetness on my head brought me to my senses suddenly wrenching me from my delirium. Wetness on my head, on my hands, my arms … Rain!

I turned over and opened my mouth to catch as much of it as I could. A few meager drops run across my tongue and down my throat. I had trouble swallowing but it was like manna from heaven.

"Tears of joy" as they say in Dominica. Let it rain! Pour out the tears. Cry for joy!

It was over as suddenly as it had begun and I was once again alone, adrift on an alien sea with only air-filled pants to support me. I was going to die and no one would know it! I would have cried if I could have but I didn't have the moisture in me.

CHAPTER 5

There was a flash of green ...
That kept coming back to me and I keep seeing it.

It was a peripheral flash and I kept trying to see who had wielded the Heineken bottle. Wonder if it broke? My head wasn't cut or at least I don't think it was. Actually I knew it wasn't because blood attracts predators and – knock on wood – so far there had not been any.

Twilight was upon me and to the southwest the sun was displaying a gorgeous yellow, red, and purple show. What is that old saying?

Red sky at night,
Sailors' delight;
Red sky in morning,
Sailors take warning.

Well, if this counted as a red sky, I don't know whether that was good or bad for me. I knew that breezes tend to lessen at night with the heat of the day gone, which means that the wave action will die down and that is not good for me. I needed the waves to keep me moving toward land. Red sky at night, ...

There was a flash of green ...
I actually ducked or tried to as far as the pants float would let me. I got my face into the water. As long as I was ducking I might as well fill the pants.

Now where was I – three – fifteen; three – sixteen; a flash of green ...
No, it wasn't a flash – it was more of a twinkle and it wasn't at the side. It was in front. I raised my head and looked as I crested a wave. There it was ... a twinkle of yellow not green, and a second, a third...

Lights being turned on! Ahead of me the islanders were welcoming the evening. They were welcoming me! I was close enough to discern the individual lights and that gave me renewed faith.

Three – twenty-five; rest. More lights coming on ... but they were to my left about eleven o'clock, or fifty-five after if you wish to be precise.

I suddenly realized that meant I was too far to the right – too far east. All afternoon I had been working to get the island in front of me and somehow I had overshot. So I had to change my tactics and move to the left.

With renewed vigor I picked up the pace: four – one; four – two; four – three ... four – twenty-five; rest. Welcome rest. My legs ached. I could scarcely get them to move. I was doing feeble flutter kicks and not making much headway. I strained to look for the lights and suddenly realized that I didn't have to strain. They were constant in front of me.

The wind had died down some time ago and slowly the waves had decreased and now there were just wavelets.

"No," I screamed. "Lieutenant Bruce, you can't let that happen. I need the wind! I need the waves! I'll die without them! Please, SIR!"

There was no answer! Of course there wasn't an answer. I might as well be praying to God for all the good it would do! I was raised as a Christian (Methodist in some form) but had given it up for Lent some year in college. What I had given up was the practice of religion. I was still a Christian in the way I lead my life; well, for the most part. It was probably my senior year when I realized that all my prayers for help with my classes weren't being answered. But that was selfish of me to ask God to help one person with his grades. That wasn't going to happen. If you want help with your grades, you'd better do it yourself. Asking the Creator of the Universe for personal help wasn't going to get it. Or at least I didn't think so and so being young and reckless, omnipotent, and completely in control of my destiny, I had given up prayer and with it the practice of religion.

Now on the verge of death, I found myself once again silently praying. I hadn't realized it but I had been praying for some time for some miracle to save me. I must have started even before the wind died down. Maybe I had prayed to be able to find the pants or to fill them with air. I can't remember but I know I had. Of course, having been away from Him for so long, I could not expect Him to answer my personal, purely selfish request to save my life. If my life was going to be saved it had to be done by me.

So I had better get to it. Taking a fix on the lights ahead, now even more, I started kicking again, with more energy and more intensity but with a prayer continually in my head:

One – one; please, God; one – two; please, God; one – three; save me; one – four; give me wind; one – five; give me waves; one – six; please, God; please, God ...

CHAPTER 6

Bright light flashed and its report reverberated like a cannon shot in the mountains. I don't know how long I had been on this current marathon of swimming (for want of a better word) but the sun was long gone below the horizon. The moon had risen sometime ago (maybe before the sun went down; I didn't keep track) and stars twinkled. Lights on the island ahead had come and gone twinkling on and off like the stars above me.

Long ago the clouds had crept in, dark and ominous, covering the stars and the moon. *To hell with 'Red sky at night,'* I thought. That was not good! For whatever reason, my cargo pant floatation device seemed to need air more often. It didn't help that in addition to kicking my feet I was using my arms and thus squeezing the legs of the pants on each stroke, undoubtedly forcing air out of the waistband hole.

I had achieved my goal of getting back on course toward the island but had continued my frantic propelling of the craft as much as I could. With the coming of the clouds announcing the impending storm, the wind had picked up with a noticeable change in direction. It was now from my seven o'clock position and was trying to push me away from the island. I thought I had made good progress while the sea was calm but I really couldn't tell. The lights on the island had been constantly growing in size or at least I thought they had. They appeared sharper than they had been originally, which should have meant they were closer.

During the next round of four twenty-fives, the wind increased in velocity and direction, slowly moving toward nine o'clock and taking control of my craft as the waves grew in size with the change of direction. I was probably only holding my own and if the storm lasted very long, I would be pushed away from the island.

Please, God. Please, God, I thought in between strokes.

But the storm continued and my silent prayer went unanswered. But what did I expect? I knew that God did not answer selfish prayers.

Suddenly rain droplets started splashing around me and on me. I turned on my back and opened my mouth trying to collect all the water I could. My parched lips welcomed the wetness but I found it difficult to swallow. The intensity of the rain increased and the amount of water in my mouth did also. Gradually I was able to swallow. The rain was the most welcome thing I had all day.

I croaked a meek "Thanks" when I thought I had enough and turned over into fighting position. Halfway through the turn I was carried to the crest of a huge wave and it was then I heard it. At first I didn't know what it was and looked frantically around but all I saw was blackness. Even the lights from the island had disappeared with the onslaught of rain. Patiently I waited for the next wave to carry me upward and I heard it again. This time I knew what it was – waves crashing on something, hopefully shore. As welcome as the sound was, it was also ominous because the waves were big, six or seven feet, I guess. The sound of the waves that size crashing signaled danger. The sound was loud enough that I knew it wouldn't be long before the waves crashed me onto whatever it was.

Quickly I maneuvered myself facing away from the sound and frantically kicked in an effort to slow my progress down and it was to no avail. Within a matter of a few minutes, I was picked up by a huge wave and dashed against something hard and terribly solid. My breath was knocked out of me and I was engulfed in the wave swallowing a mouthful of salt water as I gasped for breath. My left arm was caught between my body and the surface and went numb. I clutched at anything, my fingers searching, trying to get a grip to hold me but the surface was smooth and my deadened fingers weren't working. As the wave receded, I grabbed my pants with my left hand and sought a handhold with my good right. I felt a crevice in a rock, or between two, and thrust my bruised fingers into it but the effort was for naught. The receding wave pulled them loose and the sharp rocks sliced as my fingers slipped out.

The crush of the next wave crashing against the rock lifted me up and away from the tenuous hold and the wave smashed me into the rock and again I lost my breath. Down the rock I slid pulled by the ebbing wave, scrapping flesh against the eroded surface, and then was caught on the swell of the next and carried quickly up and once again caught between the rocks and the crashing wave. However, I was ready this time and had taken a breath. As I started slipping back, being pulled by the ebbing strength of the wave, my bruised hands felt an edge of rock and I grabbed with both hands releasing the pants with my left and holding on for dear life as the next wave hit. Fortunately it wasn't as big as the previous one and as soon as the wave started to recede I began pulling myself up, dragging my trousers with me since they had been caught between my body and the rock. I had my elbows over the top of the rock just as the next wave hit but my purchase was secure. Once that wave had hit, I scrambled up and over the edge of the rock, clutching my trousers to my chest and cowering as the next several waves crashed against the rock. Once I felt strong enough and mindless of the sharp rocks cutting both hands and feet, I continued upward until I was well above the reach of the waves.

I seemed to have reached some sort of plateau, though the surface beneath me was rough and uneven. Thankfully I breathed a prayer of relief and wondered if perhaps in some way someone had been listening. Exhausted, battered and bruised, I lay on my back and listened to the sound of the waves crashing on the rocks below and let the rain wash the salt and blood from my body and gradually sank into a deep and dreamless sleep.

CHAPTER 7

I awoke to the cry of gulls and the surf gently beating against the shore. It hurt to open my eyes so I didn't. I rolled over as best I could until the sun no longer was directly on my face and then slowly opened my eyes. At first everything was blurry but after several seconds and several blinks, things focused. Reddish-brown rock was all I saw. I tried to sit up and almost every muscle screamed in agony. I looked at my arms and saw them crimson and blistered. I knew that my face must be the same as it cracked and hurt whenever I made any kind of grimace. There was nothing else but to fight through the pain. I heard someone screaming and knew it must be me.

Finally sitting up, I slowly looked about. The first thing I saw was a small pool of water in the rocks. It shimmered slightly in the sun and was warm to the touch of my fingers. I brought the fingers to my mouth and tasted – slightly salty but not seawater. I coerced my body into moving until I could get my mouth into the water and drank deeply, or as deeply as I could with such a shallow pool. Still even after having had the rainwater of the night before to drink, I knew that I must be careful and not drink too much at one time.

Once again achieving a sitting position I looked around. In front and to both sides the land ended fairly abruptly and the rest was water. That wasn't good. I turned my head as far as I could counterclockwise and saw the same thing although it appeared that the land extended further. I turned my head clockwise and could see land elevated behind me. Quickly and ever so painfully, I maneuvered my body around until I was facing what had been behind me. The land I was atop continued for about twenty feet and then ended. Beyond that was about three hundred feet of open water and then more land. I raised my head crying out as the obviously raw skin on the back of my neck screamed in agony at what it was being asked to do. The land in front of me rose to about ten o'clock and then the reddish-brown of the rocks turned green and white and red. The white and red, I happily realized, was a white house with a red roof. Behind the house, the land continued and broadened as it went further and extended to the left as far as I could see but on the right was only the sea.

I moved my attention back to the house and tried to focus but the sun was about forty-five degrees to the right of the house and blinded my vision. I saw no movement in the area around the house. There was nothing to do but to attempt to cross the strait of water between the large island and me. Moving gingerly so as to affect as little pain as possible, I got myself into a shaky standing position. My legs protested as much as my arms but in a different way. My arms were way beyond well done but my legs were just tired and sore from the exertion I had demanded of them in the last twenty-four hours. I felt that it must be early morning as the sun was not very high in the sky, but whatever sunrise there had been was long gone. Still being early, people in the house might not be up and about. I wouldn't have been.

I tottered forward seeking purchase with each footfall, often crying out as my feet encountered sharp rocks. Finally I could see the slope in front of me. It was a jumble of flat stones of varying sizes and textures, although all were obviously of the same type. It was possible to descend but it would be tortuously slow. There might have been an easier path. To find it would require moving around the top of my small island. That would be as difficult as moving to the edge had been or even clambering down the slope in front of me.

And clamber I did. Not trusting my legs, which thanked me, I sat down with both my legs in front of me and slid and humped down the slope, using my feet to stop me when I slid on the still wet rocks. Raising my butt and using hands and feet, I moved from rock to rock and across spaces between adjoining rocks. It was slow progress and probably took half an hour but I made it down. Looking up at the house on the other side of the strait, I still could see no activity. A look to the left toward the rest of civilization revealed nothing either. I knew what I had to do to cross the water and get to the island and that is why I had not bothered to put my pants on. I checked the knots on the legs, made certain that the zippers holding the pant bottom to the shorts top were secured, that the fly was zippered and snapped at the top.

Then I gingerly eased myself into the water until my feet found a ledge or another rock on which to rest. By this time I was shoulder deep in the water but that is what I wanted. I shook out the pants, grabbed the waistband by both hands at the extremities and raised the pants above and behind my head with the legs hanging down.

"Suck on this, Lieutenant Bruce, Sir," I cried as I brought the pants over the top of my head and down to the water with all the strength I could muster. The effort caused my feet to lose their purchase on the ledge and I slid down into the water. I had enough sense this time to hold my breath. I felt myself sinking until the buoyancy of the air-filled trousers stopped my descent and I kicked my way to the surface.

The water was almost calm as there wasn't a sign of a breeze and the crossing was made without incident other than my cussing and crying out in agony as the salt water attacked my cuts and rawness and my muscles cried at the effort required. Luckily I found a landing spot of sorts on the other side and quickly scrambled up onto solid but not dry land. With a sense of decency, I untied the knots in the pants' legs and got dressed. Then I looked for a way up the steep rock strewn bank in front of me. What I would have given to have my shoes, which by now were undoubtedly in Davy Jones's Locker.

I found a path of sorts through the rocks – it zigged and zagged, snaking its way up the hill and I wondered if the inhabitants of the house had helped improve it from its natural form. I would have to ask them.

At the top of the hill I pulled myself erect and, before heading for the house, turned to the sea. As loudly and intelligibly as I could, I screamed, "Take that, you son of a bitch; you might defeat some people but you can't defeat Stuart Andrews." I know this was melodramatic and cinematic but at that point I didn't care. I was alive and I wanted the world and nature to know.

CHAPTER 8

The seaward side of the ranch-style house, which is the one I could see, was all glass on the main level with a huge deck jutting out in the middle. On the lower level to the left of the deck was a slider with a small patio in front. A path made of white stones connected the patio to the bottom of the stairs from the deck then continued on to the top of the bluff where it ended at a small terrace with a white table and four chairs which were turned over on top of the table. This was my first indication that the owner of the house wasn't home. There should have been an umbrella in the center of the table also but there wasn't. You don't leave an umbrella in the table where the wind might take it and carry it to who knows where. I saw and reasoned all this as I proceeded to the back of the house where the front door would be. People who own places like this are "terminology weird." The front of the house is the one facing the Caribbean, "We own sea-front property" but yet the front door (the one your guests use) is on the back of the house, because you would never defile the front yard of your seafront property with a drive-way and/or garage. The front "yard" as well as the side "yard" was natural and teeming with native flora that I had to be watchful of since many of the native flora are cacti-type plants.

The back of the house was very much like the front of the house only without windows. There was a carport with no cars – my second clue that the owner was not on the premises. I guessed the carport was to protect the cars from the sun and rain as well as saltwater because they certainly don't get any snow here. The front door was to the left of the carport. It was a double wooden door with huge wrought iron hinges, knobs, and knocker. I lifted the knocker and let it fall. I heard the report rebound throughout the house. Nobody came to the door because nobody was home. That was my third clue. Three clues and you're out, but I wanted in. Most people that I know have a key hidden outside in case they forgot theirs or to let friends and/or guests in when they're not home. Not under the doormat or the potted cacti on either side of the entrance. The frame around the door was big and I ran my hand across the top and didn't find anything. So I tried again letting my fingers do the walking and they discovered the key in a small depression carved just above the center of the door. It worked and the door unlocked. Before opening the door, I put the key back so I wouldn't forget to replace it and it would be there if I got locked out.

Now what if they have a security system? The cops would be here in no time and I wanted nothing to do with the police right now. I figuratively held my breath as I opened the door, stepped inside and closed the door. Immediately I was aware of soft lighting turning on near the floor, machinery hummed from within the depths of the house and I felt a cool waft of air. Looking up, I saw vents near the ceiling. I thought that the lighting must have been triggered by the door opening and maybe the air conditioning as well unless the thermostat had just activated the cooling.

After about a minute when I didn't hear any siren and hadn't seen any keypad close to the door, I figured there was no alarm system unless it was a silent alarm. I called out "Anyone home?" and was greeted with only silence.

I observed that I was in a foyer with a tile floor. The tile seemed to be a light aqua color and the walls were white. To my left and right were dark hallways and in front of me the foyer opened into what seemed to be a much larger room ending in sliders that lead out to the deck hidden behind gauzy curtains. The light aqua tile ended with the foyer and turned to a deeper greenish aqua (I never have been much of a descriptive-color person but then I am a man) and then deeper hues of blue ending in a dark blue at the sliders. The owner must have had the tile done resembling the way the water looks running from shore outward. I found the effect extremely calming. At the right end of the foyer was a dark doorway that I learned later was a stairway leading to a basement theatre or, as the hoi polloi say, a media center.

Having satisfied myself that no one was home, my first item of business was water. Where was the kitchen? I mentally flipped a coin (tails) and set off down the left hall. As I entered the hallway, floor lighting turned on. I was startled and turned around to see who was there but no one was. I noticed that the lighting in the foyer was off. I realized then that the lighting was sensor activated and turned back to the hallway. The outside wall was blank but the inside wall was decorated with pictures. There was a light switch on the wall and I used it to turn on ceiling lights. The wall was covered with autographed pictures of people, many of whom I knew by sight but not in person. Hollywood stars. They were all ages, both sexes, and all spectrums of the industry: one hit wonders, well-established stars, dead stars, young stars, producers, and directors. I assumed that the house must belong to someone of that ilk but could not discern to what part of the business the owner of the house belonged.

The tile in the hall was the same aqua as the foyer. I turned off the overhead light and continued down the hall. The first door on the right was a half bath, the next a large bedroom which extend the breadth of the house ending in windows overlooking the sea. Obviously I had chosen the wrong section of the house; this will be my second choice. The tile pattern I had noticed beyond the foyer was repeated and would be in every room in the house except for the downstairs theatre.

I retraced my steps and crossed the foyer to the other end of the house. Again the lighting turned on in front of me and off behind me. The first door on the left was another half bath and the second revealed a state-of-the-art kitchen. There was the warm glow of the floor lighting as I entered. I easily found a switch that controlled ceiling lighting. The kitchen was twenty feet wide, wall to wall, and ran the breadth of the house ending at a slider that opened onto the deck. The left wall ended short of the sliders and I assumed that the doorway formed provided access to an eating area. A clock on the wall gave the time as 7:17, which I assumed to be a.m. I opened cabinet doors until I found one containing drinking glasses. The appliances were all Viking – top-drawer stuff – and all burnished aluminum. There was an island in the center of the kitchen that had the standard four-burner stovetop, an indoor grill and two ovens. The refrigerator was one of those sub-zeroes with side-by-side doors and an inset offering cube ice, crushed ice and water. I settled for crushed ice and water and took a big gulp, which immediately I gagged on and coughed up. The icy water proved to be a mistake. My second attempt was to take a couple of little sips and those caused me to realize that I was starved. Opening the refrigerator door revealed nothing other than condiments and a rotten green pepper in one of the crispers. Aah, my fourth clue (or maybe my fifth) that no one was home and the first to indicate that no one had been here for a while. Opening the freezer door I discovered several packages wrapped in freezer paper. On one was written "OR", on another "SS", and on a third "LL." I had no idea what was what and simply grabbed the "OR" package, put it in the microwave and set it to defrost for four minutes. You can basically run any microwave by using a little common sense and reading the labels. Of course, if you have no common sense you are in big trouble.

Collecting my glass of ice water, I exited the kitchen back into the hallway from which I had entered and continued left down the hall. I found an office that also ran the breadth of the house and lastly the laundry room. I briefly considered throwing all my clothes in the trash but then I would have nothing to wear. I stripped everything completely off, threw it into the washer, added some soap and set it for a small load with warm water. Then I went in search of a shower, stopping off in the kitchen on the way. The package had thawed as the dinging of the timer told me and upon opening it I discovered it was a nice fish filet – probably Orange Roughy. That made "SS" Shark Steak, Sirloin Steak, or Swiss Steak (it was the second I would discover) but I couldn't figure out "LL." I found a suitable dish to hold the fish, turned the oven on to 325°, put the fish in to cook. Oh, I could have used the microwave to cook the fish but I consider a microwave more of a thawing/reheating convenience. Then I continued my search for a shower.

I found one in the first bedroom, its entrance on the same wall as two huge closets, one to go with each of the two king-sized beds I supposed. The bathroom faced the sea and that wall of the huge shower was all glass. The tile was continued here, as it was in the entire house, with the floor of the shower a dark blue; let's call it Caribbean Blue. There was no wall separating it from the rest of the bathroom. There were three showerheads on each end wall of the shower. I chose the left and I turned on the hot water and within a minute, steam starting to rise from the spray. I adjusted the temperature and stepped in. The water stung my cuts and sunburned areas and I had to adjust the amount of water and spray to fine mists that my body would accept. I stood in the shower, just enjoyed the water for a long time and let it wash the salt away before I bothered to wash my hair and then my body, being very careful with the sunburned areas. I don't know how long I luxuriated in the shower but the hot water never quit. I reasoned that the water heater was one of those on demand types. Finally I shut off the water and toweled myself off with one of the softest and biggest towels I had ever seen. A search of the cabinets revealed a variety of medicines, lotions, toothpaste and brushes, and what I was hoping to find – a large bottle of aloe that I liberally but carefully applied to my sunburned areas. Hanging on the back of the door was a white terry cloth robe that I donned and went to check on my food.

Using a fork, I found the fish to be flakey (if you don't know about cooking fish you can just say it was done). I put it on a plate, and wandered down to check on the laundry, eating small bites as I went. The washer was done so I put the clothes into the dryer, set it on the automatic setting and went in search of other clothes. I knew I could wear my own if needed but wanted something different in case there was a manhunt. I had already decided that I didn't want to be found for a while – a long while.

I was out for revenge and payback was going to be a bitch for the payees.

CHAPTER 9

The fact that I didn't want to be found for a long time had come to me while I was showering. There was a wall phone in the kitchen and the laundry, one on the desk in the study and the bedside table in the bedroom where I had showered. (I determined it was a guest bedroom because there were no clothes in the two huge walk-in closets.) It would have been easy to call the police but I had hesitated. I didn't know if I was even missing. The manner in which I had been "drowned" and stripped of all identification seemed to indicate that I wasn't to be identified. That didn't make any sense. One of the main motives for murder, it seemed to me, was power or money. There was no power to be gained with my death except for the company but its value without me might be questionable. I was the person who ultimately made the decisions on all sales, etc., although my staffers did most of the research and made the actual sales and investments. Thus selling the business seemed out of the question as most of my investors would pull their funds and seek out another established broker.

I had a million-dollar life insurance policy, two million in case of accidental death. How could my death at sea be considered accidental? I couldn't remember what the policy said about suicide but that didn't seem plausible. Then there was the matter of my hidden assets that only myself and Elise knew about.

I guess that fifteen million is a good enough reason to kill someone. Now I am not a Bernie Madoff – my clients actually had their own money, which had been obtained through responsible, verifiable investments. There was no problem there. I had close to one million of my own invested, that obtained completely above board and would survive any scrutiny. The fifteen million was another problem as was the more than one hundred million that Elise didn't know about.

I am not a totally honest person but it was not of my initiative. About ten years ago, after I had established a decent reputation in the investment business, a representative of some – let's say nefarious - people approached me. They needed a legitimate source through which to launder their money. I knew it was illegal but it didn't involve my investors in any way and I saw a means to secure a substantial nest egg and early retirement. I thought about it for several months. I wasn't pressured and figured out the means to do it without attracting any attention. My cut would be substantial and we had an oral agreement that I could terminate the deal at any time. I don't know whether I actually would have been able to do so but it seemed to me that now my apparent death provided the opportunity. It remained to be seen just how I had perished officially but that would be revealed to me in time.

When my unseen investors – if you want to call them that – learn of my death they will probably investigate but they won't find anything. My dealings with them have met all their requirements and they would not find anything different. My own gains had been made using their funds in the short term to be certain and, while they might find some objection to that, their investments and returns had not been compromised in any manner. Any search of my business materials would reveal nothing. I routinely change computers, hard drives, etc. and there is no trace of my actions. I am very confident of that.

As far as identity, I have had a second identity all my life thanks to my mother. Through her, I have a second passport in a different but completely legal name and no one, not even Elise knows about that. Sue me. I haven't been completely honest about everything in our marriage but then, as it is painfully obvious now, neither had she. Thus I can take advantage of this unsolicited opportunity and disappear "Without A Trace" as the popular TV show says.

The master suite was at the far end of the house – there were only two bedrooms so the owner respected his or her privacy and didn't have a lot of guests at one time. The master suite was basically a mirror image of the guest suite where I had showered but there was only one king-sized bed (speaks well if the owner was married) and the two closets were walk-in. Both suites had sliders through which to access the deck that ran the length of the house on this end and only to the kitchen on the other. In one closet there was female stuff (I don't cross-dress) but she was tall and thin judging from the gowns that were floor length or cocktail style. There were pants and suits, blouses and skirts, sports clothes and casual. Shoes of all styles. In the other was all male stuff (that meant married or a significant equal): lightweight suits, trousers, jeans, khakis, long-sleeved shirts, a tuxedo, golf shirts (but nowhere did I find any sports equipment) and shoes to go with the different styles – except no golf shoes. Whoever the owner is (and in this distinction I am admittedly being sexist), he is roughly (and thankfully) my height (6 feet 2 inches) but heavier (I weighed 200 before the start of the fishing excursion.) His underwear was too big so I had to resort to mine when it was dry, but I chose a pair of black Bermuda-type shorts and a white golf shirt with a red and blue horizontal stripe (the blue one had white stars so it was a patriotic shirt). His shoe size was bigger and wider than mine so I had to settle for some flip-flop style sandals, which were a little sloppy when I walked, but then beggars cannot be choosers (make that, housebreakers cannot be choosers.)

By this time I had finished the roughy and the first glass of water and carried the plate, fork, and glass back to the kitchen. I left the plate and fork in the dish I had cooked the fish in and set everything soaking. I refilled the glass of water and went to check on the laundry, which was dry. I put my boxers on, then the shorts that I had been carrying around (if anyone had walked in on me I would have made an interesting picture), folded my shirt and cargo pants and headed back to the kitchen. I was going to do the dishes, clean up around the place and head out, but I was hit with a huge wave of tiredness (the end of the adrenaline rush no doubt) and ended up going for a short nap on one of the beds in the guest room.

CHAPTER 10

When I awoke the room seemed awash in crimson and purple and I momentarily was confused. However, it was just a glorious sunset reflected in the full-length mirrors on the closet doors. I cursed loudly because my short-term plan had gone astray. I had hoped to make it to some town in the early afternoon and to a bank, but obviously that was not going to happen.

Somewhat chagrined at my own failure, I responded to the call from my throat and stomach and headed back to the kitchen while covering my arms with another layer of aloe from the bottle I had carried with me. I took the SS and LL packages from the freezer and flipped a mental coin. It came up heads and the LL package went into the refrigerator to thaw for breakfast and the SS into the microwave. I was going to toss out the water remaining in my glass but stopped when I remembered King Neptune. During my four years of active service in the Navy (the requirement of my N.R.O.T.C. scholarship), I had gone through the polliwog ceremony crossing the equator. It can be fun on a cruise ship but (take my word for it) no fun on a naval vessel. One of the polliwogs (people who have never crossed the equator aboard ship) threw away the water in a glass just as the ceremony was about to get underway. King Neptune had spotted this and the culprit got double the harassing for wasting part of Neptune's realm. So I added ice cubes and more water and headed in search of a liquor cabinet.

The front hallway ended at the kitchen so I turned left, bathed in the slowly darkening sunset. The hallway ended in a large room most likely referred to as a great room as it served both as a dining area and living area. The modern table seated six and in the corner behind it was a bar. There were three stools at which its patrons could sit and behind it there was a sink and a small refrigerator which, upon closer inspection, not only had ice but also many fine drink accoutrements: cherries (both red and green); a lemon and a lime (both beginning to show their age); cocktail onions; several types of stuffed olives (pimento, anchovy, almond, and jalapeño), and both green and black, unstuffed but pitted. Still not knowing what booze I might find, I selected the jalapeño stuffed olives and turned my attention to the cabinets behind the bar. One contained an assortment of drink glasses and, still not knowing but feeling confident in what I would find, I selected a fine crystal highball glass. The next cabinet contained a decent assortment of liquor, aperitifs, and cordials, all in crystal decanters. The owner of this place was no slouch. There were both Absolut and Grey Goose Vodka but no Three Olives, my personal favorite. Settling for Grey Goose, I added ice to the highball glass, several olives (not bothering with toothpicks that I was certain I would find) and filled the glass to the top.

Just as I stoppered the decanter, I heard the distinct bell of the microwave telling me that (hopefully) dinner had thawed. However, barely started with cocktail hour, I ignored it knowing that a little more thawing would not hurt. Carrying my glass and taking a tentative sip that gratefully teased my pallet and hurried its way to my appreciative stomach, I wandered the rest of the room. On the far wall (the guest bedroom wall) was one of the largest television screens I had ever seen. Below it was an entertainment center that announced the fact by a bevy of green and red lights that gleamed through the glass doors. In front of it was a semi-circle of black leather and chrome furniture. There was a three-person couch facing the TV and on either side at a thirty-degree angle were two large chairs. I noticed that both were recliners as were the seats at both ends of the couch. In the arms of the chairs and the couch were drink holders and in front of the couch was a chrome and glass coffee table, upon which was an assortment of controllers. There were so many that I decided not to even try to turn on the TV. Also it would be clearly visible through the seaward windows (there weren't any others so I don't know why I used that adjective.) There were sheers to cover the windows and help to block the glare of the sun but nothing other than that. I had discovered that all the windows were self-darkening so the sheers on all the sliders were more for modesty than blocking the sun. Being an interloper and not wanting to be discovered, as of yet, I didn't want to do anything that would raise attention.

There was a stairway behind the wall of the bar. If one came in the front door and through the foyer they could have turned right and gone right down. There was switch on the wall and I flicked it. Lighting on the steps illuminated the way down and I left it on determining to investigate after dinner.

That in mind, I hurried back to the kitchen so that I could get my meal cooked before it was dark enough to need lights and have them discernible from the water. The SS was indeed thawed and ready to be cooked. Opening the paper I started drooling at one of the biggest, thickest and juiciest looking strip steaks I had ever seen. I happily fired up the indoor grill on the center island. While waiting for the artificial coals to get heated, I carried my half-empty drink out of the kitchen and down the hall to the office that was calling me. The sidewalls were lined with books both hardbound and paperback and one entire bookcase was devoted to manuscripts, but neither they nor the books were of any interest. The only furniture in the room was a glass-topped table and large comfortable looking black leather and chrome captain's chair. On top of the table sat a computer screen and wireless keyboard. Setting my drink on the table, I made a mental note to clean up the mess it would make and turned on the computer.

In my business computers are a necessity and I was very familiar with a wide variety since I also use them in clients' offices and homes. This one was a Dell (too much hype and not the top of the heap of the PCs) loaded with Vista that caused me to shudder. I am a Macintosh man myself and have been since the first one came upon the scene (although that was years ago in my youth). The thing about Macs is that the hardware is specific to its operating system and has changed over the years. I have to hand it to Bill Gates that he has tried to improve his Windows OS while the PC hardware has remain pretty much the same except for being faster. The positive side of this is that many of the older programs still run on the PC but the software has increased in size slowing the system down and is the source of numerous crashes. But enough proselytizing.

As I had expected, the system was password protected and although there was a guest login it also required a password. Probably something simple (like the name of the owner, the name of the house if it had one, or the name of the island and I still didn't know that) but I didn't have time for guessing games. I shut the system down and carried my drink back to the bar for a refill. I wiped the decanter, olive jar, cabinet doors as well as the refrigerator door clean enough to remove fingerprints and returned to the kitchen, this time carrying with me the glass of ice water. I put the steak on the grill, turned the heat to medium, put the wrapper in the trash can in the corner, grabbed the dish rag and returned to the office where I wiped the table top, computer, and keyboard clean.

In the kitchen I found a steak knife, washed off the fork and plate I had used for the roughy, and turned the steak. I would have liked potatoes and peas but a search of the cupboards revealed nothing of interest as accoutrements to the steak. Mother Hubbard's bare cupboards but the freezer had plenty or at least enough. The steak was delicious and I devoured it standing by the sink, again not wishing to be visible in the windows any longer than necessary despite the fact that it was completely dark now.

CHAPTER 11

Having finished in the kitchen, I went to see the rest of the house. Had I not taken a nap this morning and all afternoon, I would not have had a chance to do this. But being here at this time, it only made sense. After all, this house was my salvation and I now felt the need to know it completely.

As I walked down the hall from the kitchen toward the foyer, I was in complete darkness, having extinguished the few lights I was using in the kitchen, except for the glow of the ever-present floor lighting and the glow from the lights on the stairs to guide me. If the hall had not been straight or if I had to make a couple of turns, I probably would have had trouble as I still was not in "fighting trim" and had been drinking. The closer I got to the foyer the more discernible things became.

Entering the foyer, I turned right and after a few steps the staircase was extremely visible. It was a curving staircase and by the time I reach the bottom I would have been able to view the sea if there had been windows on the wall but there weren't. I knew from my walk to the house this morning that there was a basement slider but I didn't have a clue where. I was at a doorway in the center of the theater. The seats in the theater were similar to the chairs in front of the television in the great room. There were five seats in a row and ten rows with a wide aisle between rows five and six and that was where I stood. An equally wide aisle ran completely around the perimeter of the room. To my right was a huge screen or at least huge for this room. To the left I could see a projection booth and I headed for this. The door was unlocked and I entered cautiously.

There were three different movie projectors and, judging from the looks, they must have spanned the one hundred odd years of movie making. In addition to the film projectors, there was what I judged to be a digital projector as well as a Beta tape machine, a VHS machine, DVD player as well as a Blu-ray player. In the middle of the back wall was a door. Closer inspection revealed that it was the door to a safe with a combination lock. I thought that this was probably a climate-controlled storage area for movies and the door was for security when the movies viewed were prerelease. The owner of the place was well prepared. Although he might never have many stay over guests, he certainly had some large screenings or was prepared to do so. Careful not to touch anything, and I was walking about clasping my hands behind my back, I exited the booth and closed the door using my elbow. Then I wiped the knob with my shirt.

Returning to the room's entrance, I turned off the lights and wiped the light switch before going up stairs. At the top of the stairs, I turned off the lights and again wiped the switch. Knowing that I had been a bit careless before, I walked down the hall to the kitchen and got a clean kitchen towel to carry with me. Then I went through the kitchen to the front hallway and to the slider in the middle of the great room. Opening it, a cool breeze from the sea greeted me. I walked onto the deck carefully closing the door behind me, leaving it just a bit ajar. The night was quiet enough to hear the waves lapping at the rocks below. Out at sea, I could see lights of what I judged to be a cruise ship and another set more likely a freighter. I had no idea what the rules were about lights on small fishing vessels but didn't see any other lights.

As I stood there taking in the night, I realized that the house didn't have a pool and thus knew that the owner of the house was not a beach person. Who he or she was I had no idea, but I felt that we could be friends if we might ever meet. But then I could pass him on the street and not recognize him, despite the fact that his house had a definite personality: basic but not overly pretentious. My kind of guy but, again by the use of that simple noun, I could be accused of being sexist.

Possibly it was the effect of the darkness and alcohol or just the ordeal still having its effect upon me because I felt the need to go to bed. I reentered the house, careful to wipe everything I had touched, and went to the guest bedroom. There I stripped to my shorts and set the alarm by the bed to 6:00 a.m. I had an appointment with a bank – hopefully by noon – and I had a lot to do before then so I didn't want to sleep in. Despite my nap earlier, I was asleep mere moments after my head hit the pillow.

CHAPTER 12

There was a flash of green ...

This time the dream was different like it was a television football replay. I had awakened twice during the night startled into consciousness by that vision. However this time it was happening in slow motion and I saw and heard everything with a new clarity. Well, everything that I needed to see or hear.

Quentin wrapped the line around his hand and started pulling the fish up. I pulled the rod out of the holder, my hands were shaking. Keith was on my left with my camera and was watching Quentin at work.

"Get over by the fish for a good picture," Howard, not Keith, shouted. He was on my right holding a beer – it wasn't open. The cap was still on it.

I moved a few feet toward the port side where Quentin was at work. Behind me Howard moved toward me. Just as I started leaning over to see the fish, behind me there was a blur of motion, there was a flash of green and then ...

I was lying on the deck and someone was removing my watch and my wedding ring.

"What ez going on, monsieur? Why you hit zat fella?" Quentin questioning.

"Shut up, frog faggot, and get over there to the side and don't say nothing or you'll join him feeding the fishes!" Keith.

So Howard was fleecing me. I felt my wallet being removed. Hands patted my pockets fleetingly.

"Give me a hand getting him over the side." Howard.

Hands roughly grabbed me and I felt myself scrape the gunwale and then my arms were released and I was dropping. In the brief instant before I hit the water, I somehow managed to get a breath.

As my head submerged, I struggled briefly as I thought a drowning person would and then quit. My feet were still being held. Held for an eternity I thought and then I was battered by a wave smashing against the side of the boat. One foot was released or slipped from someone's grasp. There was a pause and then the other foot was free and I slid into the water.

My lungs were bursting (for the first time that day) and I thought I was going to have to take a breath. My brief schooling in snorkeling and scuba made me slowly start releasing my breath. My lungs were on fire. I needed to breathe but had to hold it. Fire ... burning ...

My head broke the surface and I inhaled quickly as the waves turned me over. I tried not to breathe hard despite the burning ache in my lungs. I was dead and had to get them to believe that. I heard nothing ... no, there was loud shouting but I couldn't understand a thing. I felt myself being turned over by the waves and took a breath.

I floated facedown for a while, once again my lungs afire. Then the waves came to my aid again and I was turned face up, a quick breath. I heard the engines increase in pitch. They were leaving.

As I heard the engine sound begin to recede I took a breath and chanced a glance. The boat was moving away three people aboard, Quentin at the helm, all backs to me, the three of them in animated conversation with much gesturing. I felt the waves turning me over and took a breath.

CHAPTER 13

There was a flash of green ...

I woke myself with a start sitting up in bed. The room was dimly light. I was dripping in sweat and the sheets were soaked. I looked at the clock by the bed. 5:00. Dawn was surely on its way. I knew that I could sleep no more, especially since my brain kept replaying that scene. I don't know if I was dreaming or simply letting the incident play over and over in my mind. One thing was definitely clear in my mind:

On Howard's face was a malicious grin. He had enjoyed what he was doing.

Howard and I had really never been close, not even good friends but I didn't think he had a reason to hate me. Well, maybe he did. He had never been overtly unfriendly but there may have been some latent dislike because of my race. My mother was from Sierra Leone and my father was an Irish American. Looking at me you can tell about my mother (dark kinky hair, dark eyes, light to medium brown skin) but what I got from my father was my height and build. Both undoubtedly contributed to my intelligence. I was glad they were both dead because I don't know how they would have taken the news of their only child dying before them. Both were only children so there are no living relatives that I know of. Just as well because what I am going to do would not make anyone proud. Well, it was going to make me proud.

Time to get moving. I gathered the sheets, mattress cover, and pillowcases and took them to the laundry where I threw them into the washer and started it. My mother taught me how to care for myself, including laundry and cooking. Stopping in the kitchen, I started a small pot of coffee and then returned to the guest bedroom. Checking the bed, I could detect only slight dampness on the mattress but knew that would dry quickly.

I showered and shaved for the last time using a new disposable razor provided by my host and brushed my teeth using a new toothbrush and small tube of toothpaste (not my brand) again provided by my unknowing host or hostess. Once done with my ablutions, I filled the sink with hot water, pulled the plug and repeated this process several times in order to wash all trace of me away. All this time the shower had been running. Using my towel, I wiped all the surfaces of the shower, the sink area including the toilet and any surface that I might have remotely used. I repeated this procedure in the bedroom after dressing. Then I went to the master bedroom where I did the same and followed that with the living room. Then the towel went into the wash, the bedding into the dryer.

In the kitchen, I poured myself a cup of coffee (not bad) drinking it just the way it was intended to be drunk. The LL package came out of the refrigerator and was unwrapped: lasagna. "LL"? Lola's Lasagna, Lousy Lasagna (I hoped not) and settled on Leftover Lasagna. Who knew? A quick warm up in the microwave using the plate of the day before and I took my first bite. It definitely was not "Lousy Lasagna." Breakfast done, all the dishes were washed, put away using a dishtowel to handle them and all surfaces wiped with the dishtowel. I collected the trash, put a new plastic liner in the can and compacted the trash.

Moving to the laundry I took the bedding out of the dryer, put the towel in, and went to the guest bedroom to make the bed. As I left I again wiped all surfaces. Then I went to the foyer and stood there thinking about what I may have missed. The study – I couldn't remember. Once all surfaces there were wiped, I retrieved the towel that had dried quickly being the only item in the load. Surfaces, the box of detergent, and knobs wiped, I took the towel to the guest bedroom and hung it up.

Back to the foyer. On the floor was a plastic bag holding my clothes, that and the towel were the only things I was taking with me besides the clothes I was wearing and the trash. By this time it was nearly nine and I knew that by the time I got to town (I had no idea how long that would take) banks would be open. What had I forgotten? I put my hand on my head to think and realized that, although I hadn't forgotten anything, I needed something. Back to the master suite and I picked up a pair of sunglasses I had seen lying there (thankfully they were unisex) and then to the guest suite for a wide brim floppy hat bearing a Belize logo. Satisfied that I had done as much as I could, I said a silent "thank you" to the house that served as my refuge and another to my absent host. Using the towel, I opened the door, made certain that no one was around to observe me, and stepped out into the world to begin the second phase of my operation.

PART II
VANISHING

CHAPTER 14

The morning was still cool and I walked away without looking back until I had gone about a hundred yards. And there it stood, a white house with a red roof against a background of Caribbean Blue. The house at the end of the road. The house that had been my salvation. The house at the start of my new life. It was silly but I waved good-bye, knowing that within a few days I would be back to replenish what I had borrowed.

I wasn't certain what side of the road to walk on because I couldn't remember which side the steering wheels were on, but that was because I hadn't even seen the inside of a car on this island. I assumed that it was left-hand drive since many of these islands were European and walked accordingly. I found out when the first car came down the road going to one of the other houses I had passed that I had guessed correctly. Thus, this was a European island as opposed to British because cars (at least that one, and it proved to be the case for all) are right-hand drive, which means it wasn't St. Kitts or St. Nevis, which are left-hand drive. The car went by so fast I couldn't make out the license plate, although it was basically blue on white. Although other cars passed me, I chose to walk with my head down as much as possible to keep from being recognized.

After about an hour, I came to the top of a hill and could see the harbor laid out in front of me. I admit I wasn't very surprised to recognize the harbor of St. Nantes where I had departed on my fishing expedition just two days and a few hours before. That meant that I needed to be on the watch for Quentin, who was probably the only person who could recognize me, unless the news of my death or disappearance had made the papers with a picture. However if I was Quentin and I had been an unwitting party to a murder, I don't think I would be showing myself around for a few days until the uproar (if there was any) had died down. I might even cancel any fishing expeditions and I don't think I would be fishing in that same area for quite a while because who knew what the catch might be.

There was no cruise ship in the harbor so business would be slow and that suited me just fine. It took me another half hour to make it to the harbor front. Several cars had passed me going toward town but not one had stopped. I wasn't looking for a ride and wouldn't have accepted one regardless of an offer. I wanted to talk to as few people as possible. My feet were sore since my footwear wasn't the best in the world. When I got some money, shoes and socks would be my first purchase. My first stop was a trashcan and into it went the plastic bag containing trash from the house.

There are several banks in the waterfront area and I chose B.N.P.S.N. (Banque Nationale de Paris St. Nantes) on Rue de Bord de Mer fronting on the harbor because it looked to be the most prosperous. This was no time to flip a coin. I entered the bank and walked up to a teller and asked to speak to the manager. However, I had no sooner asked when I heard, "Monsieur, can I help you?"

I turned and found myself looking at a well-dressed man about my own height but heavier. He had a thin mustache, well-trimmed hair, and blue eyes that seemed to dance. He was wearing a lightweight off-white suit with a pale blue shirt and dark blue tie.

"I need to open an account."

"Certainly, Monsieur, come with me."

I followed him into a small office and closed the door behind me.

"I hope you don't mind," I said.

"Of course not, Monsieur, privacy is most important."

He indicated a chair in front of his desk and took a seat behind it. The desk was well organized but that would not been difficult as there wasn't much on it. Only a telephone and a nameplate that told me his name was Henri Flournoy.

"Monsieur Flournoy," I started. "I find myself in a bit of a predicament. I have no identification. I can give you a number to call and the person at the other end can verify who I am and provide funds to open an account. I can get proper identification papers sent but it will take a few days and I need funds until then."

"That should not be a problem, Mr. ..." Henri said.

"I'm sorry. This incident has me flustered!" Fact. "Mbayo. Dawoh Mbayo."

That's my name. Well, my Sierra Leone name. My mother was from that country and came to the United States to go to school when her father was with the Sierra Leone staff at the United Nations. She met and married my father in college. Sierra Leone approved dual citizenship in 2006 and I jumped at the chance, choosing my mother's maiden name and her maternal grandfather's first name as my Sierra Leone name. I did this entirely without my wife's knowledge. It pays to be prepared.

"Very good, Mr. Mbayo. What is the number?"

I wrote the number on the back of a business card he handed me and gave it to him. He dialed the number and waited just a minute.

"Hello, my name is Henri Flournoy and I am the manager of the Banque Nationale de Paris St. Nantes F.V.I. I have in my office a Monsieur Dawoh Mbayo who claims that you can identify him."

A slight pause.

"Yes, that's right, Dawoh Mbayo."

He handed the phone to me across the desk.

I said hello.

"Would you please punch in your account number and access code, Mr. Mbayo."

I asked Monsieur Flournoy for the phone cradle and he slide it across the desk and discretely averted his eyes as I punched in the numbers. First were six random characters followed by the account number, four more random characters followed by the access code and three more random numbers.

"Thank you, Mr. Mbayo." The voice said, "How much do you need?"

I entered the amount using the keys.

"No problem. May I speak to Monsieur Flournoy, please."

There was a brief conversation between the two and Mr. Flournoy made some notes on a piece of paper, said good-bye and hung up the phone.

"There is some paperwork to fill out. If you like, I will get you one thousand Euros to hold you until your funds arrive later today."

"That is most kind, Monsieur Flournoy. Thank you."

He left the office and returned with four different forms and left me to fill them out. Before I had completed them he returned and took a seat at his desk with a stack of Euro notes.

I completed the forms and after he perused them, he passed the money across the table. I didn't bother to count it and put in my pocket.

"If you will return here about three o'clock we can complete the necessary paperwork. Would you be needing a bankcard?"

"Yes, that will most convenient. Could you suggest a decent clothing store and a decent, but not overly expensive, hotel?"

He did and provided directions to the clothing store although the hotel he recommended was on the other side of the island and would require a taxi.

"Would you like me to make a reservation for you?"

I said yes, thanked him again, shook hands and left the bank.

CHAPTER 15

The store that Henri had recommended was set off from the waterfront and was more a store for the residents than the tourists. It was as close to a department store as one might find in the islands (at least to my way of thinking).

I first went to the shoe department and bought some comfortable walking shoes and socks. Then I bought a loose fitting long-sleeved shirt to hide the sunburn and the accompanying stares that could lead to identification, a pair of khakis and underwear and used the dressing room to change, putting my other clothes in a plastic bag. I paid for these in cash after a slight hesitation on the part of the clerk – the world is getting too accustomed to plastic. Then, almost as an afterthought, I bought another wallet like the one that Howard had taken from me. Then, with the understanding that I would be back to pay for this in the afternoon when my account opened, I selected a pair of cross trainers, more socks (both athletic and dress), a dress shirt, two more long-sleeved sports shirts, a tee shirt emblazoned with a St. Nantes logo, running shorts, another pair of Dockers, a light jacket, underwear and, to carry it when I traveled, a rolling duffel bag carry-on.

Then I went out and bought sunglasses (the reflective kind so my eyes couldn't be seen and they would also serve as a mask), a watch and a small digital camera. Acting touristy, I carefully walked the street by the waterfront, snapping an occasional photo just to have to remember the layout for future use. Despite the fact that it was early, I entered a restaurant/bar and sat at a table in the shadows. I nursed a local beer for well over an hour before ordering lunch accompanied by another beer.

Having seen nothing to arouse my suspicion (I figured Quentin to be in hiding just as I was), I paid my bill, leaving a modest tip so as not to arouse too much suspicion and went to find an Internet café. That wasn't too difficult and I logged in and entered my name into a Google search. I did this regularly about once a week just to keep tabs on what might be said in the press about my company, Andrews Investment Management, and me but found nothing that I had not previously seen. There was no notice of my death or disappearance. That was strange, I thought.

I momentarily considered logging into one of my email accounts but thought better of it. Things like that have too much scrutiny – who knew who was monitoring what? Best to let Stuart Andrews rest in peace.

Satisfied, but mystified, with the results of my Internet search, I went to an electronics store and bought a cell phone and paid for 100 minutes. Then I went outside and found a bench away from public scrutiny. I punched in the number for my banker and when the phone was answered, rather than speaking, I punched in the account number and access code using difference sequences of random numbers.

The voice on the other end of the line said "Yes, Mr. Mbayo. How can I be of service?"

"In my safety deposit box there is a sealed packet about twenty by twenty-five centimeters. It should be the top packet. I need you to send this packet express to me c/o ..." and gave him the address for my hotel. "I would like it there as soon as possible, the day after tomorrow at the latest."

"No problem, Mr. Mbayo. Consider it done. Anything else?"

"No," I said. "You have been most helpful today." and broke the connection. I turned the cellphone off and removed the battery. I wanted no GPS trace on me just in case.

I sat on the bench enjoying the coolness of the afternoon until almost three o'clock and returned to the bank. Henri Flournoy was waiting for me with two more sets of papers to sign and then handed me my bankcard and some checks to use until I ordered more although I had no intention of doing so.

"The pin is 9999," he said. "If you want to change it, use the bank machine outside to the left of our door. After you have entered the code, press the pound key, the star key and the four digits you wish your pin to be followed by the star key. However, you must use the machine here as it is the only one with that capability."

I thank him for all his help and went outside. The bank machine worked just as he said and I checked my balance. The money was there minus the one thousand Euros. That money would do until I got my packet and left the island. After withdrawing some addition funds, I went back to the clothing store and paid for the clothes I had selected using the bank debit card. Then carrying my purchases stuffed into the duffel, I hailed a cab and went to the hotel. They had my reservation and I had to do nothing except go to my room. I stripped, showered and dressed. A bellboy came to my room in response to my phone call to the desk. I gave him the clothes and dishtowel from the house at the end of the road and asked that they be washed and pressed.

The flip-flops were wrapped in my old clothes and placed in the bottom of my carry-on. I then went outside and acquainted myself with the neighborhood and all means of access and egress from the hotel.

I ate an early dinner with a good bottle of white wine, added a reasonable tip to the bill, which was charged to my room. In my room, the clean laundry was on the bed. I put it into one of the plastic bags from the electronics store where I had purchased the cell phone having wiped down the handles and other surfaces of the bag using a handkerchief when handling it.

I turned on the TV to CNN International and watched it for an hour and getting no news about me or anyone missing anywhere in the Caribbean. Intrigued, but still mystified, I turned out the light and went to sleep.

CHAPTER 16

I awoke shortly after 7:00 a.m. feeling very rested. I showered, applied aloe to my arms, dressed and went to breakfast. Afterward, dressing in my shorts, tank top, and cross trainers, I sat down at the desk to write a note:

Your beautiful house was a needed sanctuary for me after a very harrowing experience. I trust that the intrusion will not upset you very much. I left your suite alone except for the included clothes that I borrowed out of necessity.

I ate some of your food and drank some of your alcohol. I did my best to leave everything as I found it, having washed and put back that which I used. I am sorry that I had to purloin a hat and flip-flops, which I have kept and, of course, the food and liquor.

The enclosed 1000 Euros is to recompense you for the use of your beautiful house and its belongings.

The house was my salvation and I thank you for being able to use it.

Satisfied with the note, I folded and added it to the bag with the laundry. Taking it and some cash, a check written out to cash, and my bankcard for identification, I left my room and the hotel and took a cab back down to the waterfront.

In the Banque Nationale De Paris S.N., I cashed the check without the need for identification, as the teller was the one I had first approached yesterday. Monsieur Flournoy sat in his office and basically ignored me except for the nod of his head in recognition.

Putting the money in the bag, I exited the bank and went to the Internet café I had visited yesterday. I repeated the Google search I had made yesterday with the same results. Then I typed the note I had written and printed two copies. I picked up both, handling only the one underneath, folded them in half and slid the one inside untouched into the plastic bag. The handwritten note and the other printed copy I shredded in the document shredder. Then I set out for the house at the end of the road.

Via a combination of jogging and walking, I made better time than I had yesterday, despite the fact the first part of the trip was uphill. As I approached the house at the end of the road, it appeared that it was as deserted as it had been when I first saw it two days ago. After wiping the handles of the bag with a handkerchief and folding the bag over, I left it at the front door and hurried away as quickly as possible. Once back on the road, I set off jogging and alternated that with walking when needed.

I have never been athletic, actually despise exercise, but knew that my project required some physical exertion on my part and therefore I needed to get into good physical shape. Jogging was only the start.

Downtown I hailed a taxi (no sense in overdoing it) and returned to the hotel. I showered, dressed and went to lunch after checking at the desk for parcels or messages. There were none. I changed into my shorts and a tee shirt, took a beach towel provided by the hotel and walked to the beach where I rented a chaise lounge and beach umbrella. Removing my tee shirt and liberally applying sunscreen to my burned parts, I spend two hours lying in the sun, starting on my stomach and turning onto my back after an hour.

Having baked myself as much as I felt I could, I returned to the hotel, showered, put on a terry cloth bathrobe provided by the hotel and went to use the steam bath. I returned to the room rejuvenated, dressed and went to an early dinner only slightly upset that my package had not arrived. After dinner, I returned to my room and spent another hour watching CNN and learning nothing.

My sleep that night was troubled by revisiting my watery trial and strange dreams of being in a brightly lit space with no ceiling or walls and being able to get nowhere despite my best efforts.

CHAPTER 17

I awoke the next morning feeling refreshed despite the troubled dreams. I dressed in shorts and tank top and went for a run. After returning, I showered, dressed, went to breakfast and then checked the Internet. Nothing had changed. "Curiouser and curiouser!" Cried Alice ... .

I dressed for the beach and spent two hours there as I had the previous day, returning to the hotel for lunch. As I was returning to my room, the desk clerk called to me and I went over and received my package. Back in my room I called the airport and found there was space on the flight to St. Martin at 3:15 p.m. I opened the package and found, as expected, my Sierra Leone passport, two credit cards, and five thousand Euros. I dressed, packed, checked out of the hotel and took a taxi to the airport. It was a simple matter to purchase the ticket using one of the credit cards. I went through passport control and security with no problem and walked out on the tarmac and up the short ladder to the plane. At the top of the ladder I stopped and turned around to look back at the island.

I'll be back, I thought.

That same morning at the house at the end of the road, a navy and silver Smart Car turned into the carport and stopped. The car was owned by Lynette Duprey, who was the housekeeper for the house at the end of the road. She had a call from the owner saying that they would be arriving in three days and she should be certain that the house was in order.

Today she was going in to dust and clean the floors where necessary. Tomorrow she would shop for food and liquor to replenish anything that was getting low. She had been employed by the owner of the house at the end of the road for ten years. They had a good working agreement, and she was very well paid for her efforts.

She left her purse in the car, knowing that it would be safe, and carried only her key ring on which was a key to the house at the end of the road. As she approached the front door, she noticed a plastic bag lying in front of the door. She picked it up, unlocked the door, and entered. The floor lighting came on and the air conditioner turned itself on. She carried the bag to the kitchen, turned on the light and set the bag on the counter.

She got a glass, filled it with ice and water and then turned to the bag wondering what it contained. She never thought of anything bad. She dumped the contents on the counter and was surprised to see: 1) a shirt she recognized as belonging to her employer; 2) a pair of shorts belonging to her employer (both of these she recognized because she did the laundry as part of her duties); 3) a pair of sun glasses (which she did not recognize); 4) a dish towel (which she did recognize); and 5) an envelope addressed to:

Owner
The house at the end of the road

She opened the envelope and looked at the letter. Her spoken and understandable English was passable but her reading wasn't as good and "owner" was not in her reading vocabulary. It was for this reason that she couldn't read enough of the note to comprehend its contents and therefore didn't understand why the clothes were there or the purpose of the money, although she recognized its value as it was in Euros, the local currency.

One thousand Euros was a lot of money, even for an economy as well to do as this one. Her mind worked swiftly and she worked out all possible scenarios. The note and envelope were shredded and flushed in a toilet, the shirt, shorts, and towel washed, ironed and replaced (she wasn't taking any chances), the sunglasses and money were going home with her. If the owner questioned her about the package (which he wouldn't because he didn't know about it) she would plead ignorance. Once these formalities had been attended to, she went about her business noticing nothing amiss until it was time for lunch. Returning to the kitchen, she opened the freezer expecting to find her lasagna there. Akin to Old Mother Hubbard, she found the freezer was bare. She stared at the empty shelves but never made the connection with the letter.

Eventually she shrugged, closed the refrigerator, turned off the kitchen lights, exited the house making certain the front door was secure (she didn't know about the key above the door), got in her car and went home to lunch. She would return tomorrow with the food and finish the cleaning.

CHAPTER 18

MIAMI INVESTMENT
BROKER MISSING
FROM CRUISE SHIP

In the wake of Bernie Madoff, Marcus Schrenker, and Sir Allen Standford scandals, it appears that yet another financial "genius" has gone astray. Caribbean Cruise Lines announced this morning that investment manager Stuart Andrews of Andrews Investment Management, Miami, Florida, has gone missing aboard its ship, M.S. Caribbean Isle, somewhere between St. Georges, Grenada, and Willemstad, Curaçao.

A spokesman for Caribbean Cruise Lines said that all passengers had been accounted for leaving all prior ports. Passengers scan cards leaving the ship and coming aboard. The scan upon boarding pulls up a photograph so that the security personnel can verify that the person possessing the card is in fact the owner of the card. No one was late boarding in any of the ports. The ship's captain initiated an evacuation drill Saturday morning prior to arrival at Willemstad, a roll call taken by checking ship's cards and all areas of the ship thoroughly searched. There was no sign of the missing financier.

I had Googled myself yesterday in my hotel room in St. Martin where I had flown from St. Nantes the previous day and found this item in the Miami Herald. It had been quickly picked up by CNN. I had been happy to see that at this point there was no picture with the story since it was obviously just breaking news. I knew that CNN would be most likely to have the breaking story and would be the first with a picture. How good a picture would it be and whether it would make me recognizable I didn't know. This morning there was even more:

CNN: *Missing Miami financial genius Stuart Andrew's disappearance aboard the Caribbean Cruise Lines M.S. Caribbean Isle still remains a mystery. Search and rescue airplanes and vessels from the Netherlands Antilles, Grenada, and Trinidad and Tobago have been searching the seas since early morning yesterday and have found nothing.*

Andrews is reported to have disappeared sometime between departure from St. Georges, Grenada, at 5:00 p.m. local time Wednesday and 10:00 p.m. Thursday. His disappearance was reported to the ship's captain by the financier's wife Elise after a prolonged absence from his cabin where he had been in seclusion for a couple of days. At this time we have no further information but have been informed that Mrs. Andrews will issue a statement when the ship docks in Aruba this morning.

Thursday night the ship's company had made a thorough search of the ship except for passengers' cabins. Friday morning shortly before the ship arrived in Curaçao at 9:00, the captain held an evacuation drill and the cabins were searched but there was

no sign of Stuart Andrews. All other passen-
gers have been accounted for.

CNN had a picture (five years old) that had been cut from a group photo and was not that good. I was relieved.

I didn't plan on staying here long. In fact, I had a ticket that afternoon on a KLM flight to Amsterdam where I figured I could acquire some fake ID. Since Dawoh Mbayo is my Sierra Leone name, it stood to reason that someone might find it and start tracking me. Besides, I don't want that name around any of the places where I was going to be exacting payback, just in case something unexpected happened. Especially since now I was officially missed, having apparently committed suicide. However, to my knowledge, no one in the United States knew about this other identity.

One of my first thoughts was wondering if Quentin knew what had happened to me. I suspected (if he was still alive) that he would be as curious as I was about what had become of me.

The fact that I was missing after three additional days raised many questions in my mind, the most prominent of which was "How did I get aboard the Caribbean Isle since I was afloat in the Caribbean Sea?" Then "How had I managed to stay unnoticed aboard the Caribbean Isle for three days?"

Arriving on St. Martin, I had made several stops before selecting a hotel. First stop was to get a computer so I would not be seen using public computers. I selected a Vaio P Series Notebook, which is a small, easily portable computer basically used for email and formatting pictures. It is essentially 5 by 10 inches and weighs less than 1.5 pounds.

A second stop had been at a jewelry store where I had purchased a pair of diamond stud earrings as well as a plain gold stud. After purchasing some alcohol wipes and some needles at a drugstore, I had, in the privacy of my hotel room and properly anesthetized with the aid of a bottle of vodka, heated the needle to cleanse it and pierced my left ear. It wasn't that difficult and, at least in my anesthetized state, didn't hurt much. Then I had done it and had the stud in. The Internet, including several videos on You Tube, had given me the necessary methodology.

My beard grows fairly quickly and even in just two days, I was getting pretty hairy. The heat and humidity of the Caribbean is not a good place to grow a beard, but it would help to hide my identity. Wearing my sunglasses most of the time helps but you can't do that inside without looking really weird and drawing attention to yourself. So I had purchased a pair of large, really weak reading glasses in St. Nantes and had been wearing those as part of my new persona. In addition, a doo-rag had been adopted. The few hours I had spent in the sun on St. Nantes had darkened my skin but still not enough. That meant more time in the sun, although I knew I would have to be careful in my public appearances and resolved to get as far away from this part of the Caribbean as soon as possible and to stay away from the area in which I had been declared missing.

There was nothing to do but go about my business. Actually, if I were identified nothing would really happen to me as the only law I had broken (other than the breaking and entering and theft of property from the house at the end of the road) was not reporting the crime of attempted murder. Certainly Elise, Howard, and Keith were guilty of much more serious crimes. Try attempted murder for one.

I dressed for running and went out. I chose to run away from any crowds and had no problem. I doubted that there was much interest in my disappearance here as this is basically the northern Caribbean and Grenada and Curaçao are in the southern Caribbean and quite far away.

CHAPTER 19

When I got back from my run, this report was being aired:

> *CNN, Dateline Oranjestad, Aruba*
> *Elise Andrews, wife of 10 years to the missing financer Stuart Andrews issued the following statement through Caribbean Cruise Lines when the ship docked in Aruba today. Mrs. Andrews said she found that her husband was not in bed and not in their suite when she got up about 8:00 a.m. There were no breakfast dishes and the "Privacy Please" sign was in the door. She doesn't remember whether the door was locked from the inside or not.*

The picture changed to Elise standing in front of a small bank of microphones.

> *"Stuart had been acting moody since returning from a fishing excursion on St. Nantes and hadn't left the suite. He even had all his meals delivered to the room and wouldn't let the cabin attendant into the cabin. He made me leave the 'Do Not Disturb' sign in the card slot. I like to attend dance classes, art auctions, and educational lectures, and sit around the sun deck and play cards. Sometimes we met for lunch and sometimes we didn't.*
> *"When I returned to the cabin to dress for dinner (it was a formal night) he wasn't*

there. I checked and his tuxedo was still in the closet. He didn't show up for dinner. At 10:00 p.m. when I got back to the cabin after the show, there was no sign that he had been there so I contacted the ship's personnel."

The picture changed back to the CNN reporter.

Caribbean Cruise Lines has told CNN that during the night they conducted a thorough investigation of the ship and could not find him. No charges had been made using his cruise card. Thus, in the morning, the ship's Captain held an evacuation drill and all cabins were searched. There was no sign of him.

Caribbean Cruise Lines have no explanation for what has happened and have no further comment at this point. Except for the clothes he had on, there is nothing missing. He apparently left all his belongings, including his wedding ring, in the cabin. There is no note and no indication of foul play. Ship records indicate that he had not left the ship since St. Nantes.

CNN has talked to Howard Blake, Stuart Andrews's brother-in-law.

The picture changed to Howard standing in front of a nondescript building, probably part of the Aruba port.

Howard: "Stuart was in a funk when we went ashore for the fishing excursion because of the Merrill-Lynch announcement. He felt that the entire industry was in big trouble and was very worried about his clients. He wanted to cancel the excursion but Elise and I convinced him that he needed the break. He landed the first fish and after that just sat in the bow and sulked. Keith and I each caught two mahi mahi but Stuart showed no interest. When we returned to the ship he went straight to his cabin and, as far as I know, didn't leave it."

CNN: "Was he drinking?"

Howard: "No, Stuart's not a big drinker. He was depressed and sat on the porch and stared out at the sea. One time when I stopped in to see if he wanted to do something, I found him leaning against the rail just staring out at the sea. I had to touch him to get him to react to me and he told me to bug off (not his exact words) and leave him alone and so I did."

CNN: "We tried to talk to Mitchell who was also on the fishing excursion but he refused to comment."

Smart move, Keith. The fewer people talking the better. Don't want to get your stories crossed. Wonder how he got into this? He couldn't have been someone that Howard just met on the boat. Had to have been preplanned. But when, how and all those other w's?

Chapter 20

In the early afternoon I packed, checked out, and went to the airport. I had a 3:15 departure flight on KLM to Amsterdam via Paris. While a direct flight would have been preferable, there wasn't one and I wanted to get away from the Caribbean as quickly as possible. I could have opted for Paris to do what I wanted, but my contacts were in Amsterdam and that made things easier. Besides I knew the city, and I didn't know Paris.

All processes went easily. I had no baggage to check, security was a breeze as was passport control, but I was extremely nervous. There was nothing in the passport to show when I arrived in the Caribbean other than at St. Martin yesterday but no one appeared interested.

"Have a nice flight, Mr. Mbayo," the passport agent said. "Hope that you enjoyed your stay in St. Martin and come back soon."

I smiled, accepted my passport and went forward to the waiting area. I had purchased a book to read but couldn't get into it. My thoughts were racing back over the past couple of days, even months.

Elise had planned the trip and begged me to go. At first I had been reluctant but soon realized that I really needed a break. The state of the economy and the market were not going to change soon and there was nothing that I could do to really help it. My investing clients' portfolios couldn't be helped much by me being there and my offshore laundry clients had to live with the status also and that meant cutting back for the time being. They understood – they should because the partnership has been extremely lucrative for both sides.

Actually, the straw that broke the camel's back (my re-
luctance) was the fishing excursion on St. Nantes. Elise was
the one who had discovered Quentin's website and had
shown it to me. I hadn't fished in years, hadn't had a vacation in years, and that just sounded so good. I finally agreed.
She was excited, "It is going to be two weeks in paradise."

She had selected the Caribbean Cruise Lines itinerary
because it ended in Aruba and we could spend a week there
just relaxing in the sun. Admittedly it was an intriguing
trip: Fly to Puerto Rico on Saturday and board the ship; at
sea on Sunday; St. Nantes on Monday and the fishing excursion; Dominica on Tuesday; Grenada on Wednesday; at
sea on Thursday; Curaçao on Friday; and Aruba on Saturday.
Then seven days at a resort on Aruba (or seven and a half
counting that Saturday) and returning to Miami on Sunday.

It was to be a second honeymoon, a rejuvenation of our
marriage and, I agreed, it needed it. I had been working
about twelve hours a day, seven days a week prior to the
tanking of the economy in the fall and then it had changed
to eighteen hours. My business is very dependent upon the
economy and, to a large extent, the stock market as I have
much of my investors' money tied up in stocks. Collabora-
tively, we had done very well until this past fall when things
started to fall apart.

And then, I thought, Elise had brought up the cruise
idea. I had been slightly distraught over what was happening to my clients' funds. About one-third of them were retired and counting on the income to supplement their pen-
sions or social security, although a few of them were totally
dependent on the return. My silent investors weren't and I
knew that I was just one of many people laundering their
money.

And that brought another memory to the front of my
brain. About a week before Elise brought up the idea of the
cruise and just a short number of days after things started to
go south in the stock market, I had told her about the off-

shore account. Well, one offshore account, the only one that was in my name, although that would be difficult to find out. It contained about fifteen million dollars and was a combination of skimming from my silent partners and my cut of the profits from their "investments" which, for the most part, could never show up on my books. The only thing that did show up there was their legitimate investments in case the business was ever audited ... oops, which could be now.

Bringing outside authorities in when you are doing something not on the up and up – okay, illegal – is not something that one wants to do. Consider the case of Marcus Schrenker, an Indianapolis man who was under investigation. It began in January 2008 when The Indiana Department of Insurance filed a complaint against Schrenker. Seven investors claimed his actions lost a quarter million in assets because of high fees to switch annuities, a bit of knowledge he avoided telling them about. With that pressure, things began to fall apart.

In December 2008, his wife filed for divorce. The Indiana Securities Division obtained a Temporary Injunction, freezing Schrenker's personal and business assets, his Indiana state financial adviser's license expired and his home was searched for evidence of possible securities violations. At that point, Schrenker must have finally realized what was happening and thought it was time to head south, which is what he did.

He got into his plane and filed a flight plan for Destin, Florida, which was not totally unusual because he flew to Florida frequently. Near Huntsville, Alabama, he reported that turbulence had imploded one of his windshields and cut him severely. With the plane on autopilot, he bailed out. The plane flew on crashing more than 200 miles further on in a swamp in the Florida panhandle. When the wreckage was found and searched there was no sign of blood or a blown out windshield. During the plane's pilotless flight, military jets had intercepted it and had noticed the door ajar.

Police in Childersburg, Alabama, found a man wearing pilot's goggles who told them he had been in a canoeing accident and was wet enough to prove it. He was taken to a local hotel and checked in using an alias as it turned out. By the time the police learned of the crash and the resulting search for him, he had disappeared. It appeared that he had a motorcycle stored in the area and had used that to escape. He was found later in a tent in a Florida campground where he had apparently attempted suicide by slitting his wrists.

There is no telling what an audit of my business will bring – but nothing that bad. I had never stiffed any of my clients – well, make that my legitimate clients.

CHAPTER 21

Something on the TV in the KLM waiting area caught my attention. It was a CNN "breaking story."

> *CNN has talked to one of Stuart Andrews's former clients Mike Mullins (on camera): "I took my money away from Andrews Investment Management because I thought there was something funny going on. Returns hadn't been as good as in the past and I was suspicious."*

Of course returns hadn't been as good. Nobody's had. You got your money didn't you, and that was the question the CNN reporter asked.

> *Mullins: "Yes, I did but I don't know what would have happened if I had waited until now."*

You would probably have had less money because of the market downturn but then that happened to everyone.

> CNN: *"What did you do with your money?'*
> *Mullins (somewhat chagrined): "I moved it to Merrill-Lynch."*
> Great choice, Mike.
> CNN: *"And did you do any better?"*
> *Mullins (shaking his head): "No, but it was safer."*

*The reporter looked at Mullins queru-
lously.*

*CNN: " Safer? How did last week's
Merrill-Lynch announcement affect you?"*

*Mullins: "Well, in the whole shuffle, I
lost a bundle."*

CNN: "How much?"

*Mullins: "About half since I moved it
to Merrill Lynch."*

*CNN: "So how much you would you
have lost if you had kept it with Stuart Andrews?"*

Mullins didn't answer.

CNN: "How much?"

*Mullins mumbling: "Less than that,
but ..."*

*CNN: "So that was safer. Thank you,
Mr. Mullins." (Turning to the camera)
"And that is the story from one of Stuart
Andrew's former investors. He lost some
money in the downturn just as everyone
has. As of yet, there is nothing to indicate
that Stuart Andrews has done anything
wrong. However, there are still indications that Andrews Investment Management will come under closer scrutiny in the
next few weeks."*

In a way, I felt sorry for Mike. He was probably hoping
that he could make some money on talk shows but the CNN
report took the wind out of his sails. I felt good at that point
and wondered what the morrow would bring. I was certain
that some of my other individual clients would speak out as
they were certainly as concerned as Mike was. They were
probably wondering if my business was another Ponzi
scheme.

That fraudulent investment scam was named after Charles Ponzi, an Italian immigrant to the United States in 1903, but the origin can be traced back to *Little Dorrit,* an 1857 novel by Charles Dickens. Ponzi's scheme involved using the price differential in international reply coupons for postage stamps. His operation took in so much money that it was the first to become known throughout the United States.

The idea of the scheme is that the perpetrator uses the investor's own money or that from subsequent investors to pay the returns.
Envision an inverted pyramid
with the late investors at the
top, and the initial
investors at the
bottom.

A well-conducted Ponzi scheme can earn the original investors and the perpetrator huge sums but at some point it will collapse as one of the following three things will happen:

1. The perpetrator will go south taking all the existing proceeds with him/her;

2. Investment will slow, the perpetrator will have difficulty paying the promised returns, and the scheme will collapse under its own weight;

3. The perpetrator will be unable to validate his transactions when asked to either by his investors or some legal authority.

Probably the most infamous Ponzi scheme is that committed by Bernie Madoff's company Bernard L. Madoff Investment Securities LLC ("BMIS"). In 1960, BMIS provided both trading and market activities for brokers, banks, and financial institutions. During the past two decades or so, Madoff and BMIS expanded to providing investment advice to well-heeled clients including individuals, institutions, schools, and charities. Nobody seemed to question his unbe-lievable double-digit returns until the inevitable started to happen: in the fall of 2008, investment slowed.

And then Madoff made his mistake – he admitted to someone that his investment operation was a scam. Not on-ly did he admit it but he also told his two sons. They in turn reported this to the authorities on the evening of December 10, 2008, and the FBI arrested Madoff the next day.

What was the cost of his scheme to his investors? Fifty billion dollars! Madoff, age seventy, will do time, a lot of time, several lifetimes of time. If for some quirky reason he gets out, my guess is that he will go south because rumors have it that he has a lot of money stashed off shore. If it had been me, I would have gone south when it started to col-lapse and to hell with the investors.

My thoughts were interrupted by the call to board first class, business class, passengers needing assistance, people traveling with small children, … the usual announcement. I collected my belongings, got out my boarding card and joined the queue.

CHAPTER 22

I settled myself in my business class seat, happily noting that no one was sitting next to me. I had chosen business class because I didn't want to mingle with the tourists and be rude by ignoring my seatmates. I had discovered that it's a bit easier to do that in business class, at least on most flights, but then this one was leaving a vacation Mecca. I accepted a glass of champagne and continued my musing. Under the circumstances, I figured that my case was going to be most akin to that of Sir Allen Stanford.

No, I am not knighted but we both hold dual citizenships, his other being a citizen of Antigua and Barbuda and he is the first American to be knighted by that Commonwealth nation. Reports state that he is America's 205th richest man. Hmm, not even in the top one hundred.

In early 2009, he became the target of fraud investigations and SEC charged him with multiple violations of U.S. securities laws involving eight billion dollars in Certificates of Deposit. It had the ring of a Ponzi scheme, although that has been denied. The FBI raided his offices in Houston, Memphis, and Tupelo, Mississippi. Stanford's operations had been under investigation since 2008 by the FBI and other agencies for possible money laundering for Mexico's Gulf Cartel. That's close to home.

A federal judge ordered that he must surrender his passport and his assets and the company assets were frozen and placed into receivership. He tried to flee the country using a private jet company, paying by credit card, but the company would only accept a wire transfer. He was located by the FBI in Fredericksburg, Virginia, at his girlfriend's house, served with Summons and Complaint filed by the SEC and surrendered his passport. One would have thought that with all his money he would have had his own jet and been able to get away without all the hassle.

I suspect that my own assets will be frozen and my company Andrews Investment Management placed in receivership. When I founded my company twenty odd years ago, my partner at the time and I had given considerable thought to the name. We had just parted company with the Navy after serving our required four years having our college education at Cornell paid for by virtue of our Naval Reserve Officer Training Corps scholarships. I had begun to dabble in the stock market, as much as my pay had permitted, and had done well enough to figure that I could make a living at it, but had enough of working for someone else. Alan had not done as well as I had, and that was the reason that the company had my name. Because it was a partnership in name only we had thought about Andrews Investment Group but "AIG" was already taken – thank God for that in the present circumstances – and AIM had more opportunities: "Your financial security is our AIM." The partnership worked well although Alan lasted only five years and then left to pursue other ventures. I haven't heard from him in over ten years.

If receivership was in the future of AIM, I wasn't too worried. It simply meant that a court-appointed official would take charge of the company pending future litigation. During that time my books would be audited since they would not accept the audits made yearly by my own selected firm. It wouldn't matter because the firm I used was very well respected and they had never found anything untoward. All that was carefully handled by an offshore company and any link between that and me would be extremely difficult to trace. I doubted that there would be cause to look further – my accounts were completely above board. Freezing my funds of course would not freeze the fifteen million that I felt Elise wanted, again that was not attached to my company.

My clients would suffer during this time, unless they were quick enough to get the funds out before that happened, but who knew how long it would be. It would most likely depend upon how many individuals such as Mike Mullins would step forward and claim improprieties.

I couldn't worry about that now. It was all out of my hands. After all, Stuart Andrews was dead. My main concern now was to get my alter persona to disappear also. In Amsterdam, I hoped to get some fake ID and use that to completely vanish if I haven't already. I turned my face to the dark window and stared out into the nothingness wondering what tomorrow would bring. For now it is "Second star to the right, and straight on till morning."

CHAPTER 23

At 7:00 in the morning, Charles deGaulle Airport is already a bustling place. I had fallen asleep and was awakened by a stewardess as the plane was preparing to land. Somehow, we were arriving late and I was hustling to make my connection. Not having any luggage certainly helped and I breezed through passport control and then customs way ahead of the crowd. As I was making my way to the gate for my flight to Amsterdam, a story on a television monitor caught my attention.

> *...forty-eight hours the search for financial guru Stuart Andrews (Miami, USA) was called off. Officials said that there was no trace of the missing man and chances of his surviving more than twenty-four hours with no flotation devices are miniscule. It is believed that his disappearance is just another of the many shipboard suicides that have plagued the cruise line industry.*
> *Overboard Ship Deaths – Information by www.cruisebruise.com*

Deaths by Cruise Lines

American Classic Voyages	*1*
Carnival Cruise Lines	*33 (2 couples)*
Casino Cruises	*1*
Celebrity Cruise Lines	*5*
Costa Cruises	*2*
Crystal Cruise Line	*1*
Cunard Cruise Line	*6*

Discovery Cruise Line	*1*
Eastern Cruise Line (Admiral)	*1*
Holland America Cruise Line	*6*
Hornblower Cruises	*1*
Island Cruises	*1*
Norwegian Cruise Line	*6*
Norwegian Costal Cruises	*1*
Ocean Cruise Holidays – Travelscope	*1*
Oceanwide Expeditions	*1*
P&O	*8*
Princess Cruise Lines	*3*
Radisson Seven Seas	*1*
Royal Caribbean Cruise Lines	*14*
Scandinavian World Cruises	*3*
Silja Line	*1*
Silver Sea	*1*
Spirit Cruises	*1*
Star Cruises	*2*
Sundance Cruises	*1*
US Lines	*1*
Washington Ferries	*1*
Windward Isles Sailing Ship Company	*1*

Cruise Line Deaths by Years

1984	*1*
1987	*2*
1988	*1*
1997	*1*
1998	*4*
1999	*2*

2000	*4*
2001	*6*
2002	*2*
2003	*4*
2004	*8*
2005	*8*
2006	*12*
2007	*1*
2008	*4*
2009	*2*

Many of these cruise line disappearances can definitely be classified as suicides. Such is the case of a 90 year-old man and his 79 year-old wife:

When the Carnival Paradise embarked upon a five day Mexican Cruise on Monday, January 12, 2008 from Long Beach, California, an elderly, married couple from Southern California was on the ship. When it returned around noon on Friday, the couple was missing.

The missing couple was last seen was on Tuesday, January 13th. Carnival says the couple's cabin door was double locked from the inside with a "do not disturb" sign on the handle. The couple's personal belongings remained inside the cabin and the door leading from the cabin to the balcony was unlocked.

However, some of the disappearances seem suspicious:

On the last night of a West Coast cruise from Los Angeles, a woman had gone to play bingo, usually arriving early at games to get a good seat. However this night she hadn't shown up and her father went to search for her. During his search, he learned that her handbag had been found on the deck and she had been paged in order to return it to her. The bag, a small black, beaded evening bag, an overturned drink glass, and scattered papers had been discovered alongside the railing. Additionally, a security camera monitoring the deck had been covered with paper. Spots of blood and beads from her purse were found on deck near the purse, an indication that a struggle had occurred. A family member stated that a man had been harassing the woman aboard ship and that security had been notified but she had declined assistance.

Then there are the unsubstantiated stories:

A man who had taken his entire family on a cruise gathered them together for breakfast their last morning at sea. At the end of the meal he had kissed them all and left the dining room. He was never seen again.

But the reason for the disappearance of Stuart Andrews remains unresolved.

CHAPTER 24

The streets of Amsterdam were wet from an early morning rain. I had taken the train from Schiphol to the Amsterdam Centraal Station and checked my carry-on in one of the lockers. Then I set out to see if I could find the local service in which I was interested. Fifteen years ago when I used the services to get some fake ID "just in case", it had been arranged through a contact of my offshore banker, no questions asked. Now I was hoping that I could make the contact on my own, since I wanted no trace. The ID that I had gotten then in the name of "Josef Viljoen" was that of an Afrikaan, a Dutch émigré to South Africa. I had never used it and, of course, it was now out of date and nonrenewable. However, the debit card was still valid and it had been in the packet my banker had sent me on St. Nantes.

However, before I went in search of my identity, I first needed to find myself some new clothes. I was dressed in the clothes I had purchased in St. Nantes and wanted to get something looking a little more European and not quite so Caribbean tourist. I had spent several hours on St. Martin with my new laptop searching out locations in Amsterdam. The Internet is a wonderful tool and I don't how people survived without it. Well, they had so it wasn't crucial to survival. Yes, it was. It was absolutely crucial to my survival.

Leaving the Centraal Station, I headed up Damrak Straat toward Dam Square with a mental map of where I wanted to go. I was armed with credit cards and Euros from St. Nantes so money was not going to be a problem. Neither was the language – English was spoken everywhere. You can't tell it from all the cafes, bars and stores, but Damrak was a canal before most of it had been filled in

1672. A small section of it remains serving as a marina. It is here, one of many places, that tourists board "glass" covered canal boats for a tour of Amsterdam's canals. In these boats, the seats are just below water level with a low glass-covered top so that they can fit under the many bridges that cross the canals.

Damrak Straat proceeds straight from the Centraal Station to the Dam Square where the original dam was in the river Amstel and from which the city got its name "Amsteldam." "Rak" is the old Dutch term for a straight canal or river. Even at this early hour, tourists crowded the streets, frequenting the souvenir shops, moneychangers, or standing in front of bars with topless waitresses to catch a view, with the more adventuresome venturing inside for a glass of Amstel beer. For the not so adventurous, it is probably a Bud Light.

On the other side of the Damrak are residences that back up to the water – built that way to facilitate the off loading of cargo. As tourists walk down the side streets, where many original houses still stand, they will notice that the houses are leaning forward and at the top there is a protruding beam, possibly with a pulley still hanging from it. The houses are narrow in front because the property taxes were based upon frontage and thus the stairways are narrow. In order to get large pieces of furniture to the upper levels, they had to be hauled up the outside and the slant of the façade was to keep the cargo from smashing into the building's front.

Just past the Damrak Harbor and on the same side of the street is a huge colossus housing the Amsterdam Stock Market. On a prior visit, I had actually been on the floor but this time the stock market held no interest for me.

Tourists in search of the more infamous of Amsterdam's sights will turn left just past the Damrak Harbor and before the stock market and wander basically east a few blocks past sex shops and porn shows and find one of Amsterdam's three Red Light Districts. If you come upon it unaware, you will begin to wonder what the red neon lights on the buildings mean and when you take a look you will see that the front of each building is a floor to ceiling plate glass window and a door.

In the window (unless she is otherwise occupied) will be one of the "ladies of the evening," although they are there 24/7. They work in three eight-hour shifts and pay rent based on the time of day. In the daytime you will generally find the least attractive of these "ladies" – the most attractive work the night hours. If a person is interested in purchasing some time with the window's inhabitant, she will come to the door and prices are explained and negotiations begun. When a mutually satisfactory arrangement is made, the client enters the door and joins the "lady" in the bedroom behind the window display, hoping that his choice will prove satisfactory to him. At least this was the way it was explained to me.

Photography is prohibited and the ill-informed will potentially lose a camera or memory chip if spotted by one of the protectors. However, there are canal boat tours that take one past the end of the street and from there it is possible to take and keep a picture. I know because I have the picture to prove it.

At the Dam Square, I turned left and walked several blocks crossing three canals to Nieuwe Hoogstraat to Zipper, one of the best used clothing stores in the city. I spent nearly an hour buying the right clothes to fit my needs and desired style. Then, carrying my purchases, I proceeded in the same direction down the Mulderstraat to Plantage Straat and the hair salon I had chosen simply because it was the nearest. Along the way I stopped in one of the many sidewalk coffee houses for some refreshment and used the facilities to make a quick change of clothes.

I explained to the girl who greeted me in the hair salon that I had recently undergone the first of several chemotherapy sessions and had started to lose my hair (explained by the doo-rag). I wanted a wig to hide that fact and cheer me up. She helped me find one that would work (I always wanted to have dread locks) and showed to me how to put it on. That done satisfactorily, I headed back to the Centraal Station walking as far as Nieuwmarkt where I took the metro as I was beginning to wear out. Getting my carry-on out of the locker, I stowed my old clothes and the portion of my purchases that could fit. Carrying the rest in a bag I walked to a small hotel, secured a room, and set out in search of my new identity.

CHAPTER 25

The path to my "Identity Broker" took me through the Red Light District in mid-afternoon. Then I crossed the Oudezijds Voorburgwal canal and turned right. A few blocks later, I recognized the storefront housing a small bookstore. It hadn't changed. I entered the bookstore and started browsing because I was not alone. A little old man completed his purchase chatting amiably (I guess) with the sales clerk/proprietor and then turned to leave. With his purchase in one hand and cane in the other, he paused momentarily at the door. As I was near, I stepped over and opened the door.

"Dank u," he said and I simply nodded. Languages have never been my forte.

Now that's another one for you. A personal gripe instilled in me by my mother who knew the English Language better than most English teachers that I have had. If one is talking about music then it is forte, a two-syllable word "for•te" coming from Italian and is a music dynamic meaning "loudly" or "strongly." However, in other usage it is a one-syllable word "fort" coming from the French "fort" meaning "strength." To hear a sports broadcaster saying, "Tackling has never been his for•te" drives me up a wall.

"Kan ik jou helpen?" asked the clerk.

It was enough like English that I understood.

"I'm sorry, I don't speak Dutch," I replied.

"Then, can I help you," said the clerk with a smile.

"I hope so. I need the services of Pieter Devenpeck."

The clerk stared at me. "I don't know of a Pieter Devenpeck."

"He was here about 15 years ago. He helped me ... uh, find myself." I felt stupid but knew that I couldn't come right out and say, "I need some fake id."

"I have worked here for five years, and there has been no Pieter Devenpeck. There has been no Pieter at all," responded the clerk.

"Do you know anyone who offers the same services?" I was fishing but awash in a sea of uncertainty.

"I don't know what services he offered. Can you explain?"

In for a dime, in for a dollar. "I need new identity papers."

The clerk shook his head.

"I am sorry but that is something that the government handles. You will have to go ..."

"I can't," I said completely frustrated. "Look, can I leave a note ... no, forget it. I am sorry to have bothered you."

"I am sorry I couldn't help, Mr. ..."

"Viljoen. Josef Viljoen. Thank you." I turned and left.

Outside I walked to the canal and stood looking at the water with debris floating in it. A horn sounded and I looked up to see a canal boat passing under a bridge. Despite the fact that the canals are flushed daily, there is an amazing amount of debris that accumulates. In fact, at least so I was told, some of the boats, which line the sides of the canal and are lived in, do not have their toilet facilities self-contained but empty into the canal.

I don't know how long I stood there at a loss of what to do. My one hope had been dashed. Admittedly, fifteen years is a long time to expect an identity supplier to remain in business. I couldn't go back to the banker who originally referred me to Pieter Devenpeck (if that was even his name) because he is the banker who handles the account that Elise knows about and he knows me as Stuart Andrews, who is dead. I couldn't risk anyone knowing or even suspecting that I hadn't died over the side of the cruise ship or the fishing boat, depending on who the person was.

Dejectedly, I walked back toward the Damrak not knowing which way to turn. My only hope was that one of

Dawoh Mbayo's bankers could be of some help. It was too late to do anything about that now. The sun was starting to set and in the Red Light District the red lights were definitely visible and the crowd was beginning to pick up, as was the quality of the girls. The shifts must have changed.

I passed a café with a sign emblazoned "Coffee House" and felt that a cuppa might cheer me up. A drink would have been better but I hadn't eaten any lunch and would have to get some food in my stomach before I would try liquor.

As I entered the café, my senses were smacked with a strange aroma. *What the ...,* I thought and then I knew. Of course. It was Mary Jane. Coffee houses in Amsterdam are known as cannabis cafés and offer hashish and marijuana. There are web pages that tell you where the best cafés are and where there are shops selling weed, psychedelics, growing kits and everything hemp.

*Well,*I thought, *I need a pick me up. Maybe this will do it.*

CHAPTER 26

"Excuse me, sir. Are you all right?"

I looked up from the coffee I had been staring at and saw the clerk from the bookstore.

"Yes, I ..."

He pulled out a chair and sat down across from me.

"I saw you stand by the canal after you left the store. You didn't act correct. You walk away sad. I was afraid you would ..."

"No, no. It's just that I was hoping ... but you know."

He nodded in understanding. "I close the store for a few minutes and follow you. I hope that is okay?"

I nodded. Homosexuality is very much in the open in Amsterdam. I didn't think this was the case however.

"You are in some trouble, yes?" he continued.

I nodded. "Can I buy you a cup of coffee?"

"No, I must return to the store. My boss will be upset if it is close long."

He reached across the table and took my hand in a farewell gesture as he rose to leave.

"I just wanted to be certain that you were not ... that you were okay. Varwel."

He turned and left the café. As the door closed behind him, I looked at what remained behind in my hand. It was a tiny folded piece of paper. Obviously it wasn't something that he could give to me openly. I finished my coffee and left. I put the paper unopened into my pocket as though I was getting something but brought nothing out, then I put my other hand in a pocket as though I was searching for something. I smiled and pulled my hand out.

I felt better now even not knowing what was on the paper. Something had happened but I didn't know what.

Maybe it was a pickup attempt but I didn't think so. He just didn't have that look to him.

In the seclusion of my hotel room I opened the piece of paper. On it was written

Raamsteeg 3

1030

As the 24-hour clock is used to tell time in much of Europe, I knew that meant tomorrow morning. A meet? I got out the map I had picked up at the tourist information center in the Centraal Station that morning. Raamsteeg was a small narrow street several blocks from the Dam Square and on the Singel Canal.

My hopes raised after being dashed earlier, I ripped the paper into tiny pieces and flushed them down the toilet. Then I went out to get something to eat.

CHAPTER 27

I slept well and was up early as I always am and have been all my life. Even when I took a day off, I was up early. I checked out of the hotel and walked toward my goal on the back streets until I found another small hotel. I explained that I had just arrived in Amsterdam and needed a place to stay for one night. They would have a vacancy later in the day, so I registered and paid in cash as I had for the other hotel and stored my belongings for a small price. Afterward, on the way to scout out the designated spot, I picked up a cup of coffee and a Berliner, which is a European pastry. JFK's "Ich bin ein Berliner" works well for fans or foes.

Raamsteeg is in fact more of an alley than a street and number 3 is The Cracked Kettle (Gekraakte Ketel) – a wine and beer store. I walked by looking in the window and then went and walked along the Singel enjoying the crisp air and killing time until 1030.

I entered The Cracked Kettle and browsed waiting to be contacted.

"Can I help you?" A clerk asked.

"I don't know," I replied. "I think I am supposed to meet someone."

"Mr. Viljoen?"

"Yes."

"We have a package for you. Just a minute."

The clerk returned in a minute with a paper bag taped shut and handed it to me.

"Enjoy," he said and turned away to help another customer.

I walked out and found a bench along the canal. The bag was heavy and clinked as I walked. I opened it and found two bottles of Amstel Bock and something else in the bottom of the bag. A cell phone, one of those inexpensive ones you can pick up almost anywhere and use with a pre-paid minutes card.

I turned the phone on and read "One missed call" on the screen. I pressed the talk button and saw the calling number. I returned the call.

The voice on the other end said, "What is the number?"

The number? I looked at the phone to see how to find its number when something from the recesses of my mind chimed in. Years ago when I had come to Amsterdam to get my identity papers, I had been given an 8-digit number to use as identification. What was it? I thought for a moment ... whoever was on the other end of the conversation waited patiently.

"8 - 2 - 5 - 7 - 4 - 3 - 6 - 1. No – 1 - 6. 8 - 2 - 5 – 7 - 4 - 3 - 1 - 6. "

"You will be contacted." And the connection was broken.

Curiousier and curiousier, I thought.

There was nothing to do but wait so I walked and waited.

And waited and walked.

And walked and waited.

As I walked, the smell of "Vlaamse frites" (French fries) heightened my appetite and I finally stopped at a store to get a paper cone-full topped with mayonnaise, which is one of the ways they are eaten in the Netherlands. No catsup to be seen, at least in this store. There were other choices offered: curry sauce, garlic sauce, tartar sauce, chili sauce, ranch dressing, feta cheese, gravy. But in this store – no catsup.

With the cone in one hand, a couple of French fries on the plastic fork in the other and my mouth full, the expected happened – the cell phone rang. Putting the fries back into the cone and trying to chew what was in my mouth I fumbled in my pocket for the phone. Answering, I listened.

"Your book order is in."

The connection was broken. I stood there momentarily bewildered but then I understood. As I was putting the phone back into my pocket I heard a passer-by say, "Trash the phone."

I turned to see who it was but it could have been any of five different people. Turning the phone off, I put it into my pocket and quickly finished the fries. Putting the phone in the cone and crumbling it up I deposited it into a trash receptacle. I had done the same with the phone I had purchased in St. Nantes while I was walking through Charles de Gaulle although in that case I had taken the phone apart in several pieces and left them in various trash receptacles.

After a few steps, I glanced back and saw a woman putting some trash in the receptacle and retrieving the crumpled cone. With not a look at anyone, she put it into her shopping bag and walked away in the opposite direction. I turned and headed for the bookstore.

CHAPTER 28

The bell tinkled as I entered the store and the clerk looked up and smiled. "Good day, Mr. Viljoen. We have the book you wanted. That will be four Euros."

I paid him and accepted the bag he handed me and left the store followed by his cheery "Varwel."

Outside I walked several blocks before I looked at the book in the bag. I judged by the pictures in the book that it was a child's book about a girl's life on the canal. There was no note of any kind that I could find by quickly leafing through it. I didn't want to be conspicuous by shaking it to see if anything fell out. Several of the pages had childish crayon scribbling but the only readable portion was inside the front page. I could read "Allna Metternich, 9 Herengracht" in a child's handwriting.

I found the Herengracht canal on the map and headed for it as straight as I could, passing through the Dam Square on the way. I was carrying the book in my hand as I walked down Herengracht looking for number 9.

"Are you looking for someone?" a cheery voice asked.

I turned toward the canal and saw the pretty brunette who had taken my phone out of the trash standing on the deck of a canal houseboat. The hull was painted a dark blue and the cabin white with the same blue trim. Blue and white curtains were visible at the windows and window flower boxes were teeming with red, white and yellow tulips, which for the time of year I assumed to be artificial.

"Yes," I said holding the book up, "I have a book to return."

"Ah, that's my daughter's book. Please come aboard."

I did so and she pointed to the cabin's door. "She's below. Why don't you take it to her?"

I had to stoop to get through the door and was stopped rather abruptly by a man about the same height as me but twenty to thirty pounds heavier. He looked vaguely familiar as though I may have seen him today – I was certain that I had been watched today since I had gotten the phone, if not yesterday since my first visit to the bookstore. His hand was out and I gave him the book that he promptly set down.

"Please put your arms out. I must search."

I had no choice but to comply and he quickly but authoritatively patted me down, motioned to me to turn around and did the same. I then turned around and he motioned me to proceed. After I had passed him, he went topside and closed the door behind him. I found myself in a small sitting room with two chairs, one of them occupied by a white-haired elderly man I thought I recognized as "Pieter Devenpeck."

"It's nice of you to see me," I said.

He motioned me to sit down.

"I may be able to help you but I am not in the business any longer. Just so you understand. What is it you need?"

I told him that I needed two passports and accompanying documentation: One South African in the name of Josef Viljoen and another American in any given name. I could have just gone with the South African one but then I may be fingerprinted if I entered the United States legally which I thought I would have to do.

He nodded and told me that would be fifty thousand Euros each. The sum was a good deal more than those many years ago and I mentioned that.

He shrugged and said that passports were much more difficult to get nowadays and it was that or nothing.

I wasn't going to carry that much around with me but knew that there was a bank in Amsterdam through which I could access my account on St. Nantes.

"I have to get money from a bank," I said.

"Of course, you will make arrangements to get the money but we will go ahead with the preparation of your documents."

He pounded on a coffee table with his cup and the young man came into the cabin. He went straight to a cupboard and pulled out a Polaroid that he used to take several pictures of me both with and without my dreadlocks wig. When they had developed he showed them to me and I nodded my acceptance. The old man handed him a slip of paper on which he had written my request and told him about the money, at least that is what I thought he said. The young man went out on deck and came back a few minutes later. He went to a closet and brought out a green backpack.

"Buy a backpack like this – any color, this size should hold the money – and put the money in it. When you have the money go to the coffee house where Dieter talked to you at 1430. If you are not going to be able to get the money that day, don't go the coffee shop but go to the Cracked Kettle in morgen and buy two bottles of beer."

I assumed Dieter was the clerk from the bookstore.

"Put the backpack on the floor by your feet. It will be taken and replaced by another. The day after you leave the money, go to the Cracked Kettle in morgen and wait ten or fifteen minutes for someone to contact you. If no one gives you anything, leave and come back next day. The day you get something, go to the bookstore in the afternoon. Is this klar?"

I said that it was and was told to leave.

"Thank you," I said to Pieter and he waved dismissively.

As I exited through the doorway, I noticed that there were many wires running up both sides and across the top. I figured that they probably somehow scanned me for a wire and may have even done something to interfere with any eavesdropping.

The woman was nowhere to be seen as I climbed back onto solid ground. Minutes later, as I crossed the bridge headed back toward the Dam, I saw her standing looking over the railing at the houseboat. No doubt she was watching for anyone tailing me. I also had no doubt that if I would return to the houseboat I would find none of the people I had seen there.

CHAPTER 29

Four days later, Dawoh Mbayo went through passport control at Schiphol and caught a flight to Paris. He was unbejeweled, had a beard, his hair was in dreadlocks and he was wearing used clothes bought in Amsterdam. In Paris he walked into a men's restroom with his carry-on and never came out. He was called to board his flight to Sierra Leone several times but never showed. His small bag came out of the restroom carried by Josef Viljoen, a black man with relatively short hair, a shorter beard and sporting a large diamond in his left ear. He was wearing clothes for the warm weather in the islands and boarded a flight to Nassau, Bahamas. All this would have been visible on Charles de Gaulle's security cameras if anyone cared, but thankfully they didn't. Passengers not showing for flights are routine.

It had taken two days to get the money. Immediately upon leaving the canal boat I had gone to a store near the Dam and purchased a blue backpack of the size that had been indicated. Then I went back to the Herengracht Canal where I had seen an office of the BNP Paribas that I believed was associated with my bank in St. Nantes as Paribas originates from: Banque de Paris et des Pays-Bas. I was correct and I was able to access the account but was told that a withdrawal of that magnitude required two days to assemble the cash.

As I had been told, the next morning I went to The Cracked Kettle and purchased two bottles of beer, easily done as they claim to have over five hundred kinds of beer. I spent the remainder of that day walking around the city.

The next day I collected the money at 1400 and proceeded to the coffee house. I chose a table in a corner and set the bag down beside me. Soon a boisterous group of college students, all with backpacks, came in and sat at the table next to mine. Something brushed my leg and I ignored it. Soon I finished my coffee and picked up my noticeably heavier backpack. Back in my hotel room, I found that the bag was filled with textbooks. Now I had another day to kill.

I had changed hotel rooms every day and had remained fastidious about wiping all surfaces I might have touched before I checked out. Once a day, I had taken my laptop to a coffee house or other business that provided Wifi and had checked the news. Stuart Andrews's disappearance had quickly vanished from the news. Andrews Investment Management had been placed in receivership while the SEC conducted an audit, despite the fact that many of my investors had come forward asserting that their investments had been properly handled. There were a sufficient number who, like Mike Mullins, felt that there was something illegal with their investments. I was very self-assured that the audit would turn up nothing.

I had continued my fitness regimen taking long walks, running, renting a bike and riding on the numerous bike paths in the city. I also found a gym where I could do a little weight training. I could tell that I was beginning to tone up.

The morning of the third day, I had gone to the Cracked Kettle and browsed through the beers for a full twenty minutes, and although a sales clerk asked if I needed help, I shook my head and received nothing. The morning of the fourth day, after some ten minutes, a clerk asked if I was Mr. Viljoen and gave me a package containing a white wine from Austria. That afternoon I loaded the textbooks in the backpack and went to the bookstore.

"Ahh, Mr. Viljoen," Dieter greeted me as I entered. "Your book has arrived."

He placed a package on the counter and I picked it up setting the backpack on the floor.

"Any further charge?" I queried.

"No, it is full paid."

I thanked him and left the store, returning immediately to my hotel room. The passports and other documents were there as I requested. I secreted them in a computer bag I had purchased for my laptop and went in search of a Wifi hotspot, always easy to find in Amsterdam. I already knew flight schedules as I browsed them daily and quickly made reservations for Dawoh Mbayo to go home to Sierra Leone. Then I made reservations for Josef Viljoen to fly from Paris to the Bahamas.

And then I was ready to disappear like Frank Gruttadauria. He worked for Lehman Brothers in Cleveland, Ohio, and came up with an elaborate scheme to defraud his clients by sending them fake statements with transactions that never occurred and earnings that never existed. The money he skimmed was intended to be used in more profitable investments but in some ways it turned into a Ponzi scheme, in that part of the money was used to repay clients who wanted to withdraw funds that were no longer there. Most of the money was used for his personal purchases including a private jet, cars, and condominium shared with his girlfriend. He was estranged from his wife and both she and his girlfriend were forced to payback large sums of money when the scheme finally unraveled.

By all appearances he was a nice guy who attended his children's sporting events and parent-teacher conferences. He felt that students at Gilmour Academy, his high school alma mater, should learn about investments and set up a student investment program through an economics class. At his suggestion, all profit was donated to nonprofit groups of the students' choice. Wanting his children to have a good work ethic, he did not let his daughter have a cell phone and insisted that she work a part-time job when not involved in sports.

His scam lasted fifteen years and he was surprised that it lasted that long without getting caught. Every morning he could take the elevator from his office to the ground floor and buy coffee and bottled water. After finishing his coffee on the morning of January 11, 2002, he and his passport disappeared after leaving a letter confessing his scheme to the F.B.I. There was not a trace of him for a month and then, surprisingly, he turned himself in to the F.B.I.

Things being completed in Amsterdam and hopefully leaving no trace, it was time to return to the Caribbean and get on with payback.

Part III
The Weakest Link

CHAPTER 30

I had to admit overall Elise and Howard had come up with a pretty good plan to get rid of me. Officially I had disappeared some 500 miles away from where I was actually "killed." No search would ever have turned up my body. They were home free.

Almost. There were a couple of little problems – well, three that I could think of, and I had spent considerable time contemplating this.

First, there was Quentin, the fishing boat captain. Somehow he had been convinced that he needed to go along with the plan. A threat on his life or his family's lives could insure that at least for the time being. But for how long? What kind of ethics did he have to keep silent? Of course, what proof did he have? I appeared to have gotten back on the Caribbean Isle and sailed two days away before I vanished. Things like murder can eat at a person with any conscience at all. Did he have a conscience? I didn't know him well enough to know, so I had hired a person to find out. That was in progress, having been set up when I was in Amsterdam.

Second, there was Keith. He had been brought into it somehow – my guess was by Howard, and not after meeting him on the ship. I mean, after a couple of drinks to get acquainted, "Say, how would you like to go on a fishing trip in St. Nantes and help me knock off my brother-in-law?" No, that wouldn't work. He must have been in on it pretty much from the start. Probably a friend of Howard's who owed Howard a debt – a big debt. Or possibly he had a situation with which he needed help: "Look you help me kill my brother-in-law and I will help you kill your wife/girlfriend/lover." Shades of "Strangers on a Train"!

Alfred Hitchcock would love this. I also had someone working to find out about Keith.

Third, and this was something that they had no way of knowing, there was the problem of my silent investors. Those very ones who had earned me the fifteen million for which I had been killed. Elise didn't know about them. She just knew that I had been able to get the money from the business with no one the wiser – which was true. But the problem really was with the over twenty-five million that was currently in the process of being laundered. My death would probably cause my "friends" to write that off because they had been able to successfully launder close to a billion in the time we had worked together. But, and here is the crucial part, there is no body. For all they know, I faked my suicide and had gone off somewhere unknown with their twenty-five million. A fellow could live pretty well on that for quite a while.

That third part, the one that no one but my "friends" and I knew about, was the one that began to worry me as things began to settle down in Amsterdam. At first I had reasoned that all was well and nobody would come looking for me. But then I had begun to think more clearly and realized that there was this problem: With a bit of digging – and they would have the resources to do that – they would discover my other identity, Dawoh Mbayo. Then eventually they would discover that he was involved in the business overseas and that he apparently was quite alive having a bank account in St. Nantes, had flown from St. Nantes to Amsterdam and then to Paris where he seemed to have "disappeared." They were not likely to quit right there – not for twenty-five mil-lion.

So Elise and Howard had two problems: Quentin and Keith; and I had those plus my "friends" and Elise and How-ard. I had a plan, which if successful, would take care of all of these problems and leave me free and clear. Or at least as free and clear as I could possibly hope for.

First step was to take care of the weakest link – Quentin – and for that I needed a boat. A big enough boat would provide me a mobile base in the Caribbean from which to operate. That is the reason I was going to Nassau, Bahamas: to buy a yacht.

CHAPTER 31

While in Amsterdam, I had used the web to search the Caribbean area for yachts for sale. I found a boat at the East Bay Yacht Basin in Nassau, Bahamas, and that is the reason that I went there. It was a Hatteras 64 Motor Yacht that had been ordered and delivered. But in the meantime, the buyer had suffered a reversal of finances and needed to unload it quickly.

From the airport, I took a taxi to the boat basin where I met with Peter Hiller, who owned and operated the basin. We left my things in his office and walked to the slip where the yacht was docked. When I saw it I fell in love. I was not at that time a water person and, in truth, still am not. Oh, I knew how to swim because my father had made my ability to swim a requirement for getting a bicycle – no relation at all except he knew how important the ability to swim was. If I hadn't been able to swim when I got to Cornell, I would have had to take lessons because every N.R.O.T.C. midshipman had to pass a swimming test as a freshman. Not only was there a distance requirement (I can't remember how many laps but it was a struggle) but there was also the survival portion that, thankfully, Lieutenant Bruce had cajoled me through. That's not true, his urgings were in no way gentle. However, if it hadn't been for him I would not be here today – I would have drowned off the coast of St. Nantes.

We boarded at the stern – the only way to board easily. The 106-square-foot aft deck has a swim platform and a fiberglass stairwell provided quick access to the bridge. Gas-assisted cylinders lifted that stairwell for easy entrance to the engine room as well. Entry to the inside of the main deck was through a slider, three panels of which may be easily removed for an open-air feeling. The salon had two settees, large windows for viewing entertaining scenery, and a 37-inch flat-screen TV mounted under the galley counter top.

This version had a U-shaped galley and country kitchen reachable by a single step and a circular dinette with seating for six. Beyond this was the lower helm station. A ladder led from the kitchen to the flying bridge. The engine room was entered through a hatch hidden by the bridge stairway or through a door in the transom. Twin diesel engines permitted the yacht to cruise comfortably at 22 – 24 knots with a top-end of 26 – 28 knots. The master stateroom had a king-size bed with its head against one of two insulated bulkheads housing the fuel tank. This was located close to the center of buoyancy, greatly reducing engine room noise. There was a private bathroom – head – with, in this case, a shower and twin sinks. There was also a bow stateroom with a tapered queen berth with storage accessible by lifting the bed using pneumatic rams. All storage space in the living areas was cedar-lined. To port, were twin crisscross bunks perfect for young people or crewmembers. A shared head was forward. As this was going to be my home for a while when I wasn't travelling, it was perfect for my needs.

I explained to Peter Hiller my requirements in addition to the yacht and we quickly reached an agreement. So within three hours of landing in Nassau, I was owner of a 64-foot Hatteras yacht that I immediately christened "ZÀKPA."

Strange name? Not if you speak Bassa, a language spoken in Liberia, formerly called the Grain Coast of West Africa. Also there are approximately 5000 citizens of Sierra Leone who speak Bassa and one of them was my paternal great-grandmother. In her honor I had sought out this language on the web and found a Bible language dictionary. There I found the verb "Zàkpa" which means "to avenge." Actually the verb "to avenge" or "to repay" is two words "Zà kpa" but the one word works better as a boat's name and is easier for someone to figure out how to pronounce it. This was the closest I could come to "Payback" and I basically wanted to hide the name. To those who ask, I would answer, "Seeker."

CHAPTER 32

For a non-sailor getting to know how to run and maintain a yacht takes a lot of learning. Yes, I *was* in the Navy for four years, putting in the time as required by my N.R.O.T.C. scholarship that paid for my education. But you don't learn all the ins and outs of yachts doing that.

Peter Hiller had provided me with a quite able teacher: Joaquin Gagalac. Filipino in origin, Joaquin was five feet ten inches and weighed about 170 pounds. He had black hair and eyes and a tan skin color. He told me that after high school he had an urge to see the world and had worked on cruise ships in the kitchen for five years. Tiring of being trapped in a windowless environment for most of the time, he had quit that business four years before. His contract had ended when his ship docked in Nassau, Bahamas, and he had gotten a job with East Bay Yacht Basin. A fast learner with prior knowledge of boats – his father was a fisherman in the Philippines – he had become a valuable employee.

For the first three days, we had spent a lot of time studying the engines and their basic maintenance as well as the maintenance of other parts of the ship. Who knew there was so much to learn? How to empty the sewage tanks, how to keep them functioning properly, how to locate and fix sewage blockages, how to get fresh water into the tanks. There was a lot to understand.

In the course of getting to know the boat, I was also learning boating safety, the rules of the waterways. Among other finds, I discovered that the old cannonball float I had used to get rid of my shoes is now called H.E.L.P. for Heat Escape Lessening Posture. It is used when alone in the water to try to stay warm. I also learned to always have a float plan which is basically a boating flight plan you can leave with someone when you go out: when you are leaving, who is with you, where you are going, and when you're expected back. Also some helpful things like "Don't tie the anchor to the stern of the boat." Joaquin told me about four men in Florida who were out fishing on a reef and their anchor got stuck. So they tied the anchor rope to the stern and gunned the engine. The anchor didn't budge and the surge pulled the stern down and submerged it and the boat capsized. There were only three life jackets aboard and no communication devices; they were too far out for cell phones to work. By the time the Coast Guard was alerted and the boat found, there was only one survivor. Many lessons in that accident!

Then we actually went sailing for a few days. Well, there aren't any sails so we drove the yacht, learned to dock, set the anchor, etc.

I lived aboard during this time, while Joaquin had gone ashore to his own place at night. However, one day we went to San Salvador to see if I could anchor the boat and do what was necessary to go through customs, etc.

After dinner, Joaquin and I were sitting on the stern deck enjoying the kind of gorgeous sunset that you get in the islands and most likely anywhere on the water. I had come to know Joaquin fairly well over the past week and, knowing that I needed a crew, I began to feel him out.

"Do you like your job?"

"Yes, but I probably won't stay long because I want to travel. I have been saving my money and am getting close to what I need to travel for a while."

"What if you could do some traveling in the islands and earn some money at the same time?"

He looked at me. "Doing what?"

"Being the crew on this boat."

"Just me?"

"Just you and me for a while. I would pay you well."

"What's the catch?"

I laughed softly.

"Always the suspicious one. Actually there is a catch! A good friend of mine recently disappeared. Reports say that he committed suicide by jumping off a cruise ship in the southern Caribbean. However, I have reason to believe that he was killed either during the ship's visit to an island in the northern Caribbean or immediately after leaving that port.

"When he was in the northern Caribbean he was going to go on a fishing expedition with his brother-in-law and someone he met on the boat."

"How do you know all this?" questioned Joaquin.

"We were in email contact every day. We're best friends. Grew up together. We are … were like brothers. After the day of the fishing expedition there was no more email. Nothing until the news reported the suicide. "

I had thought this out in advance.

"Okay, why do you think the northern Caribbean and not the southern?"

"The news reports said that he was depressed but he wasn't. He was in great spirits and looking forward to the fishing expedition and the rest of the cruise. It was a welcome getaway with his wife as he had been working hard."

Most of that was true.

"You think that his … what … brother …?"

"Brother-in-law, the brother of his wife."

"You believe that his brother-in-law and this other guy killed him on the fishing boat?"

I nodded.

"Why would they do that?"

"I don't know for certain but I believe they did." Or tried to.

"And you think that this fishing person helped?"

"If that's what happened he had to or else he wouldn't still be alive."

"So what are you going to do?"

"I want to go to talk to the fishing guide and see if he had anything to do with the disappearance – discover what actually happen there."

"What if nothing happened? What if he says they caught fish and he got paid and … ."

"If that is the case then I will have to investigate further. This is just the first step but I have to make sure."

"What if he helped to kill your friend?"

"If he did that then he is lying about what happened and protecting the brother-in-law."

"So you are going to turn him in to the police?"

I shook my head. "If I did that, news would get out and his brother-in-law and anyone else involved would be warned and could get away."

Joaquin looked at me, stared at me straight in the eyes. "So you're going to … ."

"Yes, my friend deserves some payback … ."

He looked questioningly at me.

"My friend deserves revenge."

Joaquin thought for a moment.

Then he said, "Before I answer, I have to tell you something about myself."

CHAPTER 33

"You know that my father was a fisherman. In my junior year in high school, he was attacked and killed. The police called it a mugging and robbery but I knew that it wasn't. Two weeks before, my father had reported another fisherman to the authorities for illegal fishing practices. The incidents were investigated and the other fisherman was heavily fined.

"Although the report my father had filed was supposed to have been done anonymously, the other man made verbal threats against my father. Other than me, no one was around to hear them. A few days later my father was dead.

"I knew that I had to avenge his death. I started working out and studying martial arts. One of my teachers knew about knives and using them to kill. Two weeks before my graduation, the other fisherman's boat was found drifting with no one aboard and no sign of any violence."

"So," I said, feeling very Paul Harvey, "What's the other side of the story?"

Joaquin smiled, knowing that I would ask.

"Early that morning when he came down to his boat, I was waiting. He never knew I was there. I used an ice pick and there was no blood."

"Good teacher," I commented.

"Yes, he knew his killing." Joaquin smiled. "I took his boat out with my small fishing boat in tow alongside. No one saw or if they did, no one said anything. When we were at sea, I spread chum and when the sharks arrived, I dumped his body and the ice pick overboard and left the area. Further away I left his boat with some of the nets set out like he had been fishing. Then I left in my boat. I spent the rest of that day fishing. It was a good day for fishing. I sold most of my catch and took the rest home.

"Nobody ever questioned me about his disappearance. My mother never suspected as she had known nothing of the threats made to my father. He had not told her about reporting the other man's illegal fishing activities."

I was silent.

"I thought you needed to know," Joaquin said.

"I'm glad you did."

Joaquin smiled and with a mock salute said, "Okay, Captain, when do we get started?"

CHAPTER 34

"I don't trust that frog," Keith said. "We don't know anything about him. He could rat us out!"

"He won't," Howard said, putting his drink down on the table. They were sitting in Keith's condo in Northridge, Los Angeles County, air conditioning on although this early in the year it wasn't needed. Keith had done it to prevent eavesdropping. As though there is a reason for someone to listen, Howard had thought.

It was two weeks since their return from the ill-fated cruise. Stuart Andrews had been given up for dead and a memorial service had been held two days before. Other than the service, this was the first time the two friends had been together.

"He's got $10,000 with a promise of another $10,000 next year if he keeps his yap shut," Howard continued. "St. Nantes is an expensive island and a faggot like him can't make that much taking people out fishing. Remember that he told us that he went fishing by himself several days a week and then sold the fish to restaurants just to make ends meet?"

Keith started pacing. "But what if he blabs? He could tell them what happened and keep the money."

"It's his word against ours," Howard said patiently. "A faggot frog against two white Americans. If he blabs, what proof does he have? Nobody really paid any attention to us when he put us ashore. Were there two or three? Who can remember? Besides Stuart came back on board, remember? His cruise card proved that."

"Still ...," countered Keith.

"Besides, he knows that if he blabs, he puts his family in jeopardy. He is not going to want anything to happen to his wife or kids. No faggot frog would take that chance."

"I don't know." Keith got another beer and opened it taking a deep draught.

"You'd better cool it with the brewskis," Howard said. "You've been good recently, dried out and stayed sober for six months now. You don't want to start again."

"I just need a couple to calm down," said Keith. He was silent for a minute. "I guess you're right. It's just that he agreed awfully quickly."

"Wouldn't you have?" Howard asked. "If you knew that you would be dead in an instant if you didn't go along? I don't think we have a problem."

"I just don't ...," Keith whined.

"Look," Howard said trying to placate Keith. "We can't do anything too quickly because then it might look suspicious if he gets tied to that son-of-a-bitch black brother-in-law in any way. Let me look into having someone insure that this Quentin faggot has an accident while fishing in a few weeks. Would that make you happy?"

Keith smiled and nodded then finished his beer.

"Yeah. When am I going to get my money?"

"We have to wait until Elise gets the estate settled. Right now things are in limbo and there are too many eyes on things. The SEC is looking at Stuart's books but Elise says they won't find anything. Stuart was too good. Once that is over, funds will be unfrozen, she'll get the insurance settlement and you'll get your money."

"Okay," Keith said settling himself on the sofa. He turned on the TV and said, "Let's watch the game. The Lakers should beat the Cavs with no problem."

Later as Howard left Keith's apartment, he thought to himself, "That frog Quentin's not the weak link, you are!"

Once in his car he opened his cell phone and pressed 9 on the speed dial. The phone on the other end rang six times before being answered with a sleepy, "Hello. What time is it?"

"Probably about 2 a.m. in Florida. I'll make this quick. Keith is anxious about that faggot frog and, given the circumstances, I think it is best to go ahead with securing our story. I'll make the call and set it in motion."

There was silence on the other end.

"Elise?"

"Yeah, sure."

The connection was broken. Howard put his phone away and headed home.

CHAPTER 35

Now that I had my crew of one, and I felt that I could not trust more than that, we had several things to do before setting out. I was hoping that we weren't going to be too late. It took us a week to get done what we needed to do because several of the things required knowledge and/or skills that neither of us had. Needless to say, Peter Hiller was not happy with me hiring Joaquin out from under him and part of the time spent was getting a new hire acquainted with Joaquin's responsibilities.

Then fully provisioned and feeling confident in our ability to handle the Zàkpa, we were ready to head out. One of the things that you do when you are going on a cruise is to look at the weather. Most of it looked good, but there was a large spring storm east beyond St. Nantes and heading our way, so we would have to be prepared.

As we were headed out of East Bay Yacht Basin, I said, "And the kamikaze pilot heads out on his second mission."

Joaquin looked at me quizzically, "Kamikaze pilots ..."

I laughed. "It's a joke."

He didn't laugh.

Our first stop was Clarence Town, Bahamas, which is about one hundred eighty-four nautical miles and took us nine and one-half hours. Then on successive days our ports were: Matthew Town, one hundred eighty nautical miles and ten hours; Monte Cristi, one hundred thirty-two nautical miles and eight hours through slightly rougher seas; Las Galeras, one hundred forty-one nautical miles and eight and one-half hours. Our final stop before Genivee was to be Road Town, BVI, which was two hundred seventy nautical miles. We did this in order to bypass Puerto Rico because we

– make that I – didn't want any part of U.S. post 9/11 security at this point.

All this time, we had been keeping an eye on the weather. We knew that the storm, while not of hurricane force, was still strong and headed directly in our path. We had three options: stay in Las Galeras and wait for the storm to pass or dissipate; take a circuitous route either north or south of the storm's path; or continue on our planned course and brave the elements. Perhaps we were overly confident but we decided – okay, I decided – to continue as planned.

The first eight hours went as before, but we could watch the storm clouds darkening ahead of us. The radio had reported that winds were averaging 50 miles per hour, which according to the Beaufort scale made it a strong gale. Sir Francis Beaufort, an Irish-born British admiral and hydrographer, created the scale in 1805. Initially it referred to the effect of wind conditions on a man of war, the then work horse of the British navy. If we had been a ship of that era, the winds of this storm would have had us taking half our sails down. We had no sails but had "battened the hatches," so to speak; by making certain that everything possible was stowed and/or tied down. Taking proper precautions, we were both wearing life jackets and had moved from the lower helm station. I was sitting in the captain's chair and Joaquin was beside me.

The first rain hit us during the ninth hour and the winds began to pick up. Waves quickly increased in height from three feet to ten. For an hour or so, things were fine. We took the waves securely although some of them were breaking high against the bow and at times, when exiting a trough, one would crash across the bow. The worst thing was the visibility, which was considerably reduced by wind borne spray. We were relying greatly on our radar.

During hour ten of our trip, the wind escalated to between fifty-three and fifty-eight miles per hour and the average wave height was between fourteen and seventeen feet.

The Zàkpa shuttered when some of the bigger waves crashed into the bow. Visibility was not good and then the inevitable happened. The radar died.

"Josef, the radar just quit." This from Joaquin as the largest wave yet crashed over the bow and the Zàkpa had shuddered violently. With the bow barely visible, this was not good news.

"See if we blew a breaker or something." As I said this Joaquin was already paging furiously through the manual. The radar was our weakest link. Now I wished we had spent more time learning about it. We had dispensed with name formalities when Joaquin had signed on and called each other Josef and Joaquin.

The storm raged as Joaquin tried to fix the problem and I battled the storm at the helm. This went on for over half an hour. That's a guess – I didn't take my eyes off the storm. Joaquin had removed a panel below the radar and was inspecting the fuse box when a particularly large wave hit and he went sprawling.

CHAPTER 36

"Joaquin," I shouted, not removing my eyes from the rain swept windscreen, "are you okay?"

Joaquin pulled himself up and shouted something as he closed the panel but I didn't understand him.

There was a flash of green ...

I instinctively ducked but never released my hold of the helm. Recovering, I glanced to my left and saw the now familiar green glow from the radar screen and breathed a sigh of relief. But then I was knocked aside, actually pushed from my chair as Joaquin grabbed the helm and started turning us to port, while at the same time increasing the throttle.

"What the ..." I shouted picking myself up off the deck but Joaquin was pointing to something just beyond the bow. For a moment I could see nothing and then a huge dark shape appeared as the wind and rain lessened. I stood there petrified as the Zàkpa skewed in its course, leaning precariously to the port side, as the shape grew larger and nearer.

Joaquin increased the throttle and the engines roared. Time seemed to stand still but the black shape didn't. There seemed to be a roar and then the shape was close enough to touch and then receded, as the Zàkpa's props seemed to take a new hold and we hurtled away. Well, hurtled isn't the correct word as the distance did not increase rapidly, but the Zàkpa had regained her footing and, at least for the time being, Joaquin had control.

In the brief moments that remained before the shape disappeared in the storm, I got a clear look at the ship we had narrowly missed. It was a container ship towering massively above us. As I watched our stern draw away, I noticed movement above and watched horrified as several containers suddenly plummeted from above smashing heavily into the sea just yards behind us. The ensuing waves propelled us further and I looked at Joaquin. His face was grim and he was staring intently ahead and didn't seem to have noticed. I looked back and saw the stern of the ship just momentarily before the wind and rain blocked my vision. I think that I saw a name on the stern. Maybe I was hallucinating but what I read was "Pandora."

Joaquin continued at the helm, expertly bringing us around and back on course as much as he could because he had to take the waves at an angle. He said nothing and neither did I as the storm raged for several more hours. Finally the fury of the storm was past, the waves lessened, and things began to get back on an even keel.

"That was close," Joaquin said. "When the radar came back to life I could see the blob in front of us. I didn't realize what I had done until we were past. It was all a blur."

I told him about the ship and the containers and he stared at me incredulously.

"If you hadn't reacted the way you did, we would have hit that ship and most likely sunk or been crushed by those containers. Thanks to you, Davy Jones is short two more crew members today."

And me, for the second time in the past month. Maybe Neptune/Poseidon or Davy Jones was sending a message that the sea isn't for me.

CHAPTER 37

The voyage to Road Town should have taken us fifteen hours but it was twenty-five by the time we pulled into the anchorage. Fortunately in my planning I had allotted a day here in case the long haul had been hard on us. As it turned out, hard isn't the proper word. We collapsed into bed after going through customs and didn't wake until mid-afternoon. Then we used the remaining daylight to get the Zàkpa ship-shape.

We learned that the storm had briefly become a ten on the Beaufort scale, which put it into the category of a storm or whole gale. Fortunately it had missed all land, turning north into the Atlantic. We never learned anything about the "Pandora," if that was indeed her name.

The seventh and last day was Genivee, St. Nantes, which was one hundred sixty nautical miles and took us nine and one-half hours, arriving late afternoon. Nearing Genivee we encountered several offshore rocks and little islands as expected and took safe passage inside them. Because of our plans, we anchored off Fort Rideau, northwest of the harbor, on the seaside of the red buoys marking the channel. Once anchored, we flew the yellow quarantine flag and, having made contact with customs and immigration, waited for them to come to the boat.

When immigration arrived within half an hour, we both filled out the required immigration card and I declared my pistol. I had purchased this because of the events ahead for which I wanted to be prepared, but for all immigration events, such as this, I declared it as a protection against pirates.

Although piracy does occur rarely in the Caribbean, the most modern pirate was John Boysie Singh, usually known as "the Rajah," "Boysie" or "Boysie Singh." Born in 1908, he was a gangster and gambler before turning to piracy. From 1947 until 1956 he and his crew terrorized the waters between Trinidad and Venezuela and are credited with being responsible for no less than five thousand deaths, mostly fishermen. Their technique was generally to board fishing boats, murder the crew and steal the engine later to be sold in Venezuela. Boysie was well known to people in Trinidad and Tobago, successfully beating two charges of murder before being executed for the murder of his niece. He was held in awe and dread by most of the population and was frequently seen strolling grandly about Port of Spain in the early 1950's wearing bright, stylish clothes. Mothers and nannies would warn their charges: "Behave yourself, man, or Boysie goyn getchu, oui!"

There are many records of missing ships or ships found with no crew in the infamous Bermuda triangle, such as the yacht *Peanuts Too* that was found deserted south of Bermuda on November 25, 2003. In fact it is not uncommon for yachts to carry arms for who knows when some modern-day pirates will surface in the Caribbean as they have off the coast of Somalia.

Once through customs and immigration, we went over plans for the morning. I had already contacted Quentin Baston about a fishing excursion. I explained that I was a member of the United Nations Delegation from South Africa and was on a short break and wanted some excitement. When I said there would be only me, he was at first hesitant. I assured him that I would provide him with credentials to prove who I was and he seemed satisfied. The documents (quality suspect but hopefully Quentin would not know) had been secured in Nassau through one of Joaquin's contacts.

The plan was that early the next morning, Joaquin and I would travel by zodiac to the other side of the island where he would drop me at a hotel wharf. I would then walk to a different wharf where I had arranged for Quentin to pick me up.

CHAPTER 38

It was early morning with a clear sky and fairly calm seas. I stood on a dock near a hotel on St. Nantes and watch Quentin's boat approaching. He stood at the helm eyeing me, his eyes seeming to cast about looking for other people but there were none. He cut back the engines and eased his boat next to the dock and wrapped a line around the davit, holding the boat in place.

"Mr. Viljoen?" he asked.

"Yes," I replied. "I am Josef Viljoen. You must be Quentin Baston?"

He wouldn't have recognized me with my beard, sunglasses, and broad-brimmed hat. He nodded in answer and waved me aboard. He seemed nervous; not so that any other person might recognize it, but I knew there was apprehension. If I were in his place I would be expecting someone to come after him. He knew too much.

I handed him the papers and he looked at them, at first suspiciously and then seemed to accept them. He handed the papers back to me and I got on board, careful not to touch things but trying to be unobvious about it. He loosened the rope holding the boat to the dock and stepped to the helm. He eased the throttle forward and the boat slowly moved away from the dock.

"Have you ever been deep sea fishing before?" he asked.

"Once," I replied "but I didn't catch anything. I certainly would like to this time."

He smiled. "I will do my best."

We chatted amicably about the weather, my visit to St. Nantes, and fishing as he maneuvered the boat through the anchored fleet and out into open water where he increased the speed. We sped along for about half an hour and I watched the island recede into the distance with a feeling of déjà vu. This time I knew that neither of us would be coming back. I wondered if he felt the same.

Cutting the speed and placing the gears in neutral, he prepared the bait explaining what he was doing and how we were going to be fishing. Setting the motor in gear and getting a little speed, he let the lines out and explained how to wear the rod harness and what the procedure would be. I asked the kind of questions any rookie would and nodded understandingly when he explained things to me.

I had observed that Quentin was dressed in a different manner this time. On our first excursion, he was wearing shorts and a tight fitting long-sleeved tee shirt. Now a long-sleeved guide-type shirt with billowing sleeves and many pockets had replaced the long-sleeved tee shirt. He was wearing it outside his shorts. As he worked the tail of the shirt had flapped and I had observed that there was a bulge at the top of his shorts. Quentin was packing but that didn't bother me. I had expected it.

"Got anything to drink," I asked.

"Certainly, sir. Water, pop, or beer?"

"I'll have a beer."

He moved to the cooler, selected a Heineken, opened it with his knife, and handed it to me. "Now we fish."

The boat increased speed and I watched one of the baits as it broke surface and then disappeared in a random but (if I were a fish) enticing manner. This went on for almost half an hour.

"Fish on," I yelled as the port rod bent and the line whirred. At the same instance I had noticed this, Quentin had reduced speed and was moving toward the rod. By the time I had the rod holder harness attached around my waist, Quentin had the rod ready to insert.

As I grasped the rod, he reminded me to use the thumb to guide the line. It was a long fight, a big fish and numerous times it made a run taking the line out. However gradually I won the battle.

"It's a huge mahi mahi," Quentin said. "Quit reeling."

As before, I was grateful. As Quentin wrapped the line around his hand, I picked up my beer and moved toward him.

There was a flash of green ...

CHAPTER 39

An hour later, Joaquin pulled my boat alongside and tossed me a rope, which I tied to the divot. Quentin's boat was moving slowly with baits out and splashing along the surface behind. The last ten minutes had been spent baiting them and feeding out the line. I had used my satellite phone to call Joaquin. My message was brief: my position and heading and then I broke the connection. He had said nothing.

As soon as the boats were moving in unison, he passed the first explosives package across to me and I moved to the gas tanks and placed it. The second explosives package was placed under the console amidships. After activating the detonators, I looked around the boat and wiped any surface that I may have touched. Satisfied that I had gotten everything, I untied the mooring line, tossed it to Joaquin, and left Quentin's boat for the last time.

Joaquin moved quickly and pulled up the bumpers that he had placed over the side before coming alongside while I moved to the con and moved my boat away from Quentin's. Then I increased speed and headed away. About half a mile away, I cut the power to idle. Joaquin produced the detonator and I activated it. We looked at Quentin's boat and I depressed the button.

The two explosive packages went off simultaneously and parts of the boat went flying in every direction and fires burned on the larger pieces. Some would float and others would not and would be welcomed into Davy Jones' Locker. There might be enough pieces found to identify the boat and what had happened but there wasn't much. I had wanted no doubt about that.

With a last look, I turned to the helm and then paused. I grabbed a towel, wiped the detonator and tossed it over the side. I did the same with my satellite phone and Joaquin's after disassembling each into several pieces. Then I moved to the helm, got the boat under way, and turned it toward the Bahamas. A last look over my shoulder and I pushed the throttle to full power and the Zàkpa leapt forward eager to begin the long run.

CHAPTER 40

News of the explosion of Quentin's boat appeared in the St. Nantes weekly newspaper "Le Journal de Saint Nantes" and was translated (since at this time of year the publication is in French only) and picked up by press associations and spread around the world.

ST. NANTES'S FISHERMAN DIES IN BOAT EXPLOSION

Genivee, St. Nantes, French Virgin Islands

The search for St. Nantes's fishing guide Quentin Baston was called off Wednesday nearly 48 hours after the wreckage of his boat was reported to the authorities.

Facts surrounding the explosion are in question. While the "three-day intensive air and sea search" was hampered by a storm that came in the night after the wreckage was found, a local source reports that the search was scaled back after eight hours and was officially called off by local authorities after 24 hours.

The St. Nantes Weekly had reported the following:

Search efforts to find a 38-year old fisherman missing since sometime Tuesday were abandoned on Thursday morning, according to the Cross Antilles-Guyana, responsible for rescue at sea efforts in the Caribbean and the local sector of the Northern Atlantic. "We used all available boats and aircraft to find this man but the search was not fruitful," said Cross director Andre Éclair on Thursday. "The entire zone where he might have been found was swept by both aircraft and rescue boats, but without success. As of today, it is highly unlikely that this fisherman or his body will be found"

According to St. Nantes police, wreckage of the 25-foot fishing boat was found by another local fishing guide Patrick Laplace as he was taking some visiting fishermen on a deep sea fishing excursion. Patrick found a life ring, keys attached to a floating key fob, and other wreckage about ten miles southwest of St. Nantes. He radioed local authorities who immediately notified Cross Antilles-Guyana.

Quentin was a sixth-generation resident of St. Nantes and had been a fishing guide for over twenty years taking people either on four hour inshore fishing excursions or five-to-six hour deep sea fishing excursions. He often went fishing on days when he had no clients and sold his catch to local restaurants and residents.

His wife Celesse said that she did not believe that he had any client that morning and had left early before she or the children were up as he often did. Quentin and his wife had two children, a boy Pierre (eight) and a girl Marie (six).

In the airport waiting room on St. Martin, the article about the boating tragedy attracted the attention of at least one person who was waiting to board the next flight to St. Nantes.

"Guess I don't need to make the trip after all," he mused. "If the purchaser thinks it was my doing, the money will make it into my account. If not, then I have the deposit and am about $8,000 richer. Guess I had better see how soon I can get back home."

He put the paper into a trash receptacle and went to the ticket window.

The next day in Los Angeles, Howard read the article.

"Hmmm, quicker than I expected but it was worth it."

He picked up the phone, called Elise, and arranged to have the balance of the payment transferred.

Later on that same day, in the airport waiting room in England, a cell phone announced a text message received. Flipping the phone open, the man smiled as the deposit into his account was reported.

In Los Angeles, Keith decided a celebration was in order and headed for the fridge.

Part IV
Confession

CHAPTER 41

In Miami, a phone rang five times before it was picked up.

"Hello," a sleepy female voice answered the phone.

"We want proof he's dead and we want our money."

The line went dead.

Elise, only half awake looked at the phone for a moment, hung it up and rolled over.

"Who was that?" the man beside her asked.

"Wrong number," Elise said.

In Northridge, Los Angeles County, a phone rang. Keith answered after the third ring.

"What," he said irritatedly, his eyes glued on the TV as the Dodgers batted against the Giants in the top of the third.

"Where's his body?"

"What ...?" stammered Keith.

"We want proof he's dead."

"I don't ... ."

"We want our money."

The line went dead.

Another phone rang in Temple City, Los Angeles County. It rang five times and the answering machine picked up at the same time Howard did, standing outside his bathroom door, soaking wet with a towel in one hand.

"This had better be good," he said.

"Where's the body?"

"What are you talking about?"

"Prove that he's dead and give us the money."

"What money? " rasped Howard. "Who's dead?" he asked a dead line. He looked at the receiver and then slammed it down.

In Northridge, the phone rang again.

Keith picked it up and was greeted with silence.

"Who's there?"

"Prove he's dead."

"Who's dead?"

The question was answered with a dial tone.

Keith put the phone down, finished his beer and headed to the fridge for another one. He missed Manny Ramirez driving in Casey Blake from second with a single, tying the score at two each.

As he popped the top on the Bud-Lite he had pulled from the fridge, his cell phone rang. Walking back to the couch, he picked it up off the table and flipped it open. Whoever was calling had blocked caller id. He answered the call.

"We want our money."

Keith raised both hands as though in surrender and backed away. The phone landed on the couch. The beer can hit the floor, liquid spurting out the top and then fell over, its contents quickly becoming a puddle on the carpet.

The phone by the bed in Miami rang again. Elise rolled over and fumbled with it.

"Yes."

"Prove Stuart is dead."

"He's dead," she blurted without thinking. "He jumped over … ."

"Prove it. Prove it and give us our money."

"What money?" The line was dead.

"Another wrong number?" her companion for the night asked.

He was her first since that last night in Aruba when, after being a good "grieving widow," she had willingly, easily, succumbed to the advances of a young man staying in the same hotel. It had been a wild lustful night, her best in years.

"I don't know. They wanted … ." She stopped not wanting to say anything to someone she barely knew.

An arm went around her chest and a hand clamped on her breast, fingers tweaking her nipple sending a rush through her.

"I don't care what they want, I want you."

Elise let the phone drop and turned to face him, her hand finding him in the dark, feeling that he was ready.

"Then you got it," she said, pushing him back and climbing on top of him and guiding him home. "For tonight, you got it."

The phone rang.

The phone rang in Northridge again. Keith didn't answer. He sat on a chair in a corner and stared at it. The ringing stopped. He relaxed. His cell rang.

Howard had just put his wallet into his back pocket and grabbed his car keys when his cell rang. He answered, not looking at the screen to see who it was.

"I'm on my way, sweets," he said.

There was no answering voice from the phone.

"Hello," said Howard opening his front door.

"Where's Stuart's body?" said a disembodied voice over the phone. "We want a body and we want our money."

Howard looked at the screen and saw that the caller's number had been blocked. He closed the phone and turned it off.

CHAPTER 42

It's a simple task to pick up a pay-as-you-go cellular phone – many variety stores, super marts, drugstores or grocery stores carry them. Plunk down the money and you're good to go. Use it a few times, like one call to each of three numbers and toss it. What I did was take it apart and deposit pieces in several scattered locations. I wonder how long those numbers stay active before they are used again.

Or with the right type of cellular phone, you can get SIM cards. Subscriber Identity Module is a portable memory chip used and is easy to replace or put in a new phone. These chips hold such personal information as a cell phone number and phone book. Basically it is a mini hard disk that activates the phone in which it is installed. And you can buy them at many places too. Then you just have to take one chip out, dispose of it in a convenient place (airplane or bus toilet are good choices) and replace it with another. Couple these with a voice modulator and the calls were virtually unidentifiable.

I wasn't worried too much about my calls being traced once they really got tired of the harassing calls – all three of them quit answering their phones that first evening after the second or third. I wondered what they thought of them. I was on the way west toward Los Angeles using a variety of different modes of transportation to cover my trail. I had entered the U.S. through Dulles International in Washington D.C. using my fake U.S. passport.

"Welcome home," the passport inspector had said.

"It's good to get home," I said wondering what he thought of my dreadlocks and huge diamond earring. I had thought of getting two because that seems to be the style these days but had settled on just the one when needed. I don't like bling as a rule but felt that in this guise it was needed.

"Would you remove your sunglasses please, sir."

I did so, squinting and rapidly blinking my eyes. "I'm sorry, I have some kind of an eye infection, and the bright lights really bother them. I have an appointment tomorrow with an ophthalmologist if I can get to Memphis in time." I had made a connecting flight to get me part way to Los Angeles.

"I understand, Mr. Calhoun, but I need to be certain that it is you. You have changed a bit in the last ..." he peered at the page "nine years."

He compared me to the picture and nodded. "You are going to have to renew this pretty soon. It expires in six months."

"I know. It is on my list." I put my sunglasses back on with a sigh of relief. He probably thought it was relief from the glare but actually it was relief that he had accepted the passport, which displayed a picture of me sans earring and dreadlocks that I was wearing to help prevent identification of me as Stuart Andrews, just in case anyone was looking.

"In my business you have to keep up with the times." I said about my appearance. "I promote tours for bands."

"Any that I might know?"

"Probably not, they're mostly local. Demented Dogs, Little Green Chairs, The Dan K Theory, Barking Charlies, Bunny Carlos, The Redstone Ramblers."

"Any make it big."

"No, but I keep looking and hoping."

He stamped the passport, handed it back to me with the customs declaration, waved me through and said, "Next," while waving at the next person in line.

Having only my duffel carry-on, I went straight to the customs clerk while most of the rest of my fellow passengers were waiting for their luggage to appear on the carousels. It would be nice if all airports were like Berlin's Tegel. Passport control is right at the end of the plane's tube and right after that is the luggage carousel and then customs. From there, it is twenty or thirty feet to a taxi.

The Customs officer took my form, glanced at it and waved me through. I headed upstairs, went through the T.S.A. inspection, and went to the gate for my Memphis flight. In Memphis, I caught a taxi downtown, purchased two pay-as-you-go cell phones from two different locations, found the bus station, and caught a bus to Dallas. At rest stops, I used the two phones to make a couple of calls to each of the three conspirators. In Dallas I dumped the phones, bought a couple more. Then I went to the airport and caught a flight to Denver. There I checked into the airport hotel and caught some much needed sleep.

CHAPTER 43

Howard had turned his cell phone off after leaving his condo not wanting to be disturbed during his date. It was after three a.m. when he finally unlocked his door letting himself into his living room and dumped his wallet, keys and cell phone on the credenza where he always kept them. He bypassed his blinking answering machine and went to bed.

In the morning, he overslept and had to rush to get to Philpott and Associates, the accounting firm where he worked. He was halfway through his messages when Megan, the secretary he shared with Tim Nesbit, stuck her head in the door.

"Mr. Blake, your banker is on the phone. Line 2."

"Thanks," he responded reaching for the phone, knowing well who it was.

"Good morning, Keith, " he said after pressing the button for line 2.

"Did you get those crank …?"

"Yes, I did. This is not the place to talk about it. Meet me at Johnnie G.'s tonight and we'll talk about it."

"But …"

"Goodbye, Keith." Howard hung up the phone and sat musing for a minute.

Then he remembered his cell phone and turned it on. There were four messages waiting. Three from Keith that he deleted without listening and one from Elise just ten minutes earlier. He left his office and told Megan that he was stepping out for a minute. He took the stairway down to the rear of the building and stepped out into the alley that was used as a smoking area for the building's occupants. No one was there.

He returned Elise's call.

"I had some strange calls last night," she began.

Howard interrupted, "I did too and so did Keith. I'll talk to him tonight. They were asking for proof and demanding their money, right?"

"Yes," replied Elise.

"There isn't any proof – not on the ship or back in St. Nantes. Quentin Baston is dead and that was the only link to any proof. The ship has had several new groups of passengers by this time. Any evidence there that could have been used to show that Stuart wasn't aboard is gone."

"But aren't there tapes from the gangway."

"They never even thought to look at them and by now they are probably erased or gathering dust in some forgotten bin. The entire incident is in the past."

Silence from Elise, then "But the money?"

"Didn't Stuart tell you that the money was untraceable and was his 'payment for services rendered.'?"

"Yes, something like that."

"Then there is nothing to worry about. It is probably just someone trying to take advantage of the fact that we were involved in Stuart's disappearance."

Behind him the door opened and a man and woman stepped into the alley, cigarettes in hand. Howard started walking away down the alley.

"The best thing to do," he continued. "is nothing. If there are any more calls, just hang up. Or at least threaten to go to the police to stop the harassment."

"But we can't … ."

"I know we can't but you can threaten. If this continues, just let me know. Be calm. Our tracks are covered. The money is safe. If they knew where it was, they would tell you that they wanted that money in that account."

Silence.

"Okay, Elise?"

"Okay."

"Just be calm. We're in the clear. There are no loose ends. " He paused thinking about Keith. "I have to go. Bye."

Closing the phone, he put it in his pocket and turned around. A white man and black woman were standing close together in deep conversation with a cloud of smoke encircling their heads. They never noticed him as he opened the door and entered the building. As the door closed behind him, he muttered, "Frigging nigger lover."

CHAPTER 44

Howard got to Johnnie G.'s about 6:15. Keith, in a corner booth, was almost done with his second (according to him) beer. Howard waved at the bartender Terri, a cute petite redhead, indicating his usual. Keith and Howard were in a habit of meeting here at least once a week. In fact, this is where they had met five years ago and Terri had been the introducer.

Howard had come in on a particularly busy Friday near the end of tax season after a particularly stressful week. On the way to his apartment he had spotted the sign proclaiming "Johnnie G.'s Busy Bee Happy Hour." Trite but catchy, he had thought and found a parking place half a block away in a spot just vacated by a 50's vintage Ford. He took a seat at the bar between a man in a suit (old school banker/stockbroker type Howard had thought) and a couple who were obviously on the way to a bed somewhere and soon, or they'd wind up on the floor or bar. His tongue had to be halfway down her throat and her hand wasn't just resting on his thigh.

"I'm Terri, your tender bar tenderess," Terri had said with a wink. "What'll you have? Drinks are half price for another 20 minutes."

Howard had relaxed immediately with that greeting. "In that case give me two double Grey Goose vodka martinis up, skip the vermouth, and extra olives. Oh, and a bucket of ice water for my friends here." Indicating the couple to his right.

"On the way, but forget the ice water. They've had two already and it didn't even phase them. Bets are that he'll be off before they leave."

"Lucky him," said the fellow to his left.

"Drink up, sailor," Terri had said setting Howard's drinks on the bar in front of him. "Would you like anchovy, blue cheese, jalapeño, pimento stuffed, or unstuffed olives? No extra charge."

She set a saucer with two of each on toothpicks in front of him.

"Whatever you don't want, Keith here will eat with his beer," she said, indicating the fellow to his left.

Howard had chosen the blue cheese stuffed and shoved the plate toward Keith and then uncharacteristically stuck out his hand.

"Howard Blake," he'd said.

Keith had turned and grasped his hand while picking up a toothpick with two jalapeño stuffed olives, sticking it into his mouth and withdrawing it empty.

"Keith Mitchell," he had said through chews of olives. "YOW, THOSE ARE HOT, TERRI" grabbing his beer and draining half its contents. That seemed to startle the couple to Howard's right out of their seclusion. They finished their drinks and walked out arm-in-arm, his condition blatantly obvious by the bulge in the front of his pants.

Terri laughed. "Stuffed them myself with fresh jalapeños from my hot house. Thought you'd like them."

She set a full draft in front of Keith. "On the house. It was a dirty trick." Then to Howard "Glad you didn't try the jalapeños, but then you don't look like a spicy man to me. Hot, but not spicy." A wink and she was off.

Howard immediately set his sights on getting into her pants but after about five minutes of conversation with Keith, exchanging pleasantries, brief bios, and other mundanities, Keith had told him, sadly, that Terri was of a different persuasion and, was in fact, "married."

"Evening, Keith," Howard said cheerfully as he slid into the booth opposite Keith, followed quickly by two double Grey Goose martinis each with a toothpick laden with three olives delivered by the evening's waitperson Gary. Howard quickly checked to be certain that none were jalapeño filled.

"How many calls did you get?" Keith blurted between drinks. "I got two on each phone before I turned the cell off and put the landline on mute."

"I had as many," Howard lied. "What did they want?

"Proof that Stuart was dead."

"Shh, keep your voice down, Keith."

Keith leaned conspiratorially toward Howard, "They wanted to know where the body was and they said they wanted their money. What mon...?"

Howard held up his hand. "Hold on, Keith. Calm down. Did they use his name?"

"Yes, they ..." Keith paused. "No, they just said 'his' body."

"Right, then it's probably just a scam. Someone trying to use the fact that we were around when he died and hoping that there is money in it. He or they are just trying to coerce us into giving them money. It's just like the Internet scams or phone scams for the elderly. They're just using a recent tragic death to try to make money. It's fairly common."

Howard had no idea whether it was or wasn't, but he knew that he needed to do something to calm Keith down.

"What are we going to do?" Keith burbled in his beer.

"Relax. There's no proof. No pictures, no tapes, no fingerprints."

"What money are they talking about?" Keith asked.

"Who knows?"

Keith knew nothing of the fifteen million. Howard had roped Keith into the scheme to get rid of Stuart by promising to pay off his gambling debts of over a hundred grand. He personally had made contact with the debt holder's representative and given an advance of twenty-five thousand dollars of his own money to convince them to wait for the rest of their money. He had told them that Keith had a legacy coming due and would be able to pay them off within a month. Keith had told them the same thing, under Howard's coaching, but they had not believed him. They believed someone with no gambling ties.

"You don't have any claim to any money so stay cool. Can you?"

Keith nodded half-heartedly.

"Look, use caller ID on the cell phone and if you don't recognize the number or it's blocked, don't answer. Use the answering machine on your home phone as a screening device. I doubt these people will leave a message that the cops could use."

"Cops," Keith sputtered spewing beer halfway across the table. "What cops?"

"There aren't any and there won't be, but they don't know that. Just keep it cool. Can you do that? Can you hang tight until the weekend and if work permits maybe we can go catch a couple of Dodgers or Angels games?"

Keith assured him that he could. Howard downed the last of his second drink, put money on the table for both their tabs plus a good tip and left. He wasn't certain that Keith could ... or would.

CHAPTER 45

With Quentin safely taken care of, I had turned my attention to what I considered to be the next weakest link: Keith, mainly because he was the only remaining person in the conspiracy without a family tie. When I started considering him, I knew little about him – only what I had learned from Howard who said they had meet at the Sail Away Party leaving Ft. Lauderdale. Beyond that I had learned precious little except that he and Howard lived in the same county, but Los Angeles is a big county. The Internet is a great tool and can provide much information but nothing really in depth about a person, at least not the kind of information of the type I needed. To get that, I turned to another source – a private investigator. It was expensive but quick and the report seemed reliable. The investigator thought that the company I represented was doing a background check on a prospective client. I hadn't given him a company name explaining, "While we have our own investigators, we like to use ones outside the business occasionally to check on how well our own people were doing." I explained that this was one of those occasions. The report provided me with much useful information:

Keith Mitchell was thirty-six years old, born in Small Town, North Dakota, of parents Rachel (nee Simons) Mitchell and Richard Keith Mitchell (deceased). His father was a farmer but aspired more for his only son and sent him to North Dakota State University, where he majored in partying and business and graduated by the skin of his teeth with a 2.01 accumulative average attained after five years.

He went to work for a bank in Fargo, North Dakota (where NDSU is located and where he had worked part time during college) where he became a branch manager quickly as (despite his grades) he had a knack for the business. After five years, he got a job with a bigger bank and moved to Chicago where he spent an additional five years before making yet another career change which took him to Los Angeles. There he continued working his way up the corporate ladder becoming a second vice-president last year.

He had never married although he had been engaged during his time in Chicago. She had broken it off a month before the wedding when she found him screwing her best friend (who would have been the maid of honor) in their shared bed.

His financial history appeared to be his Achilles' heel. Apparently in Chicago he had become bitten by the gambling bug and started making monthly junket's to Vegas or Reno and had met his former fiancée on one of these. He was soon running up huge debts, one of which his fiancée's parents help to pay off so that their son-in-law to be would start married life on good footing. It hadn't taken him long to get an even larger debt and compiled that with an excessive fondness for alcohol. He had undergone treatment for both addictions and appeared to have successfully beaten both at the time of his move to Los Angeles. He stayed sober and away from the tables for two years before he succumbed and was carrying a debt again. This debt had grown to one hundred thousand dollars but there were indications that he had promised that it would be paid off soon. (*Howard to the rescue, no doubt.*) At the present time, he had been able to stay away from the gambling venues, but had fallen off the other wagon and was beginning to drink heavily. His current company seemed unaware of either of these difficulties, as he was able to sober up during most of the workweek but the weekends usually found him at the bottom of some gin barrel with increasing frequency.

Four days after Quentin's boat disaster made the news with a tie in to my death, Keith was once again heavily imbibing.

The news blurb that made the local papers and television news shows was the following:

> *The boat belonging to St. Nantes's resi-*
> *dent Quentin Baston, thirty-eight, apparently*
> *exploded approximately seven miles southwest*
> *of the island. Quentin had worked as a fishing*
> *guide in St. Nantes for thirty-five years and he*
> *had taken Stuart Andrews (missing financial*
> *genius), his brother-in-law Howard Blake,*
> *and also Howard's friend, Keith Mitchell, on*
> *a fishing excursion during the time the Carib-*
> *bean Isle was in port.*
>
> > *Police on St. Nantes believe that*
> *Quentin's boat must have had a gas line leak*
> *and most likely blew up when some spark had*
> *ignited the fumes. There is no record that*
> *Quentin had a client that morning, but often*
> *he would go out fishing by himself selling his*
> *catch to local restaurants and hotels. No*
> *body or body parts have been recovered but*
> *the area is home to barracudas and sharks.*

I would have thought that the news of Quentin's demise would have been welcome news to Keith, Howard, and Elise, but it seems to have had a different effect upon Keith.

Of course the investigator did not tie Keith's renewed "binge drinking" (the investigator's terminology) to the news report, but I certainly did. I wondered why that was but couldn't find a concrete connection although I should have. I guess I just wasn't thinking properly or should I say "con-spiratorially." Regardless, the connection was there and I thought that might give me the "in" with Keith that I needed.

I thanked the investigator and asked him to send his bill to my company (a blind drop in the Bahamas). He asked how his report had compared to the one done by my compa-ny's investigator and I told him that it was 95% on, although our investigator had not known about the bedding incident. However, our man had turned up an additional piece of information that he hadn't. He wanted to know what it was but, because of company confidentiality I told him, I was unable to give him that information. He was bit downhearted by that news but it would probably make him even more diligent in his future investigations.

As I prepared to leave Memphis, I put a letter in the mail to Keith at his office. In the envelope was a blank piece of paper folded around a four inch by six inch picture of the waterfront in Genivee that I had taken when I was there after my escape from the clutches of Davy Jones. On the back of the picture I had used a public computer and printer to write:

Four went out, three came back.
We know what happened!

I already knew from the phone calls I had continued to make that he was upset. After the first night, the other two had basically ignored the calls as I had expected – but not Keith. After seven calls in a period of twenty minutes, he had picked up one on his cell and shouted, "What do you want? I don't know anything."

Yes, you do, I thought.

CHAPTER 46

Mid-afternoon Friday, Keith had just finished with a new client who had opened a savings account, checking account, and rented one of the biggest safe deposit boxes, when his secretary brought him the afternoon mail. In it was an envelope addressed to him with no return address and marked "PERSONAL." He frowned and set it aside while he looked at the other mail and took care of it. Then he turned his attention to the mysterious envelope. Opening it he withdrew a single sheet of paper. He unfolded it and a photograph fell out.

It landed face up and upside down. He turned it around on his desk and looked at it, not recognizing the setting – a waterfront somewhere. He turned it over and read the inscription. He dropped the picture and sat staring at it as the implication slowly sank in.

Now he recognized the waterfront in Genivee from which they had departed on the fishing excursion. "Four went out," He, Howard, Quentin and Stuart. "... three came back." He, Howard and Quentin. "We know what happened!" Somebody knew they had killed Stuart. How? Who? The caller! It had to be – but who was it?

His hands shaking, he put the picture back into the paper and replaced it in the envelope, which he put in his jacket pocket. He knew that Howard was deeply involved in tax preparations as the season drew to a close, would be working all weekend despite his promise to see a ballgame or two, and wouldn't answer his cell.

Despite the fact it was mid-afternoon, he left the office telling his secretary that he had a personal appointment. She nodded and turned back to her monitor. Keith got into his car and headed for Johnnie G's.

It was well after midnight when Keith entered his condo, headed for the bathroom,and turned on the light. After relieving himself, he returned to the living room to drop his coat on the couch.

"Gud evening, mon," I said from a chair in the corner. "You kept me waiting long time."

"What!" stammered Keith, "Who are you? How'd you get in here?"

"Do it really matter, mon?" I replied, turning on a table lamp and standing up so that he could see the gun in my hand. "I be here and dat is what matter. Who I be no important. What is important why I be here."

I must have made a pretty intimidating picture with the gun, dreadlocks, beard, earring, and island clothes.

Keith sank on the couch, his jacket falling to the floor. "Why! What!"

"Why, mon? Well, 'cause we wants our money."

"I told Chas I'd pay in a few weeks. I need some time …"

"Not you gambling money, mon. We want our vestment money."

"Vestment money?" Keith stammered. "What … what … oh, investment money. What investment money?"

"The money we done gave Stuart Andrews."

"Money … Stuart. I don't have any money. Stuart's dead."

"So you say, mon. So you say. But tell me, mon, where he die?"

"He jumped off a ship in the southern Caribbean. He killed himself."

"Mon, if that be so," I continued, enjoying my role perfected by having spent several days in Nassau talking to some of the locals to try to get the island lingo down, "How he get there?"

Keith was wiping his hand on his slacks.

"On the ship, the Caribbean Isle."

"No, mon, that not so. He gone fishing in St. Nantes but not come back. How he get on the big ship?"

"No, he came back. We all did. We got on the ship and went south."

"No, mon. That no true. See, we talk to people on St. Nantes. One ole lady she member that you and dat other fella Howard, come off fishing boat but not de other fella. Den we talk to that fisher fella Quentin. He try to tell like you but he give up. He tells us that you two fella hit the Andrews mon on de head and drown him. Den give he body to de fishes."

He looked at me fear obvious on his face.

"No, that's not …"

"Mon, dis Quentin fella tells us dis to save his life. Cept he not!"

"You, you did it. Not … ."

"Not who, mon?"

"Howard did," Keith was definitely flustered. "I mean Howard paid someone to … ."

"Ah, mon. You mean we din't have to kill that mon. Someone else gon kill he?"

"No, I mean, yes … I don't know."

"Me thinks you no know what you mean, mon. But where de money?"

"Money, I don't have… I don't know about any money. Maybe Howard has the money."

"Dis Howard fella, he got our money? He got our twenty-five million?"

Keith looked at me incredulously.

"Twenty-five million? I don't know about any twenty-five million. I just know about insurance money."

"Insurance money ain't our problem less it be twenty-five million."

"I don't know how much. Howard … Elise … they … ."

Keith broke down under the stress and the lack of cognizant brain cells with which to think. I quickly took advantage.

"Mon, best you tell me de whole story. Den maybe you keep you life."

And it all spilled out.

CHAPTER 47

"Howard came to me last year. He told me that his sister Elise needed to get away from her husband Stuart. He said that he was mean to her, beat her, treated her badly. She couldn't divorce him because she would have nothing. He would probably kill her rather than have to pay alimony.

"She wasn't strong enough to kill him herself. 'Didn't have the guts', Howard said. So she asked Howard to do it. They had this plan to go on the cruise and kill him there. They were going to go fishing and drown him, then fake his suicide later. Howard didn't think that the two of them could handle Stuart and the charter captain. They knew they couldn't kill both of them because it would look too suspicious. They would have to pay the charter man to keep him quiet. They had a report that said he was struggling to make ends meet. But Howard didn't think that she could control him while Howard took care of Stuart. He knew that she couldn't do Stuart."

He paused, "Can I get a beer?" I nodded and he hurried to the kitchen and returned with his beer – I could see him the entire time. He set the beer on the coffee table and sat down.

Then he continued, "So he asked me to help. He told me that he would pay my gambling debt using the insurance money, but it would take a while for the insurance money to be released because there wouldn't be a body.

"So Howard, Stuart and I go on the fishing boat. Then Howard told Stuart that we had met at a bar on the ship so that he wouldn't know we were friends. That would be too suspicious. Stuart was a smart man."

Keith picked up his beer can and looked at it longingly.

"When Stuart was distracted when his fish was being landed, Howard hit him with a beer bottle. And I kept that fisherman quiet. He was a wimp ... faggot frog. Simply cowered in a corner, asking us not to kill him.

"Howard took all the identification from Stuart and then we held him over the side until he was dead. Then we let him go into the water. When we came back to port we landed at a different spot so people wouldn't notice but," he glanced at me, "I guess someone did."

I smiled at him displaying my fake gold tooth. He opened the beer and took a swig.

"Dis fisher fella, he go long cause you threaten he family?"

"Yes, no ... and Howard gave that frog ten thousand dollars to keep quiet."

I whistled. "Ten thousand. Boy, den I keep quiet too. Quiet like mice. So wat den?"

"Then we hooked up with Elise. She had been shopping and had all sorts of stuff, tee shirts, bobbles, just a lot of junky tourist stuff. We got on the tender and got back to the ship. Elise went first, me and then Howard. After she put her card into the machine, I stepped up to put my card in (except it was Stuart's) and pushed her. She stumbled, dropped everything spilling it all over the place and fell. Everyone rushed to help her and I put Stuart's card into the machine and then went to my cabin."

A swig, and he set the beer can on the table.

"When everything was picked up, she and Howard went to her cabin. When we were ready to leave port, the ship called my name to come to the gangway. It seemed," here he smiled for the first time, "that I had forgotten to swipe my boarding card. I explained that I had been distracted by Elise falling and they said that was understandable, as it seemed to happen quite often. Almost every port someone was called to come down because they had gotten on board without swiping their boarding pass. Some security!"

He picked the beer up again.

"We all breathed a huge sigh of relief because that was the part of the plan that was most likely to fail. Once we were safely aboard, we felt we were home free."

Another swig.

"For the next couple of days, Elise wouldn't let anyone into their cabin, not even to clean or leave clean towels. She told people that Stuart was depressed and that he wanted to be alone. She ordered meals in and she didn't leave the room much either because she didn't want someone coming in despite the 'PRIVACY PLEASE' sign."

He laughed. "There was a honeymoon couple on the trip and they had the 'PRIVACY PLEASE' sign and the cabin steward ignored it and walked in on a good old fashioned 'soixante-neuf'. Bet that was deflating."

I shook my hand and waved the pistol at him. He drained the beer and set it down.

"Well, after two days, she reported him missing. Told the captain or someone that he wasn't there in the morning and she hadn't seen any sign of him all day or in the evening. This was after a day at sea so there were many miles of open ocean or whatever.

"So they searched the ship and the water but, of course, couldn't find anything. He was thousands of miles away if any of him was still around. "

He looked at me.

"That's it. See, no money."

I stared at him, the gun still pointing at him.

"That's the truth, I swear. No money. He's dead. Just like I said, you black..."

I waved the gun at him and he shut up. Leave it to my bigoted brother-in-law to team up with another bigot. Probably made it even easier to get him to go along. *"Let's kill that black son-of-a-bitch brother-in-law of mine."*

"No money," I said. "You killed him. You and Howard? You helped Howard and Elise?"

He looked at me strangely, my island accent momentarily gone.

"Yeah," he said questioningly. "But who are you?"

"Just a mon," I said back in character. "A mon searching for me money and for truth."

"I told you the truth."

"I hope so, mon," I said, pulling the small tape recorder from my pocket that I had started with the beginning of his confession and stopped when he finished his story.

He stared at me as I pushed rewind and then play.

" *... the captain or someone that he wasn't there in the morning ...* "

Keith started at me uncomprehendingly.

"What are you going to do with that?"

"Oh, dis," I answered. "Dis is for me boss to prove that Stuart mon is dead. I think he believe there be no money. De money be gone with de Stuart mon. I think maybe, he give this to de gendarmes on St. Nantes."

CHAPTER 48

"The Gendarmes, " sputtered Keith, "but why?"

"Well, mon, with dis Stuart fella dead, my boss he no get 'is money back he been investin'. My boss he believe good Christian thing, ah what … oh, yeah, *'eye for eye.'* So no money, he want same pay."

"I'll pay, I …"

I grinned, waving the pistol. "What you pay wit' mon? You looks? You can't pay you gambling money. What be it – hundred thousand? How you going pay twenty-five million?"

Keith sagged and I think was defeated.

"Now, mon, don't you be worry about de Gendarmes there on St. Nantes. De court de be quick cause de island small and so de prison. They be quick 'guilty' and den de guillotine. Tha-WACK!" I made a downward slashing motion with my free hand onto the pistol hand. "It be over."

Keith cringed. Inwardly I was laughing and really enjoying it. St. Nantes had never used the guillotine and France doesn't use the guillotine any more, but it was used by many European counties into the twentieth century, notably Germany, Switzerland, Sweden, and Greece. France yielded to pressure from other countries in 1981 outlawing capital punishment. The death of Hamida Djadoubi in 1977 was the last by guillotine.

"Yeah, mon, wham and de head be rollin'. Tha-WACK! Plop." I made a falling over motion with my hand. "Roll … Roll." I made a rolling motion with my hands. "Me thinks tree head be rollin' real quick."

"Tree … oh."

"Now, mon, ya know that maybe there be a chance you not go guillotine."

Keith looked up, face brightening. "How?"

"De courts dey like quick trials. What dey gonna be needing is good evidence. Smart fella like you figure you write down what happen and help de gendarmes with de case. Den maybe de court ..."

I paused dramatically.

"What?" the puzzled Keith asked

"Dat fisher fella, what be he name?"

"Quentin," Keith said.

"Dat right, dis Quentin fella he be taking you fellas out fishing den dat Stuart no come back."

"But Quentin's dead. His boat blew up."

"Dat right. But dat be suspicious kinda, you dink? Dem fishing boats dey don't blow up dat quick unless helped along by some bombs. Dem gendarmes be dinking – '*Hmmm, des tree fella kill de one mon den dey say it happen miles way. Dis fisherman he be quick die in explosion, maybe explosion not accident. Perhaps these tree fella they make explosion happen.*' "

The truth hit Keith hard. "So ... ."

"Me dinks that dem gendarmes not wanna let fella go with two murders and one dem own island mon. Me dink that tree heads gwanna roll. Tha-WACK!" Always with the hand motions. "Plop! Roll... Roll. De blud ben spurt!" Fingers flexing to indicate spurting blood. "Tha-WACK! Plop! Roll ..."

Keith sagged again. "No, I can't ... too ugly. Not a good way to die."

"Be quick, mon."

"No, it'd take time, extradition, trial, sentence, then the walk to the ... . Do they do it in public?"

I hadn't thought of that. "Yeah, mon, in da town square. Make big island party. Tha-WACK! Plop! Roll ... Roll. De blud ben sprut! Hooray de people!" Arms in the air like for a touchdown. "Tha-WACK! Plop! Roll ... Roll. De blud ben sprut! Hooray de people! Tha-WACK! ..."

"I get it," Keith whined. "I can't ..." He wept.

I paused for just a moment.

"Mon, den there be other way."

"What's that?" Keith looked up at me pleading.

"You be write confession on paper and be signing. Say at end:

"I can't live with this death on my conscience. "

" Den get gun and bang."

"I don't have a gun."

"Me do," I said dangling the pistol at him on my fingers.

It took an hour and six beers for Keith to write his confession. I read it and knew it would work. Actually the recording would work. There was no evidence of coercion, no mention of gun. My voice on part of it but, if needed, that could be edited. I wouldn't want a possible voiceprint around.

I laid the confession in front of him on the coffee table and put one bullet on it. I then emptied the pistol – it was a small revolver – spun the cylinder to check and snapped it shut. Keith looked at the bullet and then questioningly at me.

"It just take one, mon," I put the revolver up under my chin pointed at the top of my head and pulled the trigger. "Bang."

Keith jumped.

I put the gun up to the side of my head and pulled the trigger. "Bang."

Keith sagged.

"It be best, mon."

I put the pistol down on the coffee table in front of the couch far enough away that he would have to move to get it. Then I went to the door.

"It be quick, mon." I showed the guillotine chop, the plop, the roll, the spurt, and then touchdown.

I opened the door and left, closing it behind me but leaving unlocked.

When I reached the end of the sidewalk I heard a single report. It had been quick.

I stripped off the latex gloves I have been wearing to eliminate my prints and put them in my pocket. Two blocks away I used the last throwaway cell phone and called 911. "There's been a gun shot." And gave the address.

I walked several more blocks hearing sirens behind me headed to Keith's condo. I dumped the torn apart cell phone in several different dumpsters separately, and the extra bullets down several sewer grates. The latex gloves would go in another city far from Los Angeles.

One killer down. Two to go. *Payback is a bitch!*

Part V

Extradition

CHAPTER 49

I took a taxi to the bus station where I had stored my duffel and computer in a locker when I arrived in Los Angeles. I retrieved these and caught the first bus out. In San Francisco I went to the airport and bought a ticket to Dallas. In the waiting area I used the laptop and pulled up the Los Angeles Times. It was small but it was there.

Local Banker Found Shot

Responding to an anonymous 911 call reporting shots fired, police went to the Northridge home of Keith Mitchell. The front door was unlocked and when there was no response to knocking, the police entered the building and found Mr. Mitchell. Police refuse to release any other information pending a further investigation.

Nothing further was found when I the checked the Times website after reaching Dallas. I went to the bus station and took a bus to Memphis where I had a return airline ticket to Washington Dulles. In the Memphis airport waiting area, there was a further update.

Local Banker's Suicide Raises Questions

Keith Mitchell, a bank manager with Federal-Chase, was found in his home in Northridge in the early hours Saturday morning. Apparently Mr. Mitchell shot himself with a pistol that police found on the floor in front of him. An anonymous police source reports that the gun bore only his fingerprints. Police say there was a handwritten note signed by Mr. Mitchell but refuse to release further information. An anonymous source in the police department told the Times that the note raises questions about another apparent suicide and implicates at least two other persons.

At Dulles, I purchased a ticket to Nassau where Joaquin was waiting with the Zàkpa. My passport was scanned and I went through T.S.A. security (shoes off; laptop out; liquids in a one quart bag; yes, Ma'am; no, sir;) and went to find a seat in the waiting area.

"Stuart, wait up."

That almost stopped me in my tracks. Who in the world could have recognized me? My slight hesitation turned into a complete stop and I let go of my bag and knelt to tie my shoe. On my right, a man passed me pulling his carry-on bag and taking long strides.

"Stuart, wait."

He never paused. I could hear someone running behind me and stood up as a woman hurried by me pulling her carry-on bag.

"Stuart, please, wait." It was her calling after the man who was obviously Stuart or Stewart. I breathed a sigh of relief and continued to the waiting area.

Someone at the Times was getting some information.

Banker's Death Connected to Financer's Disappearance

The suicide note left by Los Angeles banker Keith Mitchell apparently implicates himself and two other individuals in the disappearance and apparent suicide of Miami investment manager Stuart Andrews. Andrews reportedly committed suicide by jumping off Caribbean Cruise Lines ship m/s Caribbean Isle somewhere between St. Georges, Grenada and Willemstad, Curaçao in late February.

Unidentified police sources say that the note directly implicates himself, Howard Blake (brother-in-law of Andrews) and Elise Blake Andrews, wife of the missing financial genius. Police have stated that both Blake and the widow are persons of interest in an ongoing investigation. They won't give any more details at this time but do admit they have questioned Howard Blake who is a C.P.A. with Philpott And Associates in Los Angeles.

Andrews's widow lives in Miami, Florida and police there state they have talked to her. Both Blake and Andrews have refused to talk to a Times reporter and both have retained counsel.

The Times had good sources. Things were moving faster than I had anticipated. In Nassau I took a taxi to the East Bay Yacht Basin and boarded the Zàkpa. Joaquin was in the living area watching CNN.

> *"... our reporter in Miami.*
> *"Police here are not saying much but we have learned that this not only involves Elise Andrews, widow of missing financier Stuart Andrews, and her brother Howard Blake of Los Angeles, but has connections to an incident in Genivee, St. Nantes. You might remember a story involving an explosion of a fishing boat owned by Quentin Baston. It was this man who took financier Stuart Andrews, his brother-in-law Howard Blake, and recently deceased Los Angeles banker Keith*

*Mitchell on a fishing excursion just be-
fore Stuart Andrews's reported suicide. A
source reports that Mitchell's suicide note
contains information about the connection
between the fishing trip and explosion that
killed Quentin Baston. Our source says that
police in Genivee are very interested in both
Howard Blake and Elise Andrews.*

*"We talked to Phil Dombrey, lawyer for
Mrs. Andrews."*

The scene shifted to a man in a suit and tie standing in
front of what appeared to be a limousine with a woman sitting in the back seat. I could tell that it was Elise.

*Phil Dombrey: "At this time we have no
further comment but we do find the implications from this reported suicide note to be lu-
dicrous. Mr. Mitchell was under the care of
a psychiatrist for depression and we believe
that the accusations in the letter to be the
fantasy ravings of a very sick man."*

The sound was muted as the man turned, opened the
door of the limousine, and slid inside, closing the door and
almost catching a microphone that was being thrust at him
by some reporter.

*"CNN has attempted to locate the psy-
chiatrist but have not been able to identify
him so far."*

Joaquin muted the sound and looked at me.
"It is true," he asked.
"What I have heard and read, yes."
"You didn't …"

"No, he did it himself just like the reports say."

Then I told him what had happened. Then he asked what our next step was. He was as excited as I was that everything was working out even better than we had hoped.

"I think we need to give them more help. What do you think?"

"Let's do it, Captain."

"Then we hoist anchor and get out to sea."

CHAPTER 50

Three days later CNN's story was even bigger.

> *"Breaking news this morning as police made arrests in what is being called the Stuart Andrews Suicide-Murder Case. Warrants were issued in Miami, Florida for the arrest of Elise Blake Andrews, wife of the missing financier, and in Los Angeles,California, for the arrest of Howard Blake, his brother-in-law."*

The scene on the screen shifted from the anchor to a limousine pulling to the curb. The reporter said:

> *"In Miami, Florida, Elise Andrews turned herself in to the police accompanied by her lawyer Phil Dombrey."*

As the reporter was talking, Dombrey got out of the car and helped Elise out. She was wearing a dark veil and kept her head down. Holding her by the arm, Phil led her to the door and inside the station. He kept saying "No comment. Please, no pictures."
The scene shifted.

> *"In Los Angeles, Howard Blake turned himself in accompanied by his lawyer, Chyrise Callahan."*

The picture showed Howard accompanied by a tall African-American woman, carrying what I would describe as a barrister briefcase, walking from a big car that I thought was

a Lincoln. Reporters were bombarding them with questions.
One of the reporters said:

> *"Mr. Blake, how are you going to an-*
> *swer the charges?"*

Howard stopped and turned toward the screen. His lawyer tried to stop him by a hand on his arm but he pulled away.

> *Howard: "The charges are trumped up.*
> *Stuart Andrews committed suicide aboard the*
> *Caribbean Isle. I have no idea what happened*
> *to Quentin Baston but I had no part in it. I*
> *will fight extradition with my last breath. If I*
> *have to be tried, it will be with an American*
> *jury not a bunch of queer frogs."*

His lawyer looked astonished and chagrined and finally
pulled him away talking sternly to him as they continued into
the building.

Well, Howard, I thought, *you were right about Quentin,*
but I'll bet you think you lied about that and my supposed
suicide.

On screen the reporter continued:

> *"Howard Blake's reference to a French*
> *jury comes because the police in Genivee, St.*
> *Nantes, a member of the European Union by*
> *virtue of being a French Territory, initiated*
> *the arrest warrant. Arrest warrants went into*
> *effect on January 1, 2004, replacing the tradi-*
> *tional extradition system in the European Un-*
> *ion. While the United States is not a member*
> *of that organization, Federal Attorney's Offic-*
> *es in both Miami and Los Angeles stated that*

they had every intention of honoring the war-
rants. As of yet there has been no statement
issued by the State Department. "

We were at anchor off one of the many small-uninhabited Bahamian cays and it was late afternoon. We had been here a little over twenty-four hours after making certain that the officials in St. Nantes got the evidence they needed to tie the case up. Joaquin looked at me and gave me thumbs up.

"Do we begin the relocation program now?"

"No, we have to wait until they are actually in St. Nantes's custody. To move too early could place others and us in jeopardy. We just have to be patient."

The following day this report aired on CNN:

> *"Lawyers for both Elise Blake Andrews,*
> *widow of missing American financial genius*
> *Stuart Andrews, and her brother Howard*
> *Blake filed a response with affirmative defense*
> *in Federal Court against the extradition re-*
> *quest from St. Nantes, a French territory. In*
> *both cases, these state that the arrest warrants*
> *issued were based on the dying declaration of*
> *Keith Mitchell, Los Angeles area banker.*
>
> *"Mitchell's confession was in the form of*
> *a handwritten suicide note claiming that he*
> *and Howard Blake drowned Stuart Andrews*
> *on a fishing excursion in St. Nantes in Febru-*
> *ary. The body was left in the Caribbean off*
> *the island. Mitchell, Blake, and Blake's sister,*
> *Elise, then faked Andrew's return aboard the*
> *Caribbean Isle and for two days managed to*
> *keep his presence, or lack of it, a secret. Then*
> *following a day at sea between St. Georges,*
> *Grenada, and Willemstad, Curaçao, Elise An-*
> *drews reported her husband missing.*

"The appeals state that Mitchell was suffering from depression and was under the care of a psychiatrist and therefore the content of the deathbed confession is part of his delusional fantasies.

"CNN contacted Demarco Edwards, the aforementioned psychiatrist who told us that while he was maintaining client confidentiality at the present time, his treatment of Mitchell was not for depression.

"At the request of government officials in Paris for expedited hearings of these appeals, oral arguments have been scheduled for next month. Just to make this request clear, St. Nantes is a dependency island of Guadeloupe, an Overseas Department and Region of France. St. Nantes and neighboring St. Martin and St. Barthelémy comprise a sub-region of Guadeloupe, one of the 100 governmental departments in France each of which is governed by a prefect. The sub-region is administered by a sub-prefect who resides in St. Martin and has a representative on St. Nantes. The arrest warrant was issued by the sub-prefect but has the support of the French government all the way to the President.

"In a related event, following the disappearance and until now suspected suicide of Stuart Andrews, his company Andrews Investment Management was put into receivership because of suspected illegal financial dealings. A thorough audit of the company has been conducted and the findings were released this morning. In short, the findings are that there is no evidence of any financial improprieties. Officials at the SEC are confident that the company will be able to resume its

business within the next month but that, of course, will be contingent upon the results of the extradition appeal and, if it fails, the subsequent trial."

With this latest report, I breathed a deep sign of relief. It was what I had expected, but one never knows. This finding left me free to proceed with other business.

CHAPTER 51

The phone was picked up but nothing was said. I had expected this. Most of these conversations were one sided. I didn't know whether this one would be or not. As usual the line was secure, or as secure as I could make it and I was using a voice modulator to disguise my voice, as was the person on the other end.

"I am … ah, was … a colleague of Stuart Andrews. A working agreement with him makes this call necessary because of the recent news of his demise."

Silence at the other end.

"I am to tell you that your current order will be completed using the steps initiated in the agreement."

Nothing.

"This process will take four to six weeks."

Silence, then …

"Are you going to take future orders?"

The same voice as always or at least the same manner of speaking.

"No, I do not have the ability or facility to do that. Stuart was always the one who made the arrangements. I don't know what to do."

An audible grunt on the phone.

"Do you know anyone who can?"

"No, I'm sorry. I am just a small fish in a very big ocean. I have instructions left by Stuart on steps to follow but I have no idea how to set things up."

"What about his cut?"

"I don't know about that. My instructions are to completely vacate all accounts."

"Can't you hold some longer?"

"No, he was always moving things. I don't know where to move anything and leaving them static is too dangerous. Security investigations are just too touchy now."

A sigh on the other end. Then …"I suppose that is to be expected."

The conversation was terminated.

With this and my follow-up in a couple of weeks cleaning out accounts and leaving them to be disposed of as needed by the holding companies, my laundering partnership with – I didn't know who for certain – would come to an end. There should be no repercussions.

I breathed a sigh of relief not only because I had that financial business out of the way but also knowing or at least believing that no one would be looking for me because of a failed business agreement. I knew that the more time elapsed after my reported demise, the more likely my silent investors would come in search of their money. My act with Keith, Howard, and Elise had not been made up. I had just acted quicker than my investors had – they too were waiting until things were cool before muddying the waters.

CHAPTER 52

"Maybe we should tell them about the phone calls."

"Why?" Howard asked.

Since their arrests they had both been under 24-hour house arrest with electronic monitoring. They had surrendered their passports and posted two-million dollar bonds by mortgaging everything they could. The evening before their extradition hearing, they were conversing on prepaid cells phones bought by friends.

Elise was silent.

"Think about it, Sis, what did the caller want?"

"To prove that Stuart was dead by providing his body and their money."

"Right, how are we going to provide a body? Stuart 'died' four hundred miles from St. Nantes. How are we going to provide a body or a place to search for a body without giving ourselves away?"

Elise was silent.

"We're not. Now, that money. What money?"

"The fifteen million?"

"Maybe, if they/he really had any money to begin with. So we tell them about the fifteen million. What will happen?"

"They'll seize it – freeze it – just like they did with insurance money I don't have yet. But Stuart told me that the money had no ties. It was his profit from the business."

"But if they know about it, they will freeze it," Howard continued. "Then they'll start looking at the account. Not only will they see the withdrawals you made since Stuart's 'disappearance,' they'll find the money transfered to … uhhh … the Facilitator for causing the other problem to disappear."

"Oh."

"Yeah, that would be interesting. 'What were these two transfers, Mrs. Andrews? The ten thousand dollars and the fifty thousand dollars to this other account. Hmmm, the second is just after ... .' "

"Alright, Howard, I get it." Elise sighed on the verge of tears. "This was so perfect, you said. So easy. No one would know. Now that ... that ... other person and Keith. What are we going to do?"

"Sit tight. Don't offer anything. If they don't buy the delusional fantasy bit then we'll appeal to a higher court. We'll go all the way to the Supreme Court if we have to. That will take a while."

"You sound so confident, Howard."

He wasn't. He was as anxious as Elise but someone had to hold it together.

"Look, the only 'proof' they have is Keith's confession. He was an alcoholic and a gambler. He was deeply in debt with no way to get out."

"But we were going to ... ."

"That's part of his fantasy. He thought that we were going to help him when you got the five million for Stuart's death. Nobody is going to look at that as a reason for killing him. That policy had been in effect since you married him. If ... and that is the big IF ... if they knew about the fifteen million that's tax free, maybe that would be a consideration. That is why we have to keep silent about everything."

"But it's so hard ... this waiting ... the unknown."

"Sure, I know. But we don't have any choice at this point. Chyrise said that we have a good chance with this 'fantasy delusion' story. It's our only shot at this point. Hang tough. By this time tomorrow we'll know more."

Elise was sobbing.

"Oh, Howard ... ."

"Got to go. Hang tough. Love you."

"Me too."

Howard poured himself another stiff drink. He wasn't too confident about how many more he was going to get.

CHAPTER 53

"... It's been just about a month, 29 days to be exact, since St. Nantes, a territory of France in the Caribbean, issued a warrant for the arrests of Elise Blake Andrews here in Miami and her brother Howard Blake in Los Angeles."

We were watching CNN and the reporter, a pretty young Hispanic woman, was standing in front of James Lawrence Kind Federal Justice Building in Miami-Dade County.

"The warrant requests the extradition of the two named individuals to St. Nantes to stand trial for the murder of Stuart Andrews, husband of Elise Andrews. Ordinarily extradition hearings take months before they occur but France has requested expediency in this case citing security of their evidence as a reason. That sounds strange but we have no more information than that.
"In the courtroom of Judge Ivan Sterns of the Southern District of Florida, the initial extradition hearing for Elise Andrews is set to begin momentarily. Later this afternoon, a similar hearing will be held in the Ninth Circuit Court in the case of her brother Howard Blake."

The scene shifted to show Elise and her lawyer Phil Dombrey entering the building. She was wearing a black and white dress and had her hair pulled back in a bun. She walked proudly, stiffly, both she and Phil Dombrey ignoring the cluster of reporters held back by a few policemen. The reporters held out microphones and were shouting questions at them, which both ignored.

> *"Elise Andrews and her lawyer Miami attorney Phil Dombrey entered the Federal Justice Center approximately thirty minutes ago, both ignoring requests for an interview. We are not permitted in the courtroom and will have to wait to find out what happens. A reliable source has told us that Dr. Demarco Edwards, a California psychiatrist who had been treating Keith Mitchell, will be the only witness called by the defense and his appearance will be by means of closed circuit television. You may remember that Keith Mitchell committed suicide five weeks ago and left a dying declaration in which he said that he and Howard Blake, brother of Elise Andrews, killed Stuart Andrews by drowning him while on a fishing excursion in St. Nantes where their cruise ship had stopped. According to this letter, he, Elise Andrews and her brother Howard Blake then faked Stuart Andrews's return to the Caribbean Isle. Thereafter, supposedly secluding himself for two days, Stuart Andrews then committed suicide between St. Georges, Grenada, and Willemstad, Curaçao."*

In a courtroom inside the Federal Justice Building, James Burns of the U.S. Federal Attorneys office was making his opening statement.

"The warrant for the extradition of Elise Blake Andrews to St. Nantes to stand trial for the murder of her husband Stuart Andrews is in order. St. Nantes is unusual in that France does not have a death penalty but this territory does.

Still the State of Florida, States and the United States Government find no reason to bar extradition.

"In support of the warrant, St. Nantes offers the dying declaration of one Keith Mitchell of Los Angeles, California, in which he states that he was party to the murder by drowning of Stuart Andrews."

"Objection, your honor," Phil Dombrey was on this feet. "Hearsay."

"Your honor," responded James Burns, "the confession by Mr. Mitchell is covered under the Dying Declaration Exception to the Hearsay Rule, and the confession was written immediately prior to Mr. Mitchell's suicide."

"Has the suicide note been authenticated to verify that it was written by Mr. Mitchell?" queried Judge Sterns.

"Yes, your honor. I am submitting both the letter and the corresponding handwriting analysis into evidence as People's Exhibits One and Two." James Burns showed both documents to Phil Dombrey.

"Very well, People's Exhibits One and Two are admitted into evidence," said Ivan Sterns. "Counselor, your objection is denied."

James Burns continued. "Further, he details the subsequent cover up of that murder by faking Stuart Andrews's return on board of the Caribbean Isle and his subsequent fake suicide.

"Also the St. Nantes's government states that they have physical evidence supporting this dying declaration, as well as a witness who can attest to the fact that Stuart Andrews did not return from the fishing expedition."

Elise Andrews stiffened at the mention of a witness but said nothing.

"The Government feels that the evidence provided is sufficient for the issuance of the warrant and find no reason to block the request."

James Burns sat down and Phil Dombrey stood.

"Your honor, the basis for this warrant issued by St. Nantes, territory of the Republic of France, is the dying declaration of Keith Mitchell. It is my client's contention that Keith Mitchell was severely mentally ill and was under the care of a psychiatrist, Dr. Demarco Edwards of Los Angeles, California. We ask the Court to hear testimony from Dr. Demarco Edwards to obtain the truth about the mental condition of Keith Mitchell. We feel that you will learn that Mr. Mitchell was mentally ill and that his dying declaration is a total fantasy.

"With this fact in place, we think you will agree that the warrant issued by St. Nantes has nothing to substantiate it and we ask that extradition therefore be denied."

He sat down.

Judge Ivan Sterns looked at both parties and then said.

"This case is indeed unusual in that France, representing its territory St. Nantes, has requested that all haste be made in the execution of the extradition warrant because there is some concern as to the security of their evidence. While they are very closed-mouthed about this evidence, I do find that the warrant is perfectly proper."

Phil Dombrey started to rise.

"However, I am willing to hear the testimony of Dr. Edwards to determine if there is sufficient cause to believe that the dying declaration of Mr. Mitchell was indeed some fantasy."

CHAPTER 54

"Mr. Dombrey, are you ready to continue with this closed circuit testimony?" Judge Sterns asked.

"Yes, your honor, we are."

He nodded to a technician and a flat screen TV mounted on a mobile cart flickered to life.

Dr. Demarco Edwards appeared on the screen seated at a table in front of what appeared to be a judge's bench in a courtroom. He appeared to be middle-aged man dressed in a conservative suit and tie. His dark hair showed touches of grey at the temples.

"Dr. Edwards, I am Phil Dombrey, lawyer for Mrs. Elise Andrews. We have talked on the phone previously," Phil began.

"Yes, I recognize your voice. However, as I told you … ."

"Dr. Edwards, this is Judge Ivan Sterns of the U.S. District Court in Miami, Florida. Please wait to give your testimony until we ascertain that all has been handled correctly.

"Judge Rodriguez, are you there?"

"Yes, I am Judge Sterns," responded a female voice.

"We thank you for starting your day so early. I believe it is just after eight o'clock there on the West Coast."

The disembodied voice of Judge Consuela Rodriguez responded, "Not at all, Judge Sterns. My day usually starts at 5:00 a.m."

"I understand. Mine does too. But let's get to the point. Has Dr. Demarco been sworn in?"

"Yes, just ten minutes ago. We are ready to begin your questioning."

"Fine," said Judge Sterns. "Mr. Dombrey, he is your witness."

"Thank you, Judge Sterns." And turning to face the camera,"Dr. Edwards, how long was Keith Mitchell a patient of yours?"

On screen, Dr. Edwards shifted in his seat as though the question had made him uncomfortable.

"Five years but ..."

"Just answer the question, Dr. Edwards," Phil Dombrey admonished.

"Very well," Dr. Edwards replied.

"And for what were you treating him?" Phil Dombrey asked.

Dr. Edwards shifted uncomfortable again. "I am not happy giving out this personal information even though my client is dead. As I told you, I have never had to disclose a patient's treatment before and I find it a bit disconcerting. Even distasteful."

"Please answer the question, Dr. Edwards," Judge Sterns said. "At this point we aren't asking for details, just generalities. I am certain that can't be too intrusive into your patient-doctor confidentiality."

Demarco Edwards sighed.

"Very well. I had been treating Keith Mitchell for addiction to both alcohol and gambling."

"Anything else?" Phil Dombrey asked.

"No, Mr. Dombrey," Demarco Edwards snapped. "As I told you on the phone that was it."

"For five years?" queried Phil Dombrey.

"Mr. Mitchell was a very weak person in those areas. He made progress and for a while seemed to have everything under control."

"There was a relapse?" asked Phil Dombrey.

James Burns was on his feet immediately. "Objection, counsel is leading the witness."

"Sustained," said Judge Sterns. "Counsel, rephrase your question."

"What happened then?" Phil Dombrey asked.

"There was a relapse," answered Demarco Williams.

"Just one?" Phil Dombrey asked.

James Burns started to object and then settled back.

"Oh, there were several relapses." Suddenly Demarco Edwards was giving information willingly.

"He would be fine for a month or two and then slip back. Gambling was the big one. He just couldn't stop his wagering. Of course, when you're gambling, you drink so one would lead to the other.

"Not that the drinking led to gambling but the gambling certainly led to drinking. At least that is what Keith Mitchell told me."

"What about his fantasizing?" Phil asked.

"What fantasizing?" Demarco Edwards responded.

"About the murder of Stuart Andrews?" Phil Dombrey said.

"He never mentioned murder or Stuart Andrews. He wasn't delusional ..."

"Come, come," Phil Dombrey replied. "With all those problems, to say he wasn't delusional ..."

"I never saw any evidence of delusions." With that remark, Demarco Edwards seemed to regain control and said no more.

"But he was under stress, wasn't he?" Dombrey asked.

"There was some stress from his job but with the financial markets the way they are now that is understandable. I had seen similar patterns of stress from him at other times but nothing overpowering. He seemed to be able to handle those forms of stress quite well."

"You mean there was never any evidence of fantasies or delusions of any kind?" Dombrey needled.

"I treated Mr. Mitchell for five years meeting once a week most of the time, but sometimes when things were falling apart, two or three times. In those five years, I never saw any evidence of delusions or fantasies of the nature that you believe his dying declaration to be. I have read a photocopy of this document and do not believe that he was either delusional or fantasizing when he wrote it."

"But certainly …" Dombrey interjected.

"Mr. Dombrey," Demarco Edwards countered. "We all have fantasies, don't we? Even you."

CHAPTER 55

That last comment by Demarco Edwards ended the questioning by Phil Dombrey and James Burns had no questions. Judge Sterns adjourned the court until 2:00 when he said he would have a ruling.

Judge Sterns was five minutes late in opening the afternoon session.

"In preparation for this hearing, I consulted with officials in St. Nantes with regards to evidence in this case as well as other matters regarding the warrants. In fact I have just gotten off the phone with Huard Jubert, who is the prosecutor handling this case in St. Nantes, regarding the evidence in this case and have found nothing contrary to the warrant.

"The State Department has stated that it has no reason to bar extradition to St. Nantes because of the extradition treaty with France. Although France does not have a death penalty, the territory of St. Nantes does. However so does the state of Florida so the death penalty is not a cause for barring of the extradition request. The government of the United States does not find the death penalty reason to deny extradition.

"We had testimony this morning from California in the form of a video conference with Dr. Demarco Edwards, psychiatrist treating Mr. Keith Mitchell, deceased, whose dying declaration prompted the initial investigation by the Los Angeles County Sheriff and ultimately led to the warrant issued by France in the name of St. Nantes. He testified that he was treating Mr. Mitchell for addiction to both alcohol and gambling and that he was not depressed. He admits that while Mr. Mitchell was under some stress and that he, Mr. Mitchell, stated during one of his twice-weekly sessions the day before his suicide that was from his job. This is contrary to testimony of the defendant Elise Blake Andrews.

"In addition, the dying declaration of Mr. Mitchell is collaborated in great part by evidence obtained during the police investigation in St. Nantes, but I cannot say any more than this concerning this matter.

"With these facts in mind, I find no legal grounds to deny the extradition of Elise Blake Andrews to St. Nantes."

He accentuated this statement with a rap of his gavel on the sound block.

"Deputies please take charge of Mrs. Andrews and prepare her for extradition to St. Nantes. We are adjourned."

With a rap of his walnut gavel, he rose and departed through the door behind his bench.

Elise sat stunned as Phil Dombrey started putting his papers into his bag.

"We'll appeal immediately. I have the paperwork ready to go and will file it immediately."

Elise looked up at him, eyes like a deer caught in the headlights of an oncoming semi. "Is there a chance?" she asked.

Phil hesitated. "There's always a chance, Elise. Have faith."

"How much of a chance?"

Phil paused in his packing. "Honestly, not much."

Elise sagged in her chair as a deputy came to take her away.

Within half an hour, television stations were airing the news.

> *"In a swift decision today in the Federal District Court of the Southern District of Florida in Miami-Dade County, Elise Blake Andrews's request to bar extradition to St. Nantes to stand trial for the murder of her husband was denied and she was taken into custody for transfer to Genivee. Her lawyer Phil Dombrey stated that he had filed an appeal with the Eleventh District Court of*

Appeals from which he expected a quick reply because of the request from France that the usually long extradition process be accelerated. When asked what kind of chance this appeal had, he replied, "There's always a chance."

Much of the speculation about the extradition requests has hinged around the death penalty that is still in existence on St. Nantes but not in the rest of France's territories or France itself. And therein lies an interesting story.

In 1728 the town of Genivee – at the time known as the Village of St. Nantes – was a thriving fishing and commercial port of 1500 people centered around a beautiful wooden church named Our Lady of Protection. A young privateer named John-Paul LaPre anchored in the bay and fired a ten-gun broadside at the town killing 16. His forces then stormed ashore unhindered as the citizenry cowered behind closed doors, which did little good in stopping John-Paul's men. What could have become a murderous rampage and rape was short lived, however, as five boats of the village's small fishing fleet returned home and realized what was going on. With only fishing knives and gaffs as weapons, the ten fishermen stormed aboard the undefended privateer's ship and seized it and the captain who had remained aboard. With his own life hanging by a thread at that point, John-Paul had no choice but to have his men yield. They surrendered their weapons including the ship's cannons, which were unloaded on the future Guerre Isle. Then in an act of Christian forgiveness, they were set free.

One year to the day later, John-Paul LaPre returned with a force twice as large on a bigger ship. He bombarded the town with broadside after broadside refusing to honor a white flag of surrender. With the town afire, he and his forces landed, gathered the families of the fishermen who had seized his ship, and locked them in the church. The last woman to enter the church was Genivee Lacour. She managed to get loose from her captor and, with a knife secreted in a pocket of her dress, attacked John-Paul LaPre. She was subdued once again but only after managing to put an ugly slice on his left cheek that left an equally ugly scar. She was knocked senseless and thrust into the church that was then locked and set afire burning all the twenty-six people inside.

Leaving the burning port behind, John-Paul set sail for further pickings at sea. However, his luck failed him again within a week. As he was chasing an English merchant ship, an English man-of-war spotted him unawares and sank his ship with the loss of almost all hands. Seven of the pirates were rescued from the water. Aware of atrocity that the pirates had committed on St. Nantes, the captives were returned to that port. In a short and extremely biased trial, all seven were sentenced to death. Having no gallows handy, the masts of the English man-of-war were used and in no time the seven were "swinging from the yardarms." To this day, the gallows of St. Nantes resembles a ship's mast and on St. Nantes, seven is considered to be an unlucky number.

The surviving villagers beseeched the French government for protection and Ft. Rideau was built using as its first armaments the cannons from John-Paul LePre's first ship. The village was named Genivee in honor of the fisherman's wife who so bravely attacked and wounded LaPre.

St. Nantes remained a French Territory until the 1970's, administered by the Prefect of Guadalupe. At that time the French were making the decision to do away with capital punishment. The approximately 5800 inhabitants of the island were deeply religious (Catholicism being the main religion practiced by 90 per cent of the population) and, despite their Catholic ties and because of the incident we just discussed, had developed a strong adherence to the law of retribution, or "lex talionis" from the Latin "lex" for "law" and "talio" for "like" – the punishment is like the injury or "an eye for an eye." They could not agree with the French decision and requested that they be permitted to remain an overseas territory of France rather than become overseas department.

Two hours later, CNN aired this report.

"Shortly after the Extradition Hearing of Elise Blake Andrews to bar extradition to St. Nantes to stand trial for the alleged drowning death of her husband, her brother Howard Blake of Los Angeles was apprehended by California Highway Patrol officers, apparently as he attempted to flee the city. He was tracked by means of his electronic surveillance ankle bracelet.

"Blake is in custody in a Los Angeles jail awaiting his hearing to bar his extradition to St. Nantes to stand trial for the murder of Stuart Andrews, his brother-in-law. The decision of the Federal District Court of the Southern District of Florida will undoubtedly have an effect on what will happen in the Federal District Court of the Central District of California Pasadena hearing of Howard Mitchell's challenge to bar his extradition. It is expected that a decision denying his challenge will be issued quickly. His attempt to flee certainly doesn't help his case."

CHAPTER 56

It was 1:50 p.m. in Los Angeles, and Howard sat slumped in the chair behind the defense's table, hands hand-cuffed, feet shackled. He had been brought in by a guard from the jail and roughly seated at the table. The guard was two feet to his left and a little behind with an ugly scowl on his face. Chyrise slapped her briefcase on the table and glared at him.

"What do you have to say for yourself? What in the world made you run? You had a little chance before but now..." She sat shaking her head.

Howard said nothing.

"Well, answer me. I'm your lawyer."

Howard mumbled something.

"Speak up, Howard, you're not in an old age home."

"I panicked, alright? I saw the news report that Elise lost her case. They said that our two cases were tied, that the two judges had conferred. I figured I was a goner so I took off. I didn't think."

"You're damn right you didn't think. With that stupid move, any chance you had went right out the window. Talk about acting guilty! I wouldn't be surprised if Judge Rodriguez doesn't just by-pass all formalities and deny your appeal. I certainly would."

"But you're not facing trial by those wimpy frogs. You're not facing the gallows or potential lifetime sentence in one of their stinking faggot prisons when they railroad me to a guilty verdict. I figured that if that stupid fantasized confession of Keith's was enough to convince that Florida Judge to grant Elise's extradition then it was probably enough to convict us in their faggot court."

He was obviously angry now and he swung to face her.

"They don't even have a jury of your peers. They have nine so-called judges, three of them lawyer-types and the others – assistants or something. It's not even unanimous. Just two thirds, just six votes and you're guilty. Six faggot headed ... ."

"Shut up, Howard. You ... we aren't there yet. You have to keep a level head. You need to act like a responsible human being. If we lose, not when," she glared at him, "if we lose we will face the next part together. I don't know if I can continue as your lawyer. I haven't looked that far ahead. This has happened so quickly, I haven't had time. But ... ."

CHAPTER 57

"Order in the court," said the bailiff entering the court-room. "All rise. The honorable Judge Consuela Rodriguez presiding."

Howard stood, head down, swaying slightly as Judge Rodriguez entered the courtroom through the door behind her bench. When she had taken her seat the bailiff said. "Be seated."

Judge Rodriguez looked at the papers on her desk and then looked at Howard. "Nice that you decided to be with us today, Mr. Blake. Hello, Ms. Callahan. Mr. Rogers." She acknowledged the federal attorney.

"We are here today to consider the challenge of Howard Blake for the denial of the Application for Foreign Extradition to Genivee, St. Nantes, a territory of the Republic of France.

"Mr. Rogers, as we discussed earlier, this motion is linked to a similar motion that was considered this morning in the U.S. District Court in Miami-Dade County, Florida on behalf of Mrs. Elise Blake Andrews since France has requested that both of you be extradited to St. Nantes to stand trial for the murder of Stuart Andrews in the waters of St. Nantes.

"This morning I listened to the testimony of Dr. Demarco Edwards regarding his treatment of Mr. Keith Mitchell, deceased, who left a suicide note that implicates both parties in the aforementioned murder." And to the federal attorney, "Do the People have anything to add that has not already been considered in that case?"

"Yes, your honor. France does not have capital punishment but St. Nantes does. That may be strange, but as a territory of France and not an overseas department, that is their right. However, the State of California also has the death penalty so if the trial were to be held here, the defendant would potentially face the same penalty. There is nothing else that we would find abhorrent in having Mr. Blake extradited to face trial there."

"Ms. Callahan, as you know the testimony of Dr. Demarco Edwards about the mental health of Keith Mitchell does nothing to support your client's contention that he was mentally unbalanced and that his deathbed confession was a whimsical hallucinatory fantasy, which is the basis for Mr. Blake's appeal. You were not present at the videoconference, although I understand that you did watch it. Not being present, you had no opportunity to question Dr. Edwards. If you have questions that you think will shed a different light on his testimony, we will call Dr. Edwards to appear before this court. He is available outside this courtroom."

Chyrise looked at Howard who sat sullenly staring at the table.

"I do not have any further questions that will help my case," she replied.

Judge Rodriguez continued, "In a telephone conversation with the police on St. Nantes, I was assured that for the most part the statements in Mr. Mitchell's confession are substantiated by evidence that they have discovered."

Howard's head jerked up.

"What? What did you say? What evidence?"

Judge Rodriguez's gavel slapped sharply.

"Mr. Blake, you are out of order. Ms. Callahan, would you please talk to your client so that we may proceed."

"Yes, Judge, give me a minute."

Chyrise sat down and turned to Howard. "Howard, you have to keep quiet."

"But what does she say about evidence that those French frog faggots have? What evidence? I don't ... ."

"Howard, I don't know. We are not privy to that and neither is the judge. All that she knows is that the authorities on St. Nantes say they have evidence other than the confession that makes the confession look solid, at least for the murder of your brother-in-law. St. Nantes is different than the States and does not have to reveal all evidence prior to trial. Their system is based upon the Napoleonic Code and is quite different as you are well aware.

"This certainly puts us at a disadvantage. We will have to wait to see what the evidence is when it is presented or when we are given a chance … ."

"Bitch, you're talking like we're going to lose. That … ."

"Don't talk to me that way, Howard. You hired me because of my expertise and track record. Yes, you hired me because I am a woman and because I am African-American, like your brother-in-law. That would make a good impression, you told me. I accepted that – it's happened before – but if you want my help you're going to have to maintain control of yourself. I told you that from the very start. You are going to have to respect the court and its representatives no matter what happens. Any more outburst here or elsewhere will not be tolerated by me or any court."

"But … ."

"Don't but me, Howard. That's the way it is. That's the way it has to be. Now are we … are you clear on that?"

"Yes, but… ."

"Anything else will be handled later."

"Fine," Howard snapped slumping in his seat muttering "black bitch" under his breath and glaring through half-closed eyes at the judge. Either Chyrise didn't hear it or let it pass considering the mood that he was in.

"Ms. Callahan?" questioned Judge Rodriguez.

"Yes, your honor, we're fine," said Chyrise rising again. "However, I must object to the introduction of statements made by the police of St. Nantes to which we are not privy. That's hearsay … ."

"Ms. Callahan," said Judge Rodriguez. "I introduced no evidence but was simply making a statement in support of my decision. Your objection is overruled."

Chyrise sank into her seat.

"As I was saying, Dr. Edward's testimony does not support the petitioner's case and the case presented by the officials of St. Nantes supports the dying declaration of Mr. Mitchell.

"At this time, do you have anything else to offer in support of Mr. Blake's request?"

Chyrise looked at Howard. "Howard?"

Howard raised his head and glared at the judge. Then he lowered it and shook it side-to-side.

"No, your honor. I have nothing further to add."

"Then the Petition of St. Nantes is granted. Mr. Blake, you are remanded to custody of the sheriff's department who will see that you get transported to St. Nantes."

She slammed her gavel "We are adjourned." And left the bench.

As the door closed behind her, Howard muttered "Spic bitch."

CHAPTER 58

Both lawyers appealed the decision of the judges to grant extradition of their clients to St. Nantes. However, in short order the Federal Circuit Court of Appeals issued a Per Curiam opinion, affirming the order of the District Courts granting extradition. An appeal was made to the Supreme Court and the President of the United States. The President had his Attorney General's office consult with the St. Nantes officials as well as the U.S. District Court judges. The report to the President was that the French petition for extradition should be granted and the President responded in that manner. At approximately the same time, the Supreme Court of the United States responded that it would not consider the case.

This last piece of news dashed all hope that Howard and Elise had and officials made plans for their release to French officials. During this process, Joaquin and I had been traveling in the northern and eastern Caribbean enjoying the many different cultures and nationalities that were to be found there. We even tried fishing with the Zàkpa at very slow speeds and had some moderate success but nothing outstanding.

When the final news came that extradition had been granted, I broke out a bottle of champagne and we sat on the fantail enjoying the coolness of the evening and watching the sunset.

"To extradition," I said and and as we clinked glasses Joaquin said, "To justice."

"So, boss," Joaquin said as he finished his glass, "Is it time for relocation?"

"Yes," I responded, "it's time, but tonight we enjoy the moment. Tomorrow is soon enough."

Part VI
The Witness

CHAPTER 59

At precisely 9:00 a.m., the door on the left side of the courtroom in front of the spectator section opened and a hush fell over the assembly. Guillaume Martineau, the court's bailiff wearing a black robe and carrying a long ornate staff, entered and walked across the room leading a procession of ten people. The staff thumped quietly on the floor as he crossed the room to the second of two long tables set four feet apart and four feet in front of the low railing and floor-to-ceiling chain link fencing that separated the main part of the courtroom from the spectator section. He indicated that table to the four who had followed him and waited until they had taken up places behind the table. They were the prosecutors in the case.

Then he walked back to the first table and motioned toward it to the six who had stopped. The first of the six was a gendarme; the second was Elise looking tired and a bit disheveled, eyes to the floor as though embarrassed and I was certain she was; the third was Howard, wearing a scowl as his eyes took in the entire room sweeping only fleetingly through the onlookers; the fourth was another gendarme; the fifth Phil Dombrey; and the sixth Chyrise Callahan.

Elise was wearing a black sleeveless dress of knee length and pearl earrings and necklace. Her wedding ring was her only other jewelry. She appeared to be in mourning. She stood five feet ten inches and weighed 130 pounds and had an average figure. She was a true blond (I know) and blue-eyed. She went to school at the University of Miami (that's the one in Florida) and majored in sociology with a minor in drama of all things. In college she won several awards for her acting but, following graduation, attempts to secure roles in local amateur and professional theaters went nowhere, so she became a publicist for a local theater group after graduation. She quit working when we got married because her career was going nowhere and she "...wanted to be the best wife possible." Did that include murdering her husband?

Howard was dressed in navy slacks with a powder blue white pin-stripe shirt and white tie with red and blue stars (was he being patriotic or making his biases known?) As always he wore dark socks with black loafers. He had brown hair and eyes, stood six feet one inch, and weighed 230 solid pounds – he worked out three or four days a week. His physical condition, with which I may have had to contend, is the reason I started my fitness regimen. (I even put exercise equipment on the Zàkpa.) He also went to the University of Miami and played football four years but only got a letter in his senior year. He didn't have a scholarship and was a walk-on all four years. He played linebacker and had good hands, but not the speed necessary to keep up with receivers, and thus played mainly on special teams. He majored in accounting and got an M.B.A. He took the job with Philpott and had done well. I never knew where his bigotry came from – his sister never showed it. Or at least not to me. Of course in college he played football with many blacks – make that African-Americans to be politically correct. Perhaps the fact that he never was a starter except for senior day, and almost all the starting linebackers were African-American had something to do with it. But the hatred of the French? That is a mystery to me as it was with Keith. I should have asked him that last night.

Guillaume Martineau motioned toward the table and the gendarme in front walked Elise to the second seat behind the table, indicating that she should remain standing while the second gendarme actually pushed Howard toward the third seat. Howard stopped and glared at the gendarme, drawing another push, and he took his place. Phil Dombrey then joined them in the first seat next to Elise and Chyrise Callahan in the fourth next to Howard. The two gendarmes took places in chairs behind and to the left and right of the defense's table. The four prosecuting attorneys and the two defendants and their attorneys then picked up ear buds from boxes set on the table and put them in their ears, Howard only at the persistent insistence of Chyrise. To the right of the prosecutor's table and against the wall next to a raised section of three tables and chairs behind a low solid railing were two glass enclosed booths for translators: one English to French and the other French to English. Everyone in the courtroom, spectators included, would be given an ear bud so that they might hear all aspects of the trial in their choice of the two languages.

Guillaume Martineau had walked back to the door and had taken up a position by it. He then rapped the staff sharply on the floor and said "The Cours d'Assise …" – the Assize Court – "…of the Territory of St. Nantes of the Prefecture of Guadeloupe is called to order, the honorable Michel Villar officiating." Or at least that is what I heard over my ear bud.

Forty-five year old Michel Villar was a native born St. Nantesian who had attended Harvard undergraduate and then the University of Virginia Law School studying international law. The lure of the islands brought him back via Paris where he studied for and passed the French Bar. At six feet even, he weighed between 170 and 175, a true string bean. His black hair and eyes came from both his parents who were also tall. His father was a lawyer, who spurred his interest, and his mother a housewife – both still living. He had an older brother who died in the Twin Towers and a younger sister who was married to a doctor and lived on St. Barthelémy and had given him a niece and nephew in that order. He had been married (no children) but that fell apart quickly because of his wandering eye, hands, and private parts. He loved the good life and seemed to have found the money for it somewhere (the stock market, if rumors were to be believed). He had become judge 10 years ago and quickly achieved a good reputation as a fair but harsh jurist with a sarcastic wit that he found hard to control. You can say that he had a problem with two zippers: his fly and his mouth. He had quickly become recognized as the most prominent jurist of the French West Indies.

Guillaume Martineau then stepped in front of the door, turned toward the interior of the courtroom and led another procession of ten people, the first nine of whom wore long black robes like American judges but with long white scarves serving as collars. Michel Villar, the tenth in line, wore a red robe with the white scarf showing his status as the presiding judge. The first six followed Guillaume Martineau as he turned left to a two-level raised podium on the wall by the door. This they entered by means of a small gate in the solid railing at the near end of the platform. Three of them took seats behind a long table on the first level, and the second three ascended to the top level and took seats at a similar table. All six picked up and installed ear buds. There were two women, one middle-aged and one in her early thirties, a middle-aged black man, two middle-aged white men, and a man in his early to mid-thirties.

Guillaume Martineau returned to the four persons remaining and led them toward the raised platform on the far side of the room. The last one stopped in the middle of the courtroom just short of the witness podium, which was about six feet in front of the prosecutors' table. Guillaume Martineau and the other three continued to the near end of the raised platform. There Guillaume Martineau stopped and indicated the entry stairway to the podium waiting as they entered giving each a barely perceptible nod as they passed. These three took places behind separate tables with slightly more opulent and comfortable chairs than their six counterparts across the courtroom. They installed their ear buds and remained standing as the bailiff made his way back to the remaining figure, obviously the President of the Court Michel Villar. The three professional judges were all middle-aged white males.

The bailiff then ceremonially led the judge to the raised platform in the front center of the courtroom gesturing with a huge sweep of his arm toward a staircase on the right side. The judge ascended the staircase while Guillaume Martineau took his place to the right of the staircase. Michel Villar reached his chair, a comfortable looking high-back office chair, took his seat, placed his ear bud in his ear, nodded to the court's clerk who was previously in place at a table to his front left, rapped his gavel, and the trial had begun.

CHAPTER 60

The trial was held in a modified courtroom in Fort Rideau on Guerre Isle overlooking the port in Genivee. Guerre Isle lies one-quarter mile from the shore on the northwest and southwest sides of the harbor and is so named because of Fort Rideau, which was built atop the island. The island is about a mile long and half a mile wide with a wide beach running around the southeastern end and wrapping about half the length of the island on both sides. The fit into the harbor outline is so close that Guerre Isle almost appears to have been pulled away from the main island. The northwest end has a steep promontory atop which Fort Rideau was built to protect the island's harbor.

The fort had been expanded and improved innumerable times, the last during the Cold War when it housed equipment used to track satellites. When the French left following the island's independence, the fort was taken over by the government and used as the principal headquarters housing the office of the Prefect, the offices and meeting hall of the assembly, as well as several courtrooms and judicial offices. No cars are permitted on Guerre Isle. Two minibuses shuttle people to the fort from the ferry that runs from the harbor to the island. The ferry runs an hourly schedule during the tourist season and when the assembly is present for its quarterly two-week session and thrice-daily otherwise. The only street is cobblestone and leads from the ferry landing to the fort. Numerous footpaths lead from the ferry landing to the fort and beaches and there is an asphalted bike path that leads from the fort down the seaward side of the island and along the beach to the ferry landing. During the tourist season there are several small restaurants that open on the island, extensions of restaurants to be found in Genivee. It wasn't tourist season now but the island restaurants were open to accommodate the trial's participants.

A rush order had made the facility ready for the trial in just under a month. A permanent police force of eight officers lived on the main island near their headquarters in downtown Genivee. Usually there are four additional officers from other parts of the French West Indies on temporary assignment to the island, rotating in shifts of three months and housed in island homes. However, the anticipated number of press attending the trial and concern for security increased the number of temporary officers by eight, with six more assigned to guard Elise and Howard, who were to be quartered in rented facilities near the police headquarters because there were only two jail cells in the small police building. Each day of the trial they had to be transported from their quarters to Guerre Isle by the ferry, with no other passengers permitted, and then to the fort by van.

The French judicial system is quite different from that in the states. There are actually two judicial systems: administrative and judiciary. The administrative branch is for settling lawsuits between individuals and the French Government. The judiciary branch, responsible for civil and criminal cases, consists of three courts: Tribunaux Correctionels (Courts of Correction), the Tribunaux de Police (Police courts) and the Cours d'Assise that tries felonies and was the one handling the trial of Elise and Howard. Assise was the name of an ancient court; it derived its name from "assideo," to sit together. Appeals are referred to one of the 28 Cours d'Appel (Courts of Appeal) and ultimately the Cour de Cassation (Supreme Court of Appeals).

French judges are career professionals who attain their positions through an extremely competitive examination. The judges play a much different role in criminal trials than they do in the United States or Britain in that they conduct the questioning of the witnesses through their own questions and also those submitted by prosecuting and defense attorneys as well. There is no jury of one's peers, rather a mixed tribunal of six lay judges, who are basically like justices of the peace in the states, and three professional judges. These nine jurists convict with a minimum two-thirds majority.

The space available for the trail accounted for the physical set up. Michel Villar as the presiding judge sat on a podium at the end of the room with the three professional judges to his left and the six lay judges to his right. Interestingly, the top level of the lay judge platform was about six inches below the level of the professional judges' area and that was six inches below Villar's perch, which I judged to be about two feet off the floor.

Witnesses would enter the area through a door on the presiding judge's right. It was at the end of the lay judges area through which the judges, defense and prosecution personnel had entered. The press and interested parties sat behind the prosecution and defense, separated from them by a floor-to-ceiling link fence. The spectators entered through a door in the center of the wall at the back of the room. On the other side were stringent security measures including the latest in scanning tools: the backscatter system that can see through clothes. The French were leaving nothing to chance.

Beyond the door where the judges entered was another hallway. To the right were offices for the presiding judge, and the three professional judges. To the left was a witness waiting room and an office shared by the six lay judges, each having his or her own small cubical. At the end of the hall were two holding rooms for the two defendants and their lawyers. A hall led to the left in front of these holding rooms to another security chamber with the same stringent security measures as that for the spectators.

The security was so strict that I was forced to use my Dawoh Mbayo identity with press credentials that I had gotten from the *Awareness Times*, the largest major newspaper in Sierra Leone. I had called the editor explaining that I was in St. Nantes and interested in the trial and would be glad to provide coverage at no charge. This pass permitted me to bring in my laptop although there was no wireless access and all cell phone signals had been blocked. Security was more concerned with possible weapons being smuggled in than with information being sent. No chances were being taken. This guise as a reporter meant that I actually had to send stories in daily but that was no problem since I was able to write during the trial and could send the story as soon as I got into the harbor area. That's where there was Wifi access – most bars and restaurants had installed it for the trial, if they did not already have it.

CHAPTER 61

The judge charged the jury:

"The charges in this case against the two defendants Howard Blake and Elise Blake Andrews, both citizens of the United States of America, are that they did with premeditation kill Stuart Andrews, husband of Elise Blake Andrews, by drowning while fishing in the waters of St. Nantes and did attempt to cover that conspiracy and murder with the subterfuge of his suicide between St. Georges, Grenada, and Willemstad, Curaçao.

"You are to listen to the evidence presented by both the prosecution and defense and then to decide without reasonable doubt the guilt or innocence of both parties. There is to be no separation of guilt, both are linked to the crime by a conspiracy to commit murder: they are either both guilty or both innocent."

This is quite different from American courts. While trying two co-defendants simultaneously is quite common, no separation of guilt between the two co-defendants is certainly uncommon in American Courts. He then turned to the courtroom at large and addressed the attorneys:

"In French courts, all questioning of witnesses is done by the presiding judge, me in this case, either with my own questions or questions submitted by you to me. You motion to my bailiff Guillaume Martineau who will come to you to get your written question and will give it to me. If I feel that it is repetitive or not germane, I will not ask it.

"If you feel that you would like to address the question yourself and the request seems reasonable I will permit it but you have to keep your questions confined to the topic of the moment. It that clear?"

There was a momentary lag between the time he finished his address as it was in French and the time the translation was completed for the American lawyers. The lawyers at the prosecution table had already given their assent and about thirty seconds later, Phil Dombrey and Chyrise Callahan did the same.

"The prosecution will present its case and then the defense will have a chance to refute the testimony and evidence given with its own witnesses and evidence. The prosecution will then have an opportunity for rebuttal and then the defense. When all evidence for both sides has been presented, each side will summarize, the defense last. Is this understood?"

Again with the translation lag, all attorneys indicated their understanding. Michel Villar then addressed the press and interested parties.

"There is to be no outburst from the spectators. Any interruption will not be tolerated and the persons responsible will be escorted from this courtroom and not permitted to return. A short prison sentence could be levied to an offending party if I deem it proper. If there is continued interruption, I will have the courtroom cleared and the trial will continue without you."

He then addressed Elise and Howard.

"The same admonishment about outburst applies to the defendants also. Undue interruptions and you will find yourself watching the proceedings over television from a holding cell in this building. Is that understood?"

Elise and Howard indicated that it was although Howard's look at the judge was anything but amicable.

Michel Villar then addressed the prosecution.

"Mr. Jubert, you may begin."

CHAPTER 62

Huard Jubert, head of the prosecution's team, began with a brief opening statement to the jury. He had been born on St. Nantes but had grown up in Paris where he had gone to university and law school. He had then returned to St. Nantes to work in the prosecutor's office and had become chief prosecutor five years before. He was unmarried but shared a house with a girlfriend. He was an avid fisherman and had his own boat. Weekends, weather permitting, he would be found on the Caribbean.

"Messieurs and Mesdames, the crime which was committed by these defendants and a conspirator, who is no longer with us, is an especially egregious one as it is between husband and wife with greed and bigotry as motivations.

"On a trip to our beautiful island, Stuart Andrews, in company with his brother-in-law Monsieur Howard Blake," indicating Howard at the defense's table, "and Monsieur Keith Mitchell, deceased, departed from Genivee's port on a beautiful Caribbean morning on a fishing expedition aboard the Mahi Mahi, the fishing boat owned and operated by Quentin Baston.

"Out on the water, a fish was caught and Stuart Andrews moved to see it. In a sudden attack, Howard Blake hit Stuart Andrews with a beer bottle ..."

There was a flash of green ... unexpectedly the image came into my head.

"... rendering him unconscious. While his companion Keith Mitchell kept Quentin Baston under control ..."

Howard grunted. The judge glowered at him but said nothing.

"... Howard Blake stripped Stuart Andrews's body of all identification. Then with the help of Keith Mitchell, they hung Stuart Andrews over the side of the boat with his head under water. When he was dead, they released his body and it sank below the waves.

"They returned to the port of Genivee about the time they would have if on an actual fishing excursion, but the two Americans got off the Mahi Mahi at a different dock in order that no one could see that Stuart Andrews was not with them. Quentin Baston had been threatened with the death of himself and his family and given ten thousand dollars to keep quiet. That money has the fingerprints of Howard Blake on it."

Howard sat bolt upright with that statement. "What the…," he stammered. Chyrise reached over to grab his arm as Michel Villar rapped his gavel and Howard stopped. Huard Jubert looked at him and then continued.

"Howard Blake and Keith Mitchell joined Elise Blake Andrews and the three of them went back to the Caribbean Isle, their cruise ship, aboard one of its tenders. There they managed to divert the attention of the gangway staff and swiped Stuart Andrews cruise card to convince the ship's staff that he was back on board."

I knew that this last statement had to come from Keith's confession, as I was certain that neither Howard nor Elise would have said anything that would involve them. Of course it was not germane to the actual "murder" incident but was important as far as the cover-up was concerned.

"They managed to keep secret the fact that Stuart Andrews was not on board the Caribbean Isle for two days until, between St. Georges, Grenada, and Willemstad, Curaçao, Elise Andrews reported him missing. A futile search was conducted and at last Stuart Andrews was given up for dead. There was no chance that his body would be found and laid to rest to gain eternal salvation with our Lord."

"Monsieur Jubert," interrupted Michel Villar, "religious beliefs have no part in this case."

"Sorry, Mr. President," responded Jubert.

Michel Villar nodded and Jubert continued.

"Several weeks later the boat of Quentin Baston was destroyed in an explosion and Quentin Baston reported lost. The relevance of this incident to the murder will become clear during our presentation of evidence. It was only sometime later that the weight of these events seems to have bothered the conscience of Monsieur Mitchell and to cleanse mind and soul ..." a rap of the gavel stopped this avenue "... he wrote a detailed confession of the incidents and took his own life ... ." At this point he crossed himself but the judge could really do nothing.

"Police in California of the United States found his body and the confession and contacted the gendarmes in Genivee. Evidence was then gathered, a warrant issued, and the United States government contacted for the extradition of Monsieur Howard Blake and Madame Elise Blake Andrews to stand trial for this murder.

"When Monsieur Blake learned that his sister's request to have extradition barred had failed, his guilt made him try to flee but officials found and detained him."

Howard stirred but Chyrise's hand on his arm made him sit still.

"The evidence we will present will convince you completely of the guilt of the defendants."

CHAPTER 63

The prosecution then called its first witness.

"The prosecution calls Lt. Juliet Mills."

Guillaume Martineau went out to the witness room and returned followed by a tall redhead wearing Los Angeles Police Department Dress Blues. She stepped into the witness box and was sworn in.

"Lt. Juliet Mills," began Huard Jubert, "is a Lieutenant with the Los Angeles Police Department. She was in charge of the investigation of the death of Mr. Keith Mitchell."

He returned to his seat and Michel Villar began his questioning.

"Lt. Mills, we welcome you to St. Nantes and hope that your stay will be pleasant."

"Thank you, your honor," Juliet Mills responded.

"Will you please tell the court about the investigation of Mr. Mitchell's death."

"Early Saturday morning April 4, our department received an anonymous 911 phone call reporting that shots had been heard at the home of Mr. Mitchell. A patrol car responded to the call within fifteen minutes.

"Police Sergeant Richard Johns and Patrolman Timothy Thomas found lights on in the condo but no one responded to their repeated knocks and after they pushed the door bell several times. Officer Thomas went around to the back of the building and found a window with a curtain that was not fully closed. Looking through the curtain he could see a person slumped on the sofa to one side with what appeared to be blood on his head. He could also see what appeared to be a revolver on the floor.

"He reported this to Sergeant Johns via his radio and Sergeant Johns tried the front door which he found to be unlocked. He entered the premises and discovered the body of

Keith Mitchell with what appeared to be a self-inflicted gunshot wound to the head and a revolver lying on the floor next to him. Sergeant Johns checked for life signs and found none.

"After both officers made a quick sweep of the condominium to be certain that no one else was there, they went outside where Sergeant Johns notified the department of his findings and then the two officers waited for homicide to arrive. A thorough investigation of the building was made by myself and other homicide detectives.

"The gun had been fired once, there was only the one cartridge, and the only fingerprints on the gun and cartridge were those of Mr. Mitchell. There was gunpowder residue on his hands and the wound to the head was consistent with that of a suicide. Ballistics showed that the bullet had come from that gun.

"A note was found on the table. That note was examined for fingerprints and again his were the only prints found. The entire condominium was dusted and although there were some unidentified fingerprints found in some other parts of the house, the majority of the prints were those of the victim and the defendant Mr. Howard Blake. Mr. Blake told us that he was good friends with Mitchell and often visited him at his home. Mr. Blake was at work that night, he is a CPA and it was the height of tax preparation season. His presence at his place of business has been collaborated by other employees.

"Other fingerprints found have been identified as belonging to several female acquaintances of Keith Mitchell.

"An autopsy was performed and the findings were consistent with a self-inflicted gunshot wound and there was nothing else unusual about the body. The coroner listed the cause of death as suicide by gunshot to the head.

"Examination of the note revealed that Mr. Mitchell had implicated Mr. Howard Blake and Elise Blake Andrews in the drowning murder of Mrs. Andrews's husband Stuart Andrews on February 16, 2009, in the waters of the Caribbean off the coast of St. Nantes. The officials on the island were contacted, the note and all related evidence that our department has gathered was forwarded to them since there was no indication that Mr. Mitchell's death was anything other than suicide."

She stopped and looked at Judge Villar.

"Thank you, Lt. Mills." And looking past her to the prosecution's table, "And where is that note now?"

"Right here, your honor," said Huard Jubert rising and holding the note in a plastic bag in his hand. "We would like to have this entered into evidence as Prosecution Exhibit #1."

"Objection, hearsay," Chyrise was on her feet before Phil Dombrey had even opened his mouth.

CHAPTER 64

"The confession by Mr. Mitchell is covered under the Dying Declaration Exception to the Hearsay Rule both here and in the United States. The confession was written immediately prior to Mr. Mitchell's suicide," stated Huard Jubert.

"Is there verification that the note was written by Keith Mitchell?" Michel Villar asked, obviously impatient with this objection.

"Yes, your honor. We have the handwriting analysis submitted to us by the Los Angeles Police Department that I submit into evidence as Prosecution Exhibit #2."

"But ...," Chyrise started.

"And our next witness will provide authentication and the defense can cross-examine at that time," continued Huard Jubert.

"Mademoiselle Callahan, your objection is overruled," Michel Villar said and Chyrise sank sullenly into her seat, looked at Phil Dombrey and shook her head.

Huard Jubert continued, "At this time I would also like to introduce a written statement from Dr. Demarco Edwards attesting to fact that he was treating Mr. Mitchell for addictions to both gambling and alcohol and, in his profession opinion, Mr. Mitchell exhibited no signs of delusional fantasizing. We could arrange to have Dr. Edwards appear but since he was questioned at Mrs. Andrews's extradition hearing, we see no reason to do so. But, of course, the defense can call Dr. Edwards."

Chyrise seemed to spring to her feet, "Objection, hearsay."

Huard Jubert was quick to respond, "This statement falls under the medical records exception."

"But it is not part of Keith Mitchell's medical records," responded Chyrise.

"No, but it is a statement from his doctor as to the content of those medical records and as such is an exception to the hearsay rule," responded Huard Jubert.

"Monsieur Jubert is correct, Mademoiselle Callahan. Objection overruled. Prosecution Exhibits One, Two and Three are admitted into evidence," said Michel Villar said. "Mr. Martineau, will you please take the note in the court's possession and mark it as indicated."

Guillaume Martineau went to the prosecution's table and took receipt of the bag containing the note, the report, and the affidavit. He affixed tags to each that declared it as "Prosecution Exhibit #1," "Prosecution Exhibit #2" and "Prosecution Exhibit #3" and handed Mr. Jubert a portion of the tags that would serve as a receipt indicating the proper transmission of evidence.

Judge Villar then said, "Does anyone have any further questions of this witness?"

Chyrise Callahan raised her hand. The judge nodded to Guillaume Martineau who started toward the defense's table. But Chyrise mistook the nod for permission to ask the question.

"Lt. Mills, ..." Chyrise began.

"Mademoiselle Callahan," Michel Villars said. "Write your question and give it to the bailiff."

"Sorry, your honor," Chyrise said as she sank back to her seat. She wrote a note and gave it to Guillaume Martineau who gave it to the judge. Michel Villar read it, nodded approvingly, and then said, "Lt. Mills, isn't it unusual for the revolver to have contained just one cartridge?"

"Not really, most people who intend to kill themselves with a gun know that it just takes one bullet, or they have really screwed up." There was low laughter from the onlookers, which ended with a glare from Michel Villars.

Lt. Mills continued. "If they had to buy the gun and ammunition, there is no need to pay for more than one bullet. Most cases where there is more than one bullet, the gun was something that was handy."

She looked at Michel Villar who looked at Chyrise, who nodded her acceptance of the explanation.

Michel Villar then asked, "Does anyone have any further questions of this witness?"

This time no one did and Michel Villar said, "Lt. Mills, we thank you for coming so far to give us this testimony. You are excused, subject to recall at sometime during the rest of the trial."

"Thank you, your honor."

Lt. Mills stepped down from the witness box and followed Guillaume Martineau across the floor, her heels making a faint tac-tac sound as she walked. I could not help noticing that there were many pairs of eyes that followed the twitching of her skirt as she disappeared through the door, least of all the eyes of Michel Villar. I had the feeling that if she was around after the trial, she might be having dinner – or more – with the judge.

CHAPTER 65

Typed copies in French of Mitchell's suicide note were given to each of the judges including Michel Villar, and the actual document (probably a photocopy) was projected upon two screens pulled down on the wall behind Villar's bench, one screen at the end of each judges' stand.

"The prosecution calls Monsieur James McCoy."

Guillaume Martineau went to the door, opened it, and disappeared. He returned a minute later followed by a middle-aged black man about five foot ten and weighing at least three hundred pounds. He was dressed in an ill-fitting beige suit with a white shirt that gaped between buttonholes and a thin, somewhat disheveled black tie.

He walked – make that waddled – to the witness box where Guillaume Martineau swore him in. Mr. Jubert introduced him to the court.

"Monsieur James McCoy is a handwriting expert who works occasionally as a consultant with the Los Angeles police in California. He is here to authenticate the handwriting of Monsieur Mitchell's confession."

He then took his seat.

Michel Villar started his questioning. "Monsieur McCoy, what is your training in handwriting analysis?"

"After receiving an undergraduate degree from U.C.L.A., I studied graphology at the Sorbonne and at the University of Heidelberg."

"Impressive," remarked Michel Villar. "How long have you been working in this field?"

"For more than 25 years," answered James McCoy. "I teach courses at U.C.L.A. and am constantly working with psychiatrists, psychologists, medical doctors and other criminologists, correlating graphological characteristics with mental and physical conditions, and forensic handwriting comparison. I am a member of American Association of Handwriting Analysts."

"And how long have you been working with the Los Angeles Police Department?"

"For most of those 25 years." James McCoy smiled. "I am also an on-call consultant with more than 50 other police departments, including Scotland Yard."

Michel Villar smiled. "We are most impressed with your credentials. Would you please tell us how you came to examine the document."

"I was called by the Los Angeles Police Department to validate the writing of the document. I examined many samples of writing known to be Mr. Mitchell's and the writing on the confession is definitely his."

He then went on to point out the many examples that helped him make his decision. Some of these examples were displayed side-by-side with the confession for comparison.

"I can therefore conclude with an extremely high degree of accuracy that this document was written by Keith Mitchell."

Michel Villar then asked, "Was there any sign that this document was written under duress?"

"No, Mr. President," replied James McCoy.

Michel Villar interrupted at this point. "Judge will do fine."

James McCoy nodded and continued.

"The writing is a bit off from his standard writing probably because Mr. Mitchell may have been legally drunk at the time, at least that is what the police told me. What they said was that he was legally drunk when he took his life. However, there is no indication of stress in the handwriting. As I said, everything is consistent with the samples provided to me by the Los Angeles Police Department."

"So," said Michel Villar, "you are confident that this document was written freely without stress."

"Yes, I am"

"Is this standard with suicide notes?"

"In my opinion, it is. I have inspected many suicide notes and most do not show any kind of stress because the writer is completely at ease with his or her decision."

"Thank you, Monsieur McCoy. Does anyone have any questions?"

Chyrise Callahan raised her hand and Guillaume Martineau collected her note and handed it to the judge.

"Mademoiselle Callahan wishes to know 'Is there any indication that any part of this note is not factual?' "

"Not in my opinion but I cannot attest to the validity of content, only that it was written by Mr. Mitchell and that it does not appear to be written under stress."

Chyrise's hand went up again and Michel Villar said, "You have my permission to ask your question."

Chyrise rose and said, "Is there ordinarily a difference in the writing if someone was writing a lie?"

"Only if the lie produces stress or is written under stress. If the person writes the note freely and believes what is being written, I cannot determine whether it is the truth or a lie."

"Judge Villar, may I ask another question?"

"Yes, Mademoiselle Callahan."

"So, Mr. McCoy, this note, this confession written by Mr. Mitchell – we have to accept that fact – could actually be delusional fantasizing?"

"Objection, calls for speculation," Huard Jubert was on his feet.

"I believe that Mr. McCoy's training and consultation with both psychiatrists and psychologists qualifies him to answer the question. Objection overruled." Michel Villar looked at Huard Jubert as though to say, "*Nice try though.*"

Then to the witness, "Mr. McCoy, could the contents of the note be delusional fantasizing?"

McCoy seemed to pause, then, "Yes, I suppose they could be but … ."

"Thank you," Chyrise said to both McCoy and Villar and resumed her seat.

"Any more questions of this witness?" asked Villar.

No one raised a hand.

"You are excused, Mr. McCoy. However, please remain in the witness room until such time as you are dismissed."

McCoy nodded and stepped down from the witness stand and was led to the door by Guillaume Martineau, who opened it and led McCoy through. He returned, closed the door and stood to one side.

Huard Jubert then called his next witness.

"The prosecution calls Quentin Baston."

CHAPTER 66

"Fish on," I yelled as the port rod bent and the line whirred. At the same instant I had noticed this, Quentin had reduced speed and was moving toward the rod. By the time I had the rod holder harness attached around my waist, Quentin had the rod ready to insert.

As I grasped the rod, he reminded me to use the thumb to guide the line. It was a long fight, a big fish and numerous times it made a run taking the line out. However, gradually I won the battle.

"It's a huge mahi mahi," Quentin said. "Quit reeling."

As before, I was grateful. As Quentin wrapped the line around his hand, I moved toward him.

There was a flash of green ...

The remembrance had hit me without warning and I stumbled into Quentin and dropped the pole. He yelled and shoved me away, releasing the line in his hand and reaching behind him. As I reeled away, I knew that he was going for his gun, and put my hands up.

"Wait," I said. "It was an accident. I am a friend."

His hand behind his back grasping the gun I knew was there, he stood looking apprehensively at me. I backed away toward the starboard side of the boat reaching behind me for the gunwale. When I reached it, I sat down on it.

"Please," I said, hands out empty in front of me. "I mean you no harm. I am a friend."

Quentin stood still, not moving.

"I was a good friend of Stuart Andrews. I don't believe that he committed suicide on the Caribbean Isle."

His mouth dropped open and he sank to the gunwale and stared at me.

" I know that he, his brother-in-law Howard Blake, and Howard's friend Keith Mitchell went out on a fishing excursion with you on February 16. I have a reliable source who saw Howard and Keith disembark from your boat in the middle of that afternoon. Stuart wasn't with them." It was a lie, but true in that I did not disembark.

As I was talking, Quentin sank to the deck and I did the same.

"I don't think that you took an active part in Stuart's murder but were forced to go along with it. I don't want to hurt you. I just want justice for Stuart."

He shook his head and put his hands in front of his face for a minute. Then he looked at me and started.

"We were fishing and Mr. Andrews got ze first fish. Ee got eet to the ship and I was pulling eet up, a big mahi mahi, and ee fell against me. Ze one monsieur..."

"His brother-in-law Howard."

He nodded.

"Ee hit 'im with a beer bottle. Knocked 'im out! He shoved me away to ze other side of ze ship and then started searching Monsieur Andrews and putting 'is belongings in a bag he brought.

"I say, 'What is going on, monsieur? Why you hit zat monsieur?' Ze other monsieur ..."

"Keith, " I injected. He never questioned how I knew who had done what because he was just glad to get it out.

"Yes. Ze other monsieur said 'Shut up and get over zere to ze side and say nozing or you'll join 'im feeding ze fishes!' He pick up ze gaff I use on ze fish and was 'reatening me with eet. I had no weapon and knew zat if I tried to help I be dead, so I sat down just like now.

"The other monsieur..."

"Howard."

"Howard say, 'Gif me hand getting 'im over ze side.' So zat one with ze gaff ..."

"Keith."

"... go to help 'im. Zey picked Monsieur Andrews up and push 'im over ze ship in ze water holding by ze feet. A big wave hit ze side of ze ship and the one monsieur ... Keith... lost ze feet. He tried to grab eet again and fell against ze big monsieur ... Howard?"

I nodded.

"... and he lost his grip and Monsieur Andrews was gone."

CHAPTER 67

"Ze big monsieur … uuh, Howard, … told ze other … Keith?"

I nodded.

"… zat he was idiot. Zey kept talking at each ozer and looking in ze water trying to see Monsieur Andrews. Zen zey raised their hand and slapped each other."

"A high five," I said. Quentin stared at me and then continued.

"I zought zat maybe I could reach ze gaff and started getting up. Keith catch sight of me, said somezing to Howard and zey both turned to face me. Zey told me to sit still and listen so I did.

"Howard told me zat Monsieur Andrews was one bad monsieur, a drinker, always going after other women and always hitting his wife, Monsieur Howard's sister. She afraid of 'im and couldn't go to ze gendarmes … police … and asked Howard to help her get rid of Monsieur Andrews.

"I didn't know. I had just met zem all and other than email, I knew little about Monsieur Andrews. I had to believe 'im.

"All this time the boat was running on and beginning to act up because of the waves. I said somezing about it and Howard told me to turn us around to look for Monsieur Andrews. First I had to pull ze ozer lines in and zey both helped. Then I went to ze helm and gave ze engines gas and turn us around. We all look for Monsieur Andrews but never saw anyzing. Well, I thought I had once, but pointed to the other side afraid that if they saw Monsieur Andrews zey would want me to run him over and I couldn't do zat.

"After about ten minutes, Howard figured Monsieur Andrews was drowned and sunk. Zey told me to get out of ze area.

"We must have traveled ..."

"What about the fish?" I queried.

"Oh, monsieur," Quentin said getting up and reaching for the rod which was lying on the deck. He reeled the line in and the hook came up empty. He put the rod in the holder on the gunwale.

"Gone," he said, "just like zis one."

He moved to the helm and took control of the boat that had been underway at a slow speed the entire time but not having problems in the slight swell of the sea. Then he continued.

"We motored for a while with ze two of zem drinking beer. That Keith could really drink ze stuff. Zey threw bottles over ze side and I didn't say anyzing but it really made me mad zem trashing ze sea – it gives me life.

"After a while I asked zem what zey were going to say to ze police.

" 'Nozing', Howard said. 'You take us back to ze port, drop us at a different dock but not far away. Zen you going home and forget this ever happened.' He reached into ze bag he brought and pulled out packet of money and he thrust et at me.

"'Here's ten zousand dollars to help you forget. If you stay forget for a year, no matter what you hear, you get 'nother ten zousand. If you don't, zen your family will pay.'

"I told zem I was good with zat because I still zought I was a dead monsieur. I took the money and took zem back to port. After dropping zem I went home."

"What did you do with the money?" I asked.

Quentin laughed. "It's blood money. I put et in a plastic bag, wrap et in a rag and stuffed et in the bottom of zis compartment."

He got up, and opened a door, rummaged around, and withdrew a rag bundle. He unwrapped it and handed me a plastic bundle. I could see a bundle of bills, the top one being a hundred and bank wrapper bearing the label "$10,000."

I laughed. Howard was so stupid that he hadn't even removed the wrapper. That was good evidence and possibly held fingerprints.

"Thanks," I said. "Did you tell anyone?"

"I told my wife Celesse. I had to. She knows I was acting strange. It must have been a week or so. I had already got ze gun you noticed because I figured I would never live to see ze end of ze year. I thought about going to the gendarmes but zey had zreatened my family and my two children. I was upset and after fifteen years wiz me, she knew somezing was wrong, so I tell her. She wanted me to go to ze gendarme but I couldn't take zat chance. My kids ..."

Quentin wiped his eyes.

I had expected this was the case. I had hired a man to check out Quentin and knew about the wife and kids but I was ready just in case. I also had a pistol in the small of my back in a holster.

CHAPTER 68

"I think you're right. I don't think that you will see the end of the year. That's why I am here. I'm glad you told me the story."

Quentin and I were standing at the control console of the Mahi Mahi each with a beer in our hands.

"I feel better, monsieur." Quentin admitted. "Eet's been a bad couple of months."

"We have to do something to keep you safe until we can bring Howard, Keith, and m..." almost slipped, "Mrs. Andrews to justice. I have a plan to do just that.

"I have a bigger boat near here, actually just a phone call away. It has a couple of berths and a galley. It is a big yacht. I have a friend running it. You can stay on it until we can get them in custody."

"Ah, monsieur, I love the sea but stay on a boat ... how long and what about my family?"

"I don't know how long. Maybe we can get you a place on land somewhere, but your family can't know, it's too dangerous to involve them.

"You are going to have to die!"

"Die? But you said..." Quentin backed away and reached behind his back.

"Wait. Hold on. Bad choice of words. You are going to have to appear to have died. We are going to blow up your boat and make it look as though you were killed in the explosion."

"Blow up my ship? But eet's how I make a living"

"I know. When it's all over, I will buy you a new boat."

He looked at me strangely, unbelievingly. Then he shrugged.

"But what about me family?"

"I'll tell your wife. Better yet, you can tell your wife but not your kids. Kids talk too much."

"Ah, monsieur," Quentin shook his head and I could see tears coming to his eyes.

"I don't like it either. It won't be too long. Your wife will know how to make it good with them. If things work out, once Howard, Keith and Stuart's wife ..." (Better this time!) "... are in care of the police, we'll try to get you all together in another place. Then when it's all over, you can all come back here.

"I think that it has to be this way if we are ever going to bring Mr. Andrew's killers to justice."

Quentin was silent for several minutes. Then he raised his head and looked me straight in the eyes.

"But my family had better be kept safe!" There was a definite threat in his voice.

"They will, I promise." I would arrange for someone to watch over them just in case.

Then I called Joaquin and while we waited Quentin and I spent the next hour wiping the boat clean of fingerprints and then had Quentin touch and handle everything that he would in a normal day of fishing. We also put fishing lines out to make everything as realistic as possible.

When the Zàkpa was tied up next to Quentin's boat, he boarded it and went immediately below, because he didn't want to see his boat destroyed. I knew that he had issues with the entire plan but I couldn't see any other way. I was as certain as he was that he wouldn't last the year. I knew that if I were Howard, he wouldn't. He was a loose end, the weakest link in the chain.

When I was on the flying bridge ready to detonate the explosives, I heard a sound behind me. Quentin had come up the ladder and was looking at his boat. I offered him the detonator and he shook his head.

I turned back to the boat and pressed the button. Two explosions and a flash – the redness of fire and the blackness of smoke. The sound of the explosions hit us and Quentin disappeared.

With a last look, I turned to the helm and then paused. I grabbed a towel, wiped the detonator and tossed it over the side. I did the same with my satellite phone and Joaquin's. Then I moved to the helm, got the boat under way and turned it toward the Bahamas. A last look over my shoulder and I pushed the throttle to full power and the Zàkpa leapt forward eager to begin the long run.

But first there was a stop to make.

CHAPTER 69

Because we had only been out on a short run supposedly testing a faulty engine, we were able to anchor again without having to worry about customs, but we would have to face them eventually and that would require a fake passport for Quentin. We had prepared for that.

Joaquin dropped me at the same dock as earlier that morning before I walked to the one where Quentin was to pick me up. I was dressed in clothes more suitable for a tourist rather than a fisherman. Joaquin went back to the Zàkpa and would wait for my return while Quentin stayed below out of sight, lost in his sorrow over his boat and his family.

I walked to a nearby hotel that I entered by a side door and then walked out the front and asked the concierge to call me a taxi. He did so without hesitation.

The taxi dropped me a block away from the jewelry store where Celesse worked part-time to help ends meet with the family. I walked to the store and browsed the displays until I was in front of an attractive woman with "Celesse" proclaimed prominently on her nametag.

"May I help you, Monsieur?" she asked.

"Yes," I looked around to be certain that the other sales-clerk was not near.

"I am a friend of Quentin's and I need to talk to you in private."

She gasped and asked, "Is he …?"

"He's fine. It's just something that is confidential and needs to be done privately."

"Oh, well, I can take a break in fifteen minutes. There is a small park down the street on the other side. Is that okay?"

I said it was, thanked her for her help and left the store. As she spent many hours with tourists, her English was much better than her husband's. I spent the next fifteen minutes browsing the stores on the way to the park and was in the park seated on a bench when Celesse arrived. I could tell by the way she was walking that she was quite agitated.

She sat down next to me. "What's this with my husband?" she queried.

"Just a minute and I'll let him tell you." I had my satellite phone out (a different one) and called Joaquin.

"Give Quentin the phone," I said and handed it to Celesse.

In the next fifteen minutes, Celesse's emotions ran the gamut from elation at hearing Quentin's voice to depression and tears. The conversation was in French and so I couldn't understand what was being said, but I could tell by her emotions what it was.

First "I'm okay," (*elation and relief*) followed by the explanation of what had happened that day (*disbelief and dismay*) and then what the future held (*consternation and sorrow*).

After their fond farewells – that was easy to figure out – she handed the phone back to me and looked at me questioningly.

"I'm sorry," I said. "I don't think there is another way to guarantee his safety and that of you and your children."

"I knew it was a bad thing when he told me. I am sorry that your friend was killed and that he was a part of it."

"He didn't help in the murder," I assured her, "and he won't pay any penalty for it."

"What will we do?" She was referring to herself and her children.

"You will have to carry on the best you can just as if he was dead. You can refuse to have a funeral or anything saying that you don't believe it. Saying that might help the children also."

"Yes," she agreed, "that is what Quentin said too. How long will this be?"

"I don't know," I said. "A couple of months at most I think. When it is safe for you to join Quentin, I will contact you and pay for all expenses. I have arranged for someone to watch you and the children to make certain you stay safe. Someone will contact you once a week to see if you need anything but you will have to try to be natural."

"I understand. I have worried that Quentin might really be killed and this is much better. It will be difficult for the children, but if I believe that he is not dead then they will also."

"Can I help you in any other way now?" I asked.

"No," she glanced at her watch. "I have to get back to the shop. Thank you, uhh. I don't even know your name."

"Just called me Josef. For now that is best."

She stood up and left, never looking back walking now more resolutely. I was confident that she would be fine.

I walked away several blocks, called Joaquin and hailed a cab. I had it drop me at a different hotel and then walked to the dock where the zodiac and Joaquin were waiting. Back on the Zàkpa, I told Quentin about my meeting with Celesse.

He was quiet and subdued. He nodded in understanding and then said, "Let's go get zem, Monsieur Josef."

CHAPTER 70

We had gotten Quentin a place on Barbados where he could stay quietly until needed. As soon as the story of Keith's confession had started to break, I knew that it would get to the police on St. Nantes and knowing that Quentin was a witness would be a key factor in making arrests. We put to sea when I returned from the States and once away from land, I used a satellite phone with a voice modulator to call the authorities on St. Nantes. It took a while to get someone in authority and I had to call back half an hour after my first call. Just being safe, I used another of our phones. Perhaps in all this I was being overly cautious but I had promised Quentin and Celesse that I would keep them and their children safe.

"Who I am is not important other than I am of friend of Quentin Baston. He is not dead," I added before the official could say anything. "He was not killed in the explosion of his boat – that event was to protect him from a similar fate.

"He can and will verify the facts put forth in the deathbed confession of Keith Mitchell of Los Angeles, California. He is not on St. Nantes but in a safe location. We will make arrangements to meet with a representative of your choice and in a location that you select.

"You should not try to trace him because he will disappear if you do. He will be a witness at the trial of the murderers of Stuart Andrews.

"I will call back in twenty-four hours to get the time and a neutral meeting place that you select as long as it is not a French territory."

The next day I called again and we set up a meet in Roseau, Dominica. I chartered a private plane that picked up Quentin, Joaquin, and I in St. Lucia where Quentin had flown commercially. We arrived an hour before the two officials from St. Nantes. Joaquin met them at immigration and guided them out to the plane. They were surprised, because they had thought we would meet in some office.

Joaquin remained on the ground and I was in the cockpit with the pilot, who never saw his passengers and they never saw me. We flew for nearly three hours while the two officials talked to Quentin, fingerprinted him, took pictures, and basically grilled him the entire time. Finally they were satisfied with his story and the assurance that he would testify.

Back on the ground, Joaquin escorted the two French officials to their departure gate and saw them off. Then he came back to the chartered plane and we flew back to St. Lucia. After the plane left for its home airport, we boarded the Zàkpa bound for Barbados where we sequestered Quentin. With the assurance that we would reunite him with his family as soon as possible, we left him there and headed seaward.

CHAPTER 71

I was true to my word. As soon as Elise and Howard were in custody, I sent for Celesse and the children. They came by plane, first to St. Martin, and then to Bermuda where they spent a few days. Then they flew to Jamaica for another couple of days, and finally to Barbados where Quentin and I awaited them. We had rented a small house outside Bridgetown.

Quentin and I were in the arrival hall outside customs when they came through, dragging and carrying their bags. They had only been permitted carry-on luggage and we hadn't told them their final destination. At each airport they were met and given tickets for their next leg or taken to their lodgings. Anything they needed during their stay was purchased for them and if something couldn't fit into a suitcase, it was left behind to be destroyed. Their lodgings were thoroughly cleaned after their departure. When they were ready to depart they were taken to the airport and given tickets.

Quentin had changed his appearance in the time away from them. He had grown some facial hair and, for the time, was wearing a wig. We were both dressed in local clothes and it would be difficult to tell us from the other locals. I was behind Quentin and he had a sign with "Celesse" written on it. It was a sign like all the other signs that had greeted them at the other airports. The boy spotted it and tugged at his mother's hand. She looked at the sign and then started toward it.

She stopped, looked, and then with a cry of joy ran and flung herself into his arms. The children were momentarily stunned until recognition hit them also and they ran to greet their father.

Joaquin collected their bags and we hustled out of the airport into the waiting van. I said nothing during the ride to their lodgings because too much was happening.

"I told you I didn't think he was dead," Celesse told the children.

When we got to their residence, Celesse and Quentin finally had a moment for me while the children ran to see the house.

"Thank you," she said. "Thank you for saving him and us."

Quentin, one arm around Celesse, smiled and said, "Thank you, Josef. We'll be here until you need me."

From the start, they had both known me only as Josef and that is the way it would stay. I didn't want them ever to know that I was really Stuart Andrews or Dawoh Mbayo. When it was all over, Josef would vanish completely.

"Hopefully, there will not be a need to move you, but if there is, I will call. Someone will be contacting you to see to your needs. You have the phone and you can call me if you need to. Remember no other calls at all. No email, nothing that could possibly be traced back to here. I don't think there is a need to worry but you never know."

They both nodded assent. Quentin shook my hand and Celesse kissed my check. Then I got in the car where Joaquin waited and we drove away. When I looked back they were walking to the house hand-in-hand.

We didn't need to move them and Celesse and the children stayed on the island when Quentin left to come to the trial. He flew to Jamaica and then the Bahamas and finally St. Nantes via St. Martin. He arrived two days before his court appearance so that the prosecutors had time to talk to him prior to his surprise appearance in court but, of course, he had talked to them before.

Part VII

The Picture

CHAPTER 72

The noise in the courtroom from this revelation rose in a crescendo and would have drowned out the judge's gavel had he chosen to use it. But he didn't. Where one might have expected a look of consternation there was instead the faintest of smiles and he snuck a judicial look at the defense's table.

The two lawyers had looks of bewilderment on their faces and Elise and Howard were in deep conversation. I could imagine what was going on:

> Elise: *"You told me you had taken care of it. Sixty thousand dollars we paid and the frog is still alive? What happened, Howard?"*
>
> Howard: *"I don't know. The Facilitator told me that he would arrange for a boating accident. The newspapers reported that frog's boat had blown up with him in it. I assumed that it was the Facilitator's work and we paid him. We never agreed to contact him to see if it was he."*
>
> Elise: *"Well, he obviously isn't dead. I don't ever remember reading about a body being found. It was assumed that he was dead because of the explosion."*
>
> Howard: *"Just as everyone assumed that Stuart had died in the southern Caribbean rather than in the northern."*
>
> *Possible realization hits and there is a stunned silence. They both look around searching the courtroom ...*

But that doesn't happen. While the noise in the courtroom was reaching its maximum, Guillaume Martineau had turned and opened the door and disappeared. He reappeared, leading three people: first, a gendarme armed with an Uzi or some similar weapon; then Quentin; and then another armed gendarme. The second gendarme took a position at the end of the lay judges' dais, facing the spectators, weapon at the ready.

Quentin, clean shaven, hair freshly trimmed and wearing a navy blazer over a powder blue shirt and white sharply-creased pants and brown topsiders with no socks (I shuddered as I hadn't mentioned socks when I had told him how to dress) walked calmly to the witness box without looking anywhere except straight ahead.

In the movies, he probably would have both hands clasped above his head, shaking them in a sort of victory acknowledgement and facing the crowd drinking in their adoration. He would stop in front of the defense's table and look at both Elise and Howard, flip each of them the bird, and then continue to the witness box in his victory parade.

But that was my fantasy. The first gendarme continued past the witness podium and took up station at the end of the professional judges' dais and in front of the translators' booths – they just had to hear, not see.

Quentin stepped up into the witness box and was sworn in.

Michel Villar rapped his gavel and the courtroom plunged into silence. The testimony was given in French and, as were many of the people in the courtroom, I was hearing a translation.

"Welcome, Monsieur Baston. To paraphrase an American author 'The story of your death has been greatly exaggerated.' "

There was a murmur among the spectators quickly ending with a rap of Michel Villar's gavel.

"Will you please tell the court about your fishing charter on Monday, February 16, 2009."

"Where should I begin? When I picked them up?"

"No, start at the beginning, with the first contact."

"In late December 2008, I had an email from a man named Stuart Andrews. He told me that he was coming to St. Nantes on a cruise on Monday, February 16, and he would like to go deep-sea fishing. He said that he and his party would be able to start at 10:00 a.m. and had to be back in port to get the last tender to the ship, that would probably be 3:00 or 4:00.

"I explained to him that it would take 30 to 45 minutes to get to a good fishing area and then of course, the same to return. He replied that was fine.

"I asked how many people there would be and he said probably just two, he and his brother-in-law Howard. I asked him to contact me a week before the day just to confirm and he said that he would.

"I heard from him the Monday before, that was ... February 9, and he said he would see me on the harbor side in Genivee at 10:00, on Monday, February 16.

"That morning the sea was a little rough but the sun was out and it was a beautiful day. I had gotten my bait the evening before and I arrived at the harbor where the tenders drop the passengers just before 10:00.

"There were three of them, Monsieur Andrews," he crossed himself (I hadn't known he was religious and Michel Villar said nothing, after all Quentin was the star witness.) "Monsieur Blake, the brother-in-law, and a third man, a Monsieur Mitchell.

"We went out to the fishing area taking about forty minutes. I got the baits out and we trolled for a while, maybe half an hour, before we had a strike.

"Monsieur Andrews took the rod and he brought the fish in. When it got close, Monsieur Mitchell had a camera and he was taking pictures, I think. When the fish, it was a mahi mahi after which I name my boat," ... he paused briefly here as though remembering his boat ... "and when it was close and I could get the line, I told Monsieur Andrews to stop reeling. He did, and his brother-in-law or the other man, I don't remember, told him to get over with the fish for a picture.

"I wrapped the fish line around my hand and was pulling the fish up when Monsieur Andrews fell into me ... ."

There was a flash of green ...

CHAPTER 73

Quentin and I had talked about his testimony several times as he was trying to get things straight in his memory. It was at his request because he said that he wanted to try to remember everything because it would help if he did. No matter how many times we had talked about this incident, that *flash of green* always happened just as it did whenever I had that recurring nightmare. I was beginning to wonder if that was going to happen the rest of my life.

Quentin continued, "When he fell against me, I fell against the side of the boat and lost the fishing line. Monsieur Blake, the brother-in-law, grabbed me and pushed me to the other side of the boat. That other man, Monsieur Mitchell, he told me that I should sit down and be quiet or I would join Monsieur Andrews in 'feeding the fish.' He called me a "queer frog' or something. I don't remember. He had picked up the gaff and threatened me with it."

I knew that it was "faggot frog" but I wasn't going to correct his testimony and part of it could have been lost in translation. It was his memory. Maybe the translator wanted to avoid that derogatory term. If memory serves, the term comes from a reference to the food eaten. The French eat frogs, and the English are known in France as 'les rosbifs'. In the seventeenth and eighteenth centuries it was the Dutch not the French who were identified as frogs since the Dutch and frogs seemed to be at home in waterlogged terrain. It is true that the French were often caricatured in eighteenth-century literature and visual satires as frog-eaters, but that is not at all the same as being frogs. All Frenchmen do not look upon the term as being derogatory. In fact it has been used in levity. At one time, the London Institut Francais advertised French language courses at all levels from beginners to advanced students using a graphic poster that pictured the development of a frog in stages from egg through tadpole to full maturity.

"The other man, the brother-in-law, was going through Monsieur Andrews clothes and taking things. He took his wallet, his watch, he took off the rod holder harness, he took money ... ."

At this point Michel Villar interrupted. "What did he do with the things he took?"

"He put them into a cloth bag he had brought with him, sort of a backpack but with just cords for the straps and made of cloth, not canvas. He just threw the rod holder harness on the deck."

He looked at the judge to see if there was more to the question. Michel Villar just nodded.

"Then he told the other man, that Monsieur Mitchell, that he needed his help to get Monsieur Andrews over the side. I started to protest, to get up, but that Monsieur Mitchell kicked me and told me to sit ... uhh, squat ... like a good 'queer frog,' and made a threatening motion with the gaff."

There was a commotion at the defense table and Villar's rapped his gavel. I saw that Howard was in deep conversation with Chyrise that stopped with the gavel's knock.

"Please continue, Monsieur Baston," said the court's president.

"That Monsieur Mitchell went to help Monsieur Blake and they picked Monsieur Andrews up and put his head over the side. They held him there for a minute and then a big wave hit that side of the boat. With no guidance the boat had been turned by the waves, which were now coming against the side of the boat. Monsieur Mitchell he lost the foot he was holding. Monsieur Blake couldn't hold him and let go," he crossed himself again. "They looked into the water and then they ... uhhh ... slap hands."

He raised his right hand and gave one half of the American "high five."

"Then they came to me and told me that Monsieur Andrews was not a good husband to his wife, that he hit her,

and he went with other women for sex. The boat was starting to act crazy in the waves, the wind was bigger, and I
went to the controls to get the boat right again. They made
me turn the boat around and look for Monsieur Andrews's
body. I think that if we had seen it they would have made
me hit him with the boat."

Another commotion at the defense table. Howard and
Chyrise in yet another conversation. Another gavel rap.
Quentin continued.

"Once I thought I saw him but said nothing. I could not
do something like run the boat over a man. Then they told
me to leave and go somewhere else. They both had beers.
They drank all I had brought by the time we got back to
port."

"How many?" asked Villar.

"I had a dozen. All Heinekens. In those green bottles.
They threw the bottles into the sea."

"How did they open the bottles?"

"I have a fish knife ... big ... to cut the fish I keep. I
used it to open the bottles at first but then, they must have
thought I would use it to attack them but ... I am small and
they ... Monsieur Blake he is big. I am not a fighter."

"No faggot frog is a fighter or a lover."

That was Howard.

Villar rapped his gavel. "That's enough, Monsieur
Blake. I am trying to be tolerant, but if you continue to inter-
rupt the witness, I will have you removed."

Howard glared at him but said nothing.

"Continue, Monsieur Baston. What happened then?"

"I asked them about the police and they said there would
be no police. I would drop them at a different spot in the
harbor and go home and forget it. If I said anything they
would kill my family in front of me and then kill me. They
gave me money to be quiet."

"How much money?" Judge Villar asked.

"Ten thousand American dollars. All wrapped up."

"What happened to the money?"

"I kept it wrapped up in my boat in plastic."

"Your boat blew up. What happened to the money?"

"I took it with me."

A low exclamation ran through the crowd.

"And what happened to the money after that?"

Quentin smiled.

"I gave it to Monsieur Jubert."

Michel Villar looked at the chief prosecutor.

"Do you have the money, Monsieur Jubert?"

Huard Jubert stood up and picked up a plastic bag from the table. He held it up. It was the size of a one-gallon freezer bag. In it was a packet of bills in a bank wrapper.

"Enter that as Prosecution Exhibit #4 if there is no objection from the Defense Counsel," Michel Villar instructed Guillaume Martineau, who moved to the prosecution table and took the bag, which he then took to the defense's table and show it to Phil Dombrey and Chyrise Callahan. They nodded their agreement and he marked it with a tag, gave a portion of it to Jubert, and then placed the bag on the evidence table.

"What happened then?" asked Villar.

"I took them to the harbor in Genivee and dropped them across from the tender landing. Then I went home."

"You mentioned that ... who was it? ... Monsieur Mitchell had a camera and was taking pictures. What happened to it?"

"Oh, yes." Quentin smiled. "They forgot it. I found it the next day."

CHAPTER 74

It was my camera purchased especially for this trip. It was an Olympus Stylus 850 SW – the SW for Shockproof (from six feet or so) and Waterproof (to fifteen feet). I had stuck it in my pocket when we went ashore. I had taken a few pictures aboard ship to get the feel of it and deleted them. Ashore in Genivee, I had taken a few pictures including the lighthouse on top of the hill. Then the harbor, Quentin's boat alongside the harbor wall, Elise on the dock waving goodbye to me (for the last time) and taking a picture with her camera, Howard and Keith sitting on the bench seat against the transom drinking beer and looking … what? Quentin at the helm, baiting hooks, throwing the lines in the water. When the fish had struck I had given the camera to Keith (he was closest) asking him to get some action pictures.

There was a commotion at the defense table again, Howard severely agitated by the looks of things and both Chyrise and Elise trying to calm him down. Michel Villar rapped his gavel but the frantic consultation continued. In my mind I could hear what was happening.

> Elise: *"You idiot! You left the camera!"*
> Howard: *"Keith had it. It was that bastard Stuart's."*
> Elise: *"So! You were supposed to get all his belongings. Leave no trace, you had said."*
> Howard: *"I forgot about the camera. What's the big deal?"*
> Elise: *"Pictures! Evidence! That's the big deal. Why else do they think it's important?"*

Another rap of the gavel and order was restored although neither Howard nor Elise looked at all relaxed. They looked as their world had taken another big punch.

"Where did you find the camera?" Villar asked.

"It was in the aft starboard corner of the boat, under the fishing belt. I don't know how it got there but when I was cleaning up the next day, I was too upset to do it the previous day, I found it and put it away."

"Did you look at the pictures?"

"No, I didn't think to do so. I just wanted it out of sight. I put it with the bag with the money in it."

He had then apparently forgotten about it until we were getting ready to blow up the Mahi Mahi. Quentin had gotten aboard the Zàkpa and gone below while Joaquin and I set the charges. I was about ready to board the Zàkpa and cast off when Quentin came storming up from below.

"I forget ze camera," he had shouted as he literally vaulted onto the Mahi Mahi. He had gone to the compartment where the money had been and pulled out the small camera. He offered it to me but I refused worried about my fingerprints over his and Keith's. He stuck it in his pocket, boarded the Zàkpa and went below.

Later when things had calmed down and we were underway to the Bahamas, St. Nantes and his family behind, we had looked at the camera but after those many weeks, the battery was dead. We got a charger in Nassau and looked at the pictures. That is when we knew we had the piece of evidence that would slam the door on the case. There was probably enough at this point – Quentin, the money and its fingerprints, the camera and its damning pictures – but I had wanted more. I had wanted to hear it from them, from one of them and to get answers to some questions I had. Thus I had gone after them and eventually gotten to Keith.

"Where is the camera now?" Michel Villar asked, the mere trace of a sarcastically triumphant smile on his lips.

"I gave it to Monsieur Jubert," Quentin said.

Huard Jubert stood up at the prosecution table holding a bag with the camera in it.

"I would like to enter this as Prosecution Exhibit #5," he said and gave it to the Guillaume Martineau. The camera was shown to Phil Dombrey and Chyrise Callahan who accepted it as evidence and then it was appropriately marked and the receipt given to Huard Jubert.

CHAPTER 75

"And the pictures?" Michel Villar asked.

Huard Jubert stood again holding a stack of pictures. "To be marked Prosecution Exhibit #6a - 6k, if it please the court," Jubert said handing the stack to Guillaume Martineau. The photographs were shown to the defensive counsels. Howard grabbed the photographs and flipped through them. At the last one, he stared and then started to get up but was contained by Chyrise and Elise, but he sat there visibly agitated.

Guillaume Martineau marked the photographs and gave the receipt to the prosecutor.

Then Huard Jubert said, "If it please the court" and indicated the screens. Villar nodded and again turned to the small computer screen on his desk.

A picture flashed onto the screens above the judges' daises. It was the one I had taken of the lighthouse on top of the hill overlooking the port of Genivee and the cross on the hillside below (#6a). Then the picture of the port (#6b); the Mahi Mahi (#6c); Elise waving goodbye (for the last time) (#6d); Howard and Keith drinking beer (plotting?) (#6e); Quentin at the helm (#6f), Quentin baiting (#6g), Quentin placing the starboard rod in its holder (#6h); and me holding the rod, a look of concentration on my face (#6i); me pulling the rod up and making the line feed onto the reel with my thumb (#6j); and an oddly tilted shot of a slightly out of focus Howard identifiable by his red and blue tropical shirt, beyond him me and barely Quentin (#6k). In Howard's right hand raised above my head...

There was a flash of green ...

"It's a fake. You friggin' frogs Photoshopped it. You ... ."

Now Howard was up and trying to climb over the table, Chyrise rising and grabbing at him, the two gendarmes positioned behind the table moving to constrain him, the armed gendarmes more alert with weapons ready, Villar's gavel smashing repeatedly on its sound block.

"Order, Order" came over the ear buds. "Guards, remove the defendant to his holding cell for the duration of the trial."

The room was in an uproar, flashes popping, Howard yelling, swinging at the gendarmes, Elise, Chyrise, and Phil trying to get out of the way. It was several minutes before the gendarmes had Howard under control enough to get him out of the courtroom. He was still fighting as he went through the door screaming "You frigging French frog faggots ... ."

The defendants' table was in a shambles as chairs were overturned, papers scattered, and the table moved several feet from its original place. It took several minutes to set it to rights and then get settled again. Chyrise Callahan raised her hand and Michel Villar nodded at her.

"If it please the court, I would like to have few minutes with my client."

"I deem that quite appropriate, Mademoiselle Callahan. We will recess for fifteen minutes and then hopefully finish the testimony of Monsieur Baston before breaking for lunch."

He rapped his gavel and led to the recession of judges in reverse order of their arrival following Guillaume Martineau to their chambers followed by the prosecution and then the defendants. As soon as they were gone the doors at the rear of the public room were opened and we all exited although not nearly as orderly as the judges. We went out a door on the courtroom side of the security barrier into a large fenced-in area.

As soon as they were outside, many of the press and spectators lit cigarettes. While smoking is a no-no in many of the states, no smoking areas aren't so prevalent in Europe or the Caribbean. There is no such thing as non-smoking sections in restaurants in most of Europe although bans have taken place in Ireland, Italy, Malta, Norway, Sweden and Scotland and many places in Germany. It is interesting to walk past a restaurant with outdoor seating and finding ashtrays on the tables and blankets on the chairs so that the customers can wrap up while smoking.

Also there was an immediate turning on of cell phones and other devices as the press contacted home offices with updates on the trial. I called Joaquin and reported on the progress.

"So that Howard Blake really flipped out when he saw the picture?" Joaquin asked.

"Yes, as they say in the states, 'He went ballistic.' Judge Villar threw him out and I doubt that he will let him back in. He was casting aspersions at the French right and left. Not at all politically correct."

"What?" said Joaquin but he was used to my Americanisms by now.

"It means that it is not the correct thing to say in the current political climate, but its use is more widespread. In this case, it basically means you don't go making bad comments about the French when you are on trial in a French courtroom."

"I understand," said Joaquin. "I will remember 'politically correct.' "

One of the guards shouted, "Court is in session." Cigarettes were extinguished, cell phones turned off or muted, and we all hastily returned to our seats.

CHAPTER 76

The return procession was not with all the original pomp and circumstance but with all groups in one long line led by Guillaume Martineau: the prosecutors; the defense team sans Howard, with Elise looking forlorn; the lay judges; the professional judges; and the President of the Court, Michel Villar. Once in place, they all remained standing and Guillaume Martineau announced that the court was in session and Michel Villar rapped his gavel smartly and everyone was seated. At the defense table, Chyrise Callahan remained standing and Michel Villar acknowledged her, "Mademoiselle Callahan?"

"If it please the Court, my client Howard Blake has asked me to issue his most abject apologies" *yeah, right* "and begs the Court's forgiveness. He begs the Court to consider the reinstatement of his rightful place at the defense table."

Michel Villar, elbows bent, folded his hands in front of him with index fingers up like he was playing "Here's the church … ."

"Mademoiselle Callahan, as you have undoubtedly noticed, French courts are quite different from American courts. That fact that we have permitted you to represent your client without French counsel is a formality we have indulged in at the request of you and Monsieur Dombrey.

"In France, at least for major crimes like this one being tried here today, justice is swift. We do not dally as you do in the United States. If we did your two clients would be, how do you Americans say 'Rotting in jail?' They would be waiting for their day in court because we certainly would not permit them to run free and give them the chance to escape as you Americans did with your client.

"We do not tolerate interference with the actions of the court as your client indulged in this morning. However, we do understand that this is a matter of great importance and understand that your client has a right to 'his day in court.' At least for the remainder of this day, Monsieur Blake will remain in his holding cell watching the proceedings via closed-circuit television. When we reconvene in the morning we will be willing to consider his request."

"Thank you, your Honor," Chyrise responded as she assumed her seat.

"However," Michel Villar continued, "We make no promises." And he smiled. A little sardonically, I thought. *He is enjoying this.*

Chyrise was doing her best but she was young and inexperienced. She had grown up in the L.A. projects and gone to U.C.L.A. after two years at Los Angeles Community College. Her ambition to be a lawyer was promoted by the inequality she saw while growing up. She took the LSAT and, although doing well, received no offers other than from Thomas M. Cooley Law School in Lansing, Michigan. While successful, she didn't like the cold Michigan winters and sought a law school in warmer climes. She was accepted by Florida State University and Tulane University and chose Florida State because she felt Tulane, being in the recently devastated New Orleans area, would not offer her the best physical environment. She graduated with honors and secured a job as an Assistant State Attorney with the State Attorney's Office for the Florida Eleventh Judicial Circuit, serving Miami-Dade County, Florida. Three years there, working in a courtroom setting for the last two years convinced her that she wanted to be a litigator. Done with the obligation, which helped pay for her law school student loans, she headed back to Los Angeles. She established her own law office near the projects where she grew up and worked pro bono much of the time, finding enough paying cases to live on, but it wasn't easy. Her big break came when she successfully defended an indigent white man accused of robbing and raping three black women. It turned out to be a case of badly mistaken identity since the true perpetrator was a black man. But it made her name and paying clients poured in. Howard had been one of these.

CHAPTER 77

"Please bring in the witness," Michel Villar instructed Guillaume Martineau, who went to the door, opened it, entered and returned leading Quentin to the witness box. As he passed the defense table he glanced to see that Howard wasn't there and smiled ever so slightly. He, too, was enjoying his role in this.

"Monsieur Baston, several weeks after the incident of February 16, you appeared to have died in the explosion of your boat. Would you please explain this to the court."

And Quentin began. "I felt that even though I had been given the ten thousand dollars in 'blood money,' my life was in danger. I had told my wife about these events and she was worried and agreed with me. We were both very worried about her safety and that of our two children. I had secured a pistol that I carried with me and, whenever I went out fishing with clients, I tried to do a good check on them, identities and so on. If I were at all suspicious I would not accept the trip; there weren't many of those. I also would check my boat thoroughly each day to be certain that nothing had been tampered with.

"However, even so, the threat weighed heavily on me and Celesse. I had taken a friend into my confidence and we decided that it would be best if I disappeared."

This wasn't exactly true but was close enough to the truth that Quentin felt comfortable with it – this was the only part of his testimony that I had any part in the wording.

"On that day I went fishing alone and he meet me with his boat away from the island. We rigged my boat to explode and went a safe distance away and blew it up." I could almost see a tear coming to his eye, as he had really loved that boat.

"Then I 'disappeared' until I heard about the arrests of the people involved here.' "

With his arm he indicated the defense table.

"Then I made my existence known to the gendarmes in Genivee. We met and I told them my story and gave them the money and the camera. I stayed in hiding, now with my family because I felt it was safe to bring them away, but I didn't want the fact that I was alive to be known as I felt that there still might be a chance they would try to kill me. Then I returned to St. Nantes for the trial."

"Thank you, Monsieur Baston. Your experience was indeed a difficult one for you and your family. I have no further questions. Does anyone else?"

Chyrise and Phil Dombrey both raised their hands and Guillaume Martineau moved to the defense table. After a brief conference, Phil wrote a note and handed it to Martineau who gave it to the judge. Michel Villar read the note, and then said to Chyrise and Phil, "I will ask the question although I will rephrase it slightly and if you do not feel that it is the question you wished to ask, you may try another approach."

Then to Quentin "To your knowledge, was there ever an attempt on your life that you believe came because of the event about which this trial is concerned?"

I couldn't imagine how the original question was stated but I was willing to bet that the word "alleged" was included somewhere.

Quentin answered immediately. "Not that I know of."

Phil Dombrey indicated another question by the paper in his raised hand. The question was retrieved and given to Villar, who upon reading it frowned. "I think this is a repetitive question."

Phil stood. "If it please the Court, the context of this question is to absolve my client of any involvement of this particular aspect of the court's investigation."

Villar considered it then "Very well. Monsieur Baston, to your knowledge did Elise Blake Andrews ever initiate any attempt upon your life."

"Not to my knowledge, sir," was the quick response.

Apparently satisfied, Phil Dombrey sat down. He was a seasoned lawyer although criminal defense was not his forte. He specialized in immigration law and why Elise had chosen him as her lawyer I had no clue. He was a partner in a prosperous Miami law firm. He had also graduated from Florida State University Law School and had been an undergraduate there. He had immediately joined his current firm and worked his way up. He had married his college sweetheart who had worked to support them during the three years of law school. They had three sons, one of whom had died as an infant. The youngest was still in college at the University of Miami (bet Phil loves that) and the oldest, who had graduated from West Point, was a captain in the Army currently serving in Afghanistan.

"Are there any other questions?"

Heads were shaken. "Then you are excused, Monsieur Baston, subject to recall at a later time. The Court thanks you for your testimony and extends its gratitude that you are alive."

"Thank you, your Honor."

Quentin stepped down from the witness box and was guided back to the witness waiting room by Martineau.

"We will take a one-and-one-half hour break for lunch. Court will reconvene promptly at 1:00."

Michel Villar rapped his gavel on the sound block and Guillaume Martineau led the recessional before we were permitted to exit.

CHAPTER 78

Promptly at one o'clock the doors to the public seats were locked barring the few tardy unfortunates and Guillaume Martineau led in the two processions. Michel Villar rapped his gavel calling the court to order and nodded at Huard Jubert who rose.

"The prosecution calls Philippe Canton."

A short chubby man wearing a somewhat shabby tan blazer over a black tee shirt, blue jeans and flip-flops followed Guillaume Martineau to the witness box and was sworn in.

Michel Villar was obviously a little upset with the man's dress but said nothing (after all he was a witness for the prosecution).

"Monsieur Canton, what is your occupation?"

"I am, I guess you would say, a photograph expert. I work with both digital and film negative photographs, but mostly work in the digital field."

"And what is your training?"

"I am basically self-trained. For fifteen years, I have owned a photography shop and have been interested in cameras all my life."

"Have you ever testified in a case like this before?"

Canton smiled. "Oh, yes, many times. It helps the bank account and my reputation."

"By your bank account, I assume that you are paid for your testimony?"

"Oh, yes, but just expenses and a slight fee to cover my time. Well, I should say that is what I get when I testify for the prosecution. When I testify for the defense, I really rack up the big bucks." He chuckled. "I really am pretty much in demand, if I do say so myself."

"So what is it that you do for your clients in cases like this?"

"Oh, I authenticate photographs. That is, I look at photographs to determine whether or not they have been altered."

"I guess that means you determined whether or not the photograph has been," here he smiled and chuckled a little, "as we heard earlier today, 'Photoshopped'?"

"Yes, but that is only one of many programs that people use to doctor photographs by switching heads, bodies, removing redeye, airbrushing to remove blemishes. There are a wide variety of things that can be done using modern computer technology."

"So, did you have an opportunity to look at these photographs, Prosecution Exhibit #6?" At his wave, Guillaume Martineau handed the plastic envelope containing the pictures to Philippe Canton.

He took the envelope and started to undo the zipper lock, then looked at the judge, who nodded his assent. Philippe opened the envelope, shook the pictures onto the lectern mounted on the witness box, and sorted through them.

"Are these in the same or similar condition as when you first saw them?" Michel Villar asked.

"Yes."

"And what did you do when you saw them?"

"I examined these pictures, as well as the camera and memory chip which contained them."

"And what did you discover?"

"The pictures on the chip were put there as part of the camera saving procedures. All the markings are there to indicate that. Also the pictures here," and he indicated the photographs he had been given, "are the ones that are on the memory chip."

Michel Villar once more played "Here's the church." "And in your expert opinion, have these pictures ever been," he smiled that sardonic smile, " 'Photoshopped?' "

"Not 'Photoshopped' or changed by any other process," responded Philippe confidently as he tapped the stack of photos into order and started to replace them in their plastic envelope.

"We are particularly interested in the one #6k," Canton has paused in this replacement of the pictures and looked at the screen to his right on which was being displayed Prosecution Exhibit #6k, the atilt picture of Howard swinging the Heineken bottle at me. He found the picture in the stack and put it on top.

"Out of focus or blurry images when using a process like Photoshop are very difficult to work with if they are the pictures being moved. There are too many edges that have to be smoothed into the transition. Plus, you have to get a picture of the beer bottle and blur it just right and adjust the person's grip to hold the larger portion of the bottle, not the neck. It would be very tedious, take some time, and require a real expert.

"In this picture, the most in-focus person is in the foreground but is basically just a little out of focus as though he was moving away from the camera. The other person – the other two people – are further away and seem to be more stationary but out of focus as they are further away. The person in the foreground appears to be one of the two in #6e – I am judging this by the dress and the date and time of the pictures – and the other person the one in the two previous pictures #6i and #6j; the third person is too hidden I think to be identifiable."

As he was talking, from the open doorway leading to the witness room came a muffled sound that we all knew was Howard once again letting his outrage at being tried by "frigging frogs" using "Photoshopped photographs" be known. Guillaume Martineau hastened to the door that he had forgotten to close after leading Philippe Canton through or Philippe Canton had forgotten to close after being led through by Guillaume Martineau. Having closed the door he crossed to his position to the left front of Michel Villar's dais mumbling, "Sorry, your Honor" as he passed by, but you could tell by the look on Villar's face that Guillaume had lost any points he had accumulated that day and also that Howard would not be rejoining us tomorrow or anytime soon.

Guillaume Martineau (age 65) had been gendarme sergeant major on St. Martin and had come to St. Nantes at age 60 when he retired. He and his wife Yvette have two daughters both married and living on St. Martin. The oldest (second married) had given him two grandsons and the youngest was still childless but pregnant. At six feet one inch, he weighed 230 pounds, which was 20 pounds more than at retirement. He blamed it on being less active but swam daily when not in court. He played tennis regularly with Michel Villar and the two have been "senior" doubles champions two years in a row. Villar was also singles champion six times, five years in a row before being upset two years before by a new senior (aged 40). Where Guillaume Martineau got his red hair and grey-green eyes is a mystery since his mother was blond and blue-eyed and his father had brown hair and was blue-eyed and neither has any red hair in their ancestry. (Was it the postman or the butcher?) Regardless, his striking resemblance (other than hair and eyes) to his father gave no one cause to question his paternity.

CHAPTER 79

During this time it took Guillaume Martineau to close the door and resume his post, Philippe Canton had placed the pictures back into their plastic envelope and then looked at Judge Villar expectantly.

"I have no further questions of this witness, does anyone?"

Immediately Chyrise shot to her feet, hand in the air. Villar recognized her and said, "Ask your question but be careful what you say, Mademoiselle Callahan."

"Thank you, your Honor," Chyrise said in a tone that made you think she wanted to say "your Holiness" rather than "your Honor."

"Monsieur Canton, have you ever been fooled by a photograph?"

Philippe said, "I don't ..."

"Let me rephrase that. Have you ever seen a photograph that had been 'Photoshopped' and not known it?"

"No, but perhaps if it had been done by the world's best, I could be fooled," He held up the envelope of pictures. "But then, I did not 'Photoshop' any of these and neither did anyone else." His smile was definitely confident and wicked.

For a few seconds Chyrise digested his statement, tossed it about in her mind, and must have decided that nothing further was to be gained. "Thank you," she said and resumed her seat looking a little defeated.

"I have one other question," Michel Villar said. "Let us assume that someone did 'Photoshop' the picture. Could it then be replaced on the memory chip to appear that it was the original?"

"Not to my knowledge," said Phillipe Canton. "In fact, I contacted the manufacturer of the camera to determine this. I was told there is a great risk that the chip could be contaminated making access difficult. Also, more than likely the camera would not recognize the picture as being there. However, the camera in question recognizes all the pictures on the chip and the chip is not contaminated."

"Any other questions," Villar asked. There being none, he continued. "Thank you, Monsieur Canton, for your expert testimony. You are excused but please remain available to be recalled during the remainder of this trial. We thank you for your time and ...," he was going to say something else but didn't and waved him away.

Guillaume Martineau led Philippe back to the witness room, closing the door firmly but quietly behind him as they left. Then he came back through the door, closed it and took up his post next to it, looking a little chagrined.

CHAPTER 80

Huard Jubert stood up and said, "The Prosecution calls it next witness, Sergeant Marin Paulhus."

Guillaume Martineau opened the door, entered, and closed it behind him. Shortly thereafter the door opened and he reappeared leading a man of medium height, dressed in a uniform of a French gendarme (a pale-blue shirt, and dark-blue trousers with a black stripe, black boots) carrying a manila folder. He paused just past the open door while Guillaume Martineau closed the door (obviously Sergeant Paulhus had been told to wait) and then led him to the witness stand where he was sworn in.

Without being told, Guillaume Martineau brought Prosecution Exhibit #4, the stack of money.

Michel Villar then started the questioning. "Sergeant, what is it that you do with the gendarmerie?"

"I work in the evidence division."

"And what in particular?"

"While I do many different things, my specialty is fingerprints."

"I see. Have you ever seen Prosecution Exhibit #4 before?"

Marin Paulhus picked up the plastic bag containing the stack of money and looked at it. "Yes, I have, there is a sticker on the bag bearing my initials and the date I examined it."

"And what did you find?"

"While there were a number of fingerprints, mostly smudges, on the money, the two outside bills and the band itself had four fingerprints that were good enough to be used for comparison."

"And did you identify the fingerprints?"

"Three of them fairly immediately. One set belonged to a Quentin Baston, resident of St. Nantes; one set was that of a Howard Blake, resident of Los Angeles, California, in the United States; and the third was that of an Elise Blake Andrews, resident of Miami, Florida. I received the fingerprints of Quentin Baston from the prosecutor's office, those of Howard Blake from the Los Angeles Police Department, and those of Elise Blake Andrews from the Miami, Florida, police."

"And was there any doubt about the match?"

"Not in my opinion. Those of Howard Blake and Quentin Baston each had fourteen points for comparison, while one print of Elise Blake Andrews had sixteen points for comparison. I think that almost all fingerprint experts would agree with my identification."

"Objection," Chyrise rose. "Speculation."

Michel Villar smiled that sardonic smile of his. "Sergeant Paulhus is testifying as an expert and offering his opinion, which he is permitted to do. Overruled."

Chyrise shrugged and sat down.

"Sergeant Paulhus, you said that you believed that 'almost all fingerprint experts would agree' with your identification. But not all?"

"Well, I don't believe there is any room for doubt. I myself am one hundred percent certain of the matches but others might not agree as completely. Therefore I do not say 'all'."

"And does the wrapper bear any identifying marks?"

"It bears a stamp on the back of it identifying it as being packaged at the Bank of America, 5000 Biscayne Blvd, Miami, Florida."

"Where there any other identifiable fingerprints on the wrapper?"

"Yes, having identified the bank from which we believe the money came, we requested the Miami police send us fingerprint cards of all the employees of that branch. They did and I identified the print as belonging to Alice Goodwin, a senior teller. My superior and I talked to her on the phone. We asked her about this particular bundle and she said that she remembered giving Elise Andrews a bundle a week before the cruise date. She said that Mrs. Andrews told her that the money was a surprise birthday present for her husband."

She was prepared, I thought. My birthday is, or was, in August.

Marin Paulhus continued, "Beyond that we can't actually be certain that this is the bundle she gave Mrs. Andrews but it would seem that it was."

"Does anyone else have any questions?" Michel Villar asked looking at the defense's table, his chin resting on top of his church's steeple.

Chyrise raised her hand with a folded paper in it. Guillaume Martineau retrieved it and handed it to the judge, who opened it and read it, raising one eyebrow in the process.

"Sergeant Paulhus, could you make any determination of the order in which the fingerprints were put on the wrapper or bill?"

"I can make an educated guess but can't be exact. There is a fingerprint I identified with 8 points of certainty as that of Elise Andrews under one I identified as belonging to Quentin Baston with nine points of certainty. Likewise there is a print of Howard Blake (seven points) over laying a print of Elise Andrews (six points) and that print of Howard Blake is under a print of Quentin Baston (ten points).

"So I guess I would say, and this is only a guess," Sergeant Paulhus said, "Elise Andrews handled the packet first, Howard Blake second, and Quentin Baston third. In my opinion, there is no way of determining when Alice Goodwin handled the packet."

Chyrise had another question that Guillaume Martineau retrieved and gave the judge.

"Were there any prints that could possibly be those of Stuart Andrews?"

"Not with any degree of certainty. Almost all the other prints were smudges and identification next to impossible."

Michel Villar looked at the defense's table for more questions, but there were none. I thought that Chyrise's line of questioning hurt more than it helped.

"Sergeant," Michel Villar asked. "Given all these prints, would you hazard a guess as to whether or not Stuart Andrews ever handled the packet?"

"Given the information I have, if I had to guess and it would only be a guess, I would say that he never handled the packet."

Part VIII

The Defense

CHAPTER 82

Sergeant Marin Paulhus was the last witness for the prosecution.

"At this time," Huard Jubert added.

Michel Villar then adjourned court until nine a.m. the following morning when the defense would begin.

Chyrise and Phil requested time with their clients before they were transported back to their lodgings.

Once they were alone in their conference room, Chyrise turned on Howard.

"Howard, when you came to me looking for help in the extradition case, I was skeptical ... not certain that I would be comfortable working with you because of your biases, that was the way you put it. Actually you said, 'I don't like nig... African-Americans, or chinks, or spics. I don't trust those French frogs because they have no spines.' That alone was reason for me to say no, but I didn't.

"You said that you were being railroaded for something you didn't do. You said that Stuart Andrews was alive after leaving St. Nantes and he had committed suicide by jumping overboard between Grenada and Curaçao. I never asked you if you were innocent because you made this statement to me.

"However, today not only has the evidence been damning and woven into one nice package, but your actions have been damning as well. You lost your cool and made such a bad impression that I don't know if we can recover.

"I don't know what you think our defense can be. But we'll discuss that after Phil gets his say."

Phil cleared his throat.

"Elise, we have known each other for a while and I would never have thought you capable of doing what we heard in court today. Even though you didn't have a direct hand in these purported actions, you are as guilty as though you were there.

"You are an accomplice to a conspiracy and by the laws of the United States and St. Nantes, as perversely enforced as I feel the latter to be, you are just as guilty as Howard … ."

Howard railed, "What do you mean 'as guilty as Howard'? I have told you that I didn't … ."

Phil interrupted holding up his hands. "If I may continue … as guilty as Howard, if he is found to be guilty by this jury of judges, not a jury of your peers as we have in the states …"

Howard muttered, "None of these stinking frogs could be my peers, ever."

"… but a jury of judges, three of whom are supposed to be at least as qualified as Michel Villar. Even if Howard is found to be not guilty … ."

"Not 'if', when," Howard interjected.

"… when Howard is found to be not guilty, you could be found guilty of some other associated crime as solicitation and conspiracy just as …," and he looked straight at Howard, "… Howard could. Therefore it behooves you both to be as straightforwardly honest with us as you can be. We cannot conduct a defense with nothing, which is what we have now. There are issues to be addressed: the money, the picture, etc., but we can only get at their validity and that will be extremely difficult.

"We have Jonni Dillon from Caribbean Cruise Lines who can testify about gangway security but we don't know how strong his testimony will be as far as showing that Stuart came back aboard as you have said. He wasn't there and the cruise staff and ship's staff who were don't remember, so it is basically useless in getting them. We had thought we might be able to use the tapes from the ship's gangway to show that Stuart came back on board the Caribbean Isle as you said he did. However, as you know there were no tapes because the ship was anchored and the gangway cameras only run when the ship is docked.

"I … we …," he looked at Chyrise apologetically, "… can do little with the testimony of Quentin Baston. He is an eyewitness and although his intent could be questionable because of the money, there is not much that we can do to impugn it. At least at this point… ."

The last comment was made directly at Howard who looked as though he was ready to begin another of his tirades.

"So, we feel that the two of you need some time to confer between yourselves and decide what you are going to let us use as a defense. As of now we really have nothing to use other than the story about Stuart disappearing and no body ever being recovered. We have to be ready in the morning to present a defense, although we will ask for a delay in order to bring some of our own experts to testify, but we don't have a lot of hope to be honest. The only thing we can see that can possibly help is your testimony. So you had better get your stories straight."

"And be completely forthright with us," Chyrise said as she picked up her brief case and exited the room through the door held open by Phil who didn't look back but at her slight wiggle as he followed her and shut the door.

In the room there was silence.

"Howard, what …," Elise started.

"Shut up, Sis, let me think."

Howard stared at nothing for a few minutes while Elise tore the tissue she held into tiny pieces. Then …

"We use the frog's testimony."

"What?"

"He said something like 'he was not a good husband to his wife and hit her and got sex from other women.' I don't know if there is anything we can do with the latter but we certainly can do something with his hitting you. You must be the battered wife who strikes back in self defense."

"But I didn't … ."

"No, you didn't because … because you're too weak. He threatened you with bodily harm. He hurt you; you have those photos of that bruising you got falling while roller blading. You broke your fingers in the car door but they don't know that – Stuart did it to you."

Elise was silence. "You're right, Howard. That could work. The battered wife ... but ... what about us faking his suicide? I mean we did, but we don't want to risk your imprisonment for manslaughter, which is the least it could be, if they have that in this stinking rat hole. We can't have them think that you killed Stuart on that fishing boat. We can't have them thinking that you did anything that drastic!"

"Right, it was Keith ... Keith who killed him protecting you on the ship. They can't prove that he wasn't on the ship and they only have that friggin' frog's word that we killed him. We can use that. We can beat them."

CHAPTER 83

"The Defense calls Jonni Dillon."

I cannot say what had gone on with Elise and Howard and their lawyers after court had adjourned when Sergeant Paulhus finished his testimony but in court that next morning, the defense had asked for a two-week recess but had only been granted one week to be able to refute some of the surprise testimony of the preceding day. Chyrise had requested that Howard be permitted to return during the defense's presentation, and that was granted, but Michel Villar had warned her that any additional outbursts would have him permanently removed even when giving his testimony.

Phil Dombrey had given the opening statement for the defense.

"Ladies and gentlemen of the jury, what you have heard so far is a excellent combination of prefabricated bullshit, if I may be so blunt."

Michel Villar frowned but didn't object; after all he was not really in church although his fingers were.

"Everything has been blended together to make a fantastic story beginning with the so-called dying declaration of an obviously delusional man; then a witness being resurrected from his 'watery grave'; a package of money from who knows where although the wrapper appears to be from a bank in Miami, Florida; to a camera with a purported picture of the 'murder' of Stuart Andrews... ." He used his hands to indicate the quotes around "watery grave" and "murder."

"However, as our witnesses will show they are all obviously 'Photoshopped'." No quotes indicated this time.

"The truth is that Stuart Andrews died in the waters of the southern Caribbean not the waters of St. Nantes. He returned from the fishing trip to board the Caribbean Isle in

the port of Genivee, secluded himself in his cabin for several days before falling to his death.

"But you don't have to let me tell you about it, we will let our experts tell you the facts about the evidence and let the eye witnesses to Stuart Andrews' demise tell you what happened."

Guillaume Martineau opened the door to the hallway and disappeared briefly and returned leading a dark-skinned man about six foot four wearing a white naval type uniform. He entered the witness box, was sworn in and Phil Dombrey introduced him to the court.

"Jonni Dillon is the chief security officer for Caribbean Cruise Lines. He served ... ."

Michel Villar interrupted. "Mister Dombrey, in addition to asking the questions I will determine the man's qualifications."

Looking stunned at being rebuked for trying to introduce his witness, Phil Dombrey sat down.

"Mister Dillon. Where are you from?"

"I work out of Port Ever..."

"No, where were you born?"

"Oh, Jamaica."

"I thought so. You are chief security officer for the Caribbean Lines, as Mr. Dombrey told us."

"Yes, sir, I ... ."

"Just answer the questions, Mr. Dillon, I am certain that Mr. Dombrey doesn't want you to elaborate any more than I do."

Jonni Dillon said nothing.

"Were you on the Caribbean Isle when it was in port in Genivee on February 16 of this year?"

"No, I ... ."

"So you weren't on board at that time. I don't see what you can possibly have to say ... ."

"If I may, your honor," Phil Dombrey was standing and moving his hands in an obviously irritated way. In one of them, he held a piece of paper.

"I guess that even, courtroom veteran that I am, I forgot that it is you who asks our questions."

"Yes," Michel Villar replied obviously not happy and motioned to Guillaume Martineau to get the paper. With that in his hands, he studied it momentarily, put it down, went to church, contemplated for a moment and then said, "Mr. Dombrey, why isn't the security officer or the person who was on duty at the gangway during this incident here to present this information?"

"He is currently on leave and has gone home to the Czech Republic. We have not been able to contact him. Mr. Dillon as chief security officer for Caribbean Cruise Lines has all the available information and will be able to answer your questions."

"Very well." He motioned for Phil Dombrey to sit down and then asked, "Mr. Dillon ... Jonni – J ... O... N ... N ...I. Interesting spelling, how did you get this name?"

Phil Dombrey started to get up but Michel Villar came out of the church and held his hand up and Phil sat back down.

"Never mind, Mr. Dillon. Did you see Stuart Andrews come back on board the Caribbean Isle in the port of Genivee?"

"I wasn't ... ."

"Answer the question, Mr. Dillon. That is the question that needs to be answered. Did you see Stuart Andrews come back on board the Caribbean Isle in the port of Genivee on Monday, February 16 of this year?"

"No."

"Then what do you know?"

CHAPTER 84

The courtroom was astir with this exchange.

Jonni Dillon seemed unfazed by the exchange. He placed a folder he had been carrying on the podium and opened it.

"First, if I may?" he glanced quizzically at Michel Villar.

Michel Villar, attending church again, nodded and I noticed that sardonic smile again.

"My mother's name was Nina and my father Jonathon. Neither of them liked Jonathon. My father is called Jon and I wasn't a girl so they combined the names."

"Interesting," said Michel Villar. "So inventive. Please continue and tell me what Mr. Dombrey wishes the court to know."

"When a passenger leaves the ship, in this case the Caribbean Isle, he or she swipes his or her cruise card – they're like credit cards with a magnetic strip containing the passenger's name, stateroom and other information – in a card reader and the time of departure is recorded on the computer.

"Mr. Stuart Andrews, Mr. Keith Mitchell, Mr. Howard Blake and Mrs. Elise Andrews, swiped their cards at 9:18 on the morning of February 16 of this year leaving the ship to board a tender in the port of Genivee, St. Nantes."

"All at precisely the same time?" asked Michel Villar incredulously, but that sardonic smile was there.

"No. Mr. Andrews at 18 minutes and 27 seconds, Mr. Mitchell at 18 minutes and 29 seconds – there are two card readers – Mr. Blake at 18 minutes and 40 seconds and Mrs. Andrews at 18 minutes and 15 seconds."

"Okay, so they all left the ship in the morning. Do people ever leave the ship without swiping their cruise card?"

"No, sir. All cruise staff and ship's company swipe their cards also. Since 9/11 the only way to leave the ship without swiping your cruise card is by going over the side and it's a long way down."

"So to leave the ship, everyone wipes his or her cruise card?" asked Villar.

"Yes, sir," Jonni Dillon answered.

"Has anyone ever died on a cruise ship?"

"Unfortunately yes, and I assume that you mean that died onboard, not jumped overboard and died in the water."

"Yes, that is what I mean."

"Then again the answer is 'yes'."

"Then how does that person swipe his or her cruise card as he or she is carried off the ship?"

"In that case someone else, family or cruise staff member, swipes the decedent's card."

"So, to be clear, there are cases where someone other than the card owner swipes a person's cruise card."

"Yes, but only in the case when the person would not be able to do so."

"Such as not being there?" Villar asked.

"No, the person would have to be there, dead or alive." Jonni Dillon answered emphatically.

Villar churched and then said, "What if the person disappeared on shore or disappeared on the ship?"

"In that case, a notation is made in the computer log to indicate why the person couldn't swipe the card."

"When coming aboard or going ashore, a card is swiped and what happens?"

"I don't ... ."

"I mean does the computer say, 'Have a nice time ashore' or does a picture of the person appear ... ."

"Nothing happens when the person goes ashore other than the computer recording the time and that the person is ashore. Just the card is swiped to indicate that the person is off the ship."

"So another person could swipe someone else's cruise card and leave the ship and no one would know?"

Jonni Dillon was quiet for a moment.

"Well," said Michel Villar.

"Yes, I suppose but why ..."

"Oh, any number of reasons. Now what about when a person comes back on board?"

I could sense that Villar knew the answer.

"When a person comes aboard the first time, a picture is taken after the person's cruise card is swiped. After that when a person comes aboard and swipes the cruise card, that person's picture appears and a member of the security staff verifies that the person who swiped the card matches the picture."

"But not when going ashore?"

"No, not when going ashore."

"But when coming aboard?"

"Yes, when coming aboard."

"So it is impossible for a person to swipe someone else's card when coming aboard?"

"Yes, it is. Well, someone could swipe another person's card but when the picture didn't match the person, action would be taken."

"But going ashore."

Dillon shrugged.

"Make that a 'no'," Villar instructed the clerk.

Phil Dombrey stood. "I don't understand this line of questioning."

Michel Villar glared at him. "Well, I am asking the questions both mine, yours and Monsieur Jubert's and I do understand the line of questioning and, believe me, it is relevant. Sit down, Mr. Dombrey or you will join Mr. Blake."

CHAPTER 85

Phil Dombrey sat, looked at Chyrise and shrugged.

"Now, Mr. Dillon. Would you kindly tell the court when your infallible computer reports that Mr. Andrews's cruise card was swiped indicating that he had returned aboard from the port of Genivee on February 16 of this year?"

"It was 4:11."

Michel Villar waited.

"Oh," Jonni Dillon said and looked at his paper. "... and 17 seconds."

"And Mrs. Andrews?"

Jonni Dillon consulted the paper. " 4:10 and 57 seconds."

"So she was first and then the swiper of Mr. Andrews's card?"

"Yes, she preceded Mr. Andrews by about 20 seconds."

"You are certain that it was Mr. Andrews?"

"It had to be because of the match between the picture and person who swipes the card."

"So you said," Mr. Villar said. "And you can't get aboard without swiping your own cruise card?"

"No, sir, you can't. We have a very secure system. I designed it myself."

"Good, then you can answer my other questions. When did Mr. Blake swipe his card?"

Jonni Dillon consulted his papers. "At 4:14 and 27 seconds."

"Quite a delay there. Tell me, and I hope you have the information there, did anyone else swipe a card between the time when Stuart Andrews's card was swiped and Mr. Blake swiped his card?"

I knew what he was getting at.

Jonni Dillon looked down at his paper, then the next, and then looked up at Michel Villar.

"I have two lists, one by passenger name and one by boarding time. The boarding time list" he glanced toward the defense table, "shows that no one swiped a cruise card in the intervening time."

Phil Dombrey's shoulders seemed to sag. He hadn't expected Jonni Dillon to be so prepared or maybe he hadn't expected that Villar would be this exacting.

"What is the explanation for this?"

"I don't have one. Mrs. Andrews's was the tenth person off that particular tender, you can tell by the time differential for ten to fifteen minutes between tenders and with the last tender from shore at 4:15, I would expect that this was a full tender and indeed there are 70 people who swiped cards coming off that tender."

"So there is no way for a person to come on board without swiping his or her card?"

"No, sir," Dillon answered.

"And you can't come aboard with someone else's card?"

"No, sir, you can't."

"You are certain?"

Jonni Dillon's back seemed to stiffen and he replied, "Yes, sir, I am."

"Good," said Michel Villar and settled back in his chair as though finished.

Jonni Dillon must have thought that he was finished as well because he closed his folder.

Michel Villar suddenly straightened up, made his church and said, "Mr. Dillon. Mr. Jonni Dillon. Tell the court if you would, what time did Mr. Keith Mitchell swipe his card coming aboard on that day?"

Jonni Dillon opened his folder ran his finger down the page and stopped. Then he ran his finger down the next page and the next and the next and then it stopped. He looked at the number as though in disbelief and then said "4:55 and 38 seconds."

"4:55 and 38 seconds," Michel Villar mused. "That's quite a delay. I guess he took the last tender?"

"No, sir, the last tender came along side at 4:30 and the last passenger, Martin Crenshaw, swiped his card at 4:38 and 22 seconds."

"Then how did Mr. Mitchell come aboard? Did he swim, use a canoe?"

"No, sir, you can't get close enough to the ship swimming or in a boat since 9/11."

"Then how do you explain it, Mr. Dillon?"

Jonni Dillon was silent. You could almost hear the gears grinding. Then as though sensing the truth, which he must have known but was hoping he wouldn't have to admit, he said, "He must have come on board without swiping his card."

"Without swiping his card, you say. But that is impossible, isn't it, Mr. Dillon?"

"Yes ... no ... I don't understand."

"But Mr. Dillon, doesn't it happen a lot? Aren't cruise ship's always calling passengers' names after the last tender or when the gangway has been closed?"

"Yes, sir, but usually those people are late."

"Usually but not always."

Jonni Dillon's composure seemed to sag even more. "Yes, not always."

"So then, assuming that your security system is as good as you say, in order for Mr. Mitchell to get on board without swiping his card, there must have been something to distract the gangway security staff?"

"Yes, sir, I would have to say that something like that must have happened."

"And, Mr. Dillon, if Mr. Mitchell could get aboard through your security without swiping his cruise card, isn't it possible that someone – even Mr. Mitchell – could have used this distraction to swipe Mr. Andrews's cruise card to indicate that he had come aboard."

Jonni Dillon seemed totally defeated. "Yes, I guess," he said.

CHAPTER 86

No one had any further questions and why should they? The defense had fumbled the ball and the offense had scored against the defense. What else did they have to throw up?

Michel Villar waited until Guillaume Martineau was back at his post beside the door after escorting Jonni Dillon out before asking Phil Dombrey. "Who is your next witness?" The way he said it, you could tell he meant "next sacrificial victim."

Chyrise rose and said, "The Defense calls Carrie Miller."

She was petit, say 5 feet 4 inches in her stocking feet, couldn't have weighed much more than 100 pounds if you cut off about two feet of the kinky black hair. She was wearing blue jeans (they were clean) and a pink tee shirt proclaiming "Computers aren't just are for geeks, they're for adults too." I guess you just can't get some people to dress up even when they go "courting."

"Miss Miller," Michel Villar said and you could tell he was intrigued. "Why are you here?"

Carrie turned toward the defense table, pointed at Chyrise and said, "She asked me to come."

"No, dear," Michel Villar said, "what is your field of expertise?"

"Oh, sorry," she said. Maybe the hair was dyed and she was blond. "I am a photographer. I do a lot of work with Photoshop. Have you seen those pictures of a cardinal with the Pope's head, or the Portuguese Waterdog with the President's head or ..."

"We get the idea. Did you do those?"

"Some of them," she said. "Can I show you?"

Michel Villar nodded and the first of the described photographs appeared on the screen.

"Are things like this difficult to do?"

"Yeah, for the average person." Carrie Miller replied. "But if you're good ..."

"And you are?" Michel Villar asked.

"Yes, I am," she replied. No lack of confidence there. "Let me show you. Next."

The picture of Keith and Howard in the back of the Mahi Mahi showed up but their heads had been switched. The size differential made things look funny, as Keith was smaller than Howard and so was his head. Then the picture of Quentin baiting, but his head was that of a fish and it look as though it had flowed evenly from his shoulders.

"Very nice," Villar said. "Did you do anything with 6k?"

That was the off kilter one of Howard and the upside down bottle and it was flashed on the screen.

"I tried," she admitted and another picture was displayed with Howard's head from 6e in place of his head. It looked funny because it where the back of his head should have been. In addition, it wasn't blurry like the rest of the picture and didn't seem to blend in.

"We usually don't work with blurry images. Much easier to work with distinct ones."

"But you could?"

"Yes, but it would take a long time and why go to the trouble?"

Michel Villar looked at the list of questions, this time properly supplied by Chyrise. "To try to convince some one that another person was the killer?" It was a statement but Michel Villar made it sound like a question.

"Oh, yes, well, I suppose you could but it's a lot of work."

Michel Villar looked at his sheet of questions. "Well, could you, for example, replace the bottle in Mr. Blake's hand (he's the one in the picture with the upside down bottle) with one upright and open."

"You mean like this?"

The picture flashed on the screen showed the bottle in Howard's hand now upright and open but something about it didn't look quite right. However, the picture did raise a murmur among the spectators.

"Interesting," Villar said. "You have to get the picture out of the camera in order to do that, correct?"

"You mean off the chip and on a computer? If that is the question, then yes."

"Could you then put it back on the chip and make it look like it was taken that way with the camera?"

"Maybe someone could. I mean, I could put it back on the chip but I don't know if it would look like it had been taken with the camera." She looked toward Chyrise and sort of shrugged.

"Any further questions of this witness," Michel Villar asked.

No one had any.

"The witness is excused."

He looked at the defense's table. "Call your next witness."

Chyrise stood, "The defense calls Jesse James."

CHAPTER 87

Jesse James was a tall pimply-faced kid of no more than sixteen. He was wearing khaki trousers with a black Grateful Dead tee shirt, and tennis shoes with a hole in the left one. Obviously his mother hadn't dressed him. He was accompanied by a table on wheels holding a laptop computer, a camera the size of mine, and what looked to be a projector. Guillaume Martineau took a long extension cord from the table and plugged it in to a plug underneath Michel Villar's dais. Then he swore Jesse James in.

Chyrise started to give an introduction and Michel Villar waved her aside.

"Jesse James. Any relation to …"

"No, sir," the young man said, "My father just had a fascination with outlaws of the old west."

Michel Villar glared at him. He didn't like being interrupted but held his cool.

"My younger brother is named Frank," continued Jesse James.

"Interesting but not relevant," Michel Villar snapped. Then he paused, gained control and asked. "You are a computer expert, Mr. James?"

"Yes, I …" Michel Villar stopped him with upraised hand.

"And you are here to do what?"

"I am going to demonstrate how a picture can be taken off a camera's memory chip, altered and put back on the chip so that no one can tell it was removed."

A buzz ran through the gallery.

"Proceed," said the judge, obviously interested.

Jesse moved from the witness stand to the table and picked up the camera.

"Here we have the same make and model of the camera involved in this case and it contains the same type of memory chip. Currently there are no pictures on the camera. With the court's permission."

Without waiting Jesse started taking pictures: the lay judges, the judge who winced at the flash, the professional judges, the translators, the prosecutors, the defense table and then started taking pictures of the crowd. At this point I ducked down to get something. Peering between the people in front, I could see him turn and take a final picture of Guillaume Martineau.

"That's eleven, just the number on the other camera."

He put the camera on the table, attached a cable to it, and turned the laptop. A few keystrokes and thumbnail-sized pictures appeared on the screens behind the judges' daises.

"You can see the pictures. Now I am going to download the last one." Key strokes and then the picture of Guillaume Martineau appeared on the two screens.

"Let's do something simple."A red handlebar mustache appeared on Guilluame's face. Another couple of key strokes and he had glasses.

"Now I'll save it and put it back on the camera." He was busy tapping keys.

"How are you doing that," Michel Villar asked.

"Doing what?" Jesse answered without looking up.

"Putting the picture back on the camera," Michel Villar sounded exasperated.

"With a program I wrote."

"So this is not commercial?"

Jesse stopped typing and looked up. "Oh, no. This requires expertise. It isn't something many people would want to do."

"But you do?"

"Only because Mr. Dombrey," and he indicated the defense table with a wave of his arm, "asked me to."

"I see," said Michel Villar. "Please continue."

Jesse did. Then he looked up.

"First I put the picture back on the camera using the method most programs do to save a picture. Here is the result."

The screen behind the judges' daises now showed the picture Jesse had altered but it was different than previously viewed on the camera. It was smaller and there was a wide black border.

"That's the way it would look. Obviously you can tell it wasn't put there by the camera.

"Now let's do it using the program I wrote."

He bent over the laptop and typed some keys.

"It's back on the camera."

The screens on the wall now showed the camera's screen and Jesse picked the camera up, cable extending from it to the computer.

"Now let's see the picture on the camera."

He pressed some buttons on the camera and the screen changed.

PICTURE ERROR showed on the screen.

"What?" Jesse said frowning. "I don't ..." He started tapping keys on the laptop again.

"Hold on, young man," Michel Villar said with a sharp rap of his gavel.

Jesse jumped and stood straight, hands on the keyboard.

"What are you doing or attempting to do?" Michel Villar asked.

"I am trying to fix the problem," Jesse said and went back to typing.

"What problem?" Michel Villar asked.

"The problem with the picture."

"Stop." And Jesse stopped.

"You mean you put the picture back and it's not there correctly?"

"Yes, but I ... ."

"No 'buts' please. You're done."

Phil Dombrey rose "Your honor ... ."

"The demonstration is over. It failed. The picture is faulty … ."

Jesse had resumed typing and picked the camera up again and pressed a button.

CARD ERROR appeared on the screen.

"Young man, I told you to stop. What does that mean?" his waving hand indicated the screen.

"It means that the memory card is faulty and can't be used."

"Well," said Michel Villar. "We're glad that it wasn't the actual card we have admitted for evidence because you would have destroyed the evidence. Obviously you have demonstrated to the court that the picture could not be re-moved, changed and replaced.

"Does anyone have any other questions of this witness," he said looking at Phil Dombrey who had shrunk back into his seat.

No one did.

"The witness is excused."

He glanced at his watch. "It is now 11:30. Rather than calling another witness, we will break for lunch. We will reconvene at 1:00."

CHAPTER 88

The consensus among my fellow "reporters" gathered at the Blue Dolphin Bar and Grill near the ferry landing on Guerre Isle was that the defense had scored some points with Carrie Miller, but not done as well with Jonni Dillon. Of course, Jesse James's demonstration had done irreparable harm to their case.

"She made a good argument about the Photoshopping of that picture but it's still questionable about putting it back on the chip and making it look natural. I don't know if it can be done." A reporter from the L.A. Times made this comment.

"It really doesn't matter, does it?" said a reporter from the Washington Post. "No matter how good you Photoshop the picture, you can't get it back on the camera."

"At least Jesse James couldn't," retorted the L.A. Times.

"I know about Jesse," said the Plain Dealer. "He is the best. If he can't do it, no one can."

There were murmurs of agreement. I simply nodded.

"The judge really led that Jonni Dillon along, didn't he," a female reporter from the Miami Herald said. "He was so smug about that security system and then wham. You almost have to believe that the judge is working for the prosecution and not the defense."

"I don't agree," said the local reporter. "Judge Villar is being fair with both sides. He just looks to see where the argument is weak and then homes in."

"Who do you think we'll hear this afternoon?" queried the Washington Post. "Think they'll go after Quentin Baston's testimony?"

"I'm thinking the suicide note," said the L.A. Times. "The extradition hearing was based on Keith Mitchell being delusional but the psychiatrist treating him said he wasn't having problems like that. His problems were alcohol and gambling. I say they call in another guy to go that way or attack the handwriting."

"Be difficult to get another psychiatrist to make a judgment based on that letter if you ask me," countered the Miami Herald. "What do you think?"

This one was directed at me. Fortunately I had my mouth full of fish at the time and just shrugged.

"You never say anything in these discussions," said Miami Herald. "Why not?"

I finished my mouthful, smiled apologetically and said, "I am trying to be like the jury. Getting all the information and then make a decision." This didn't answer the question but I didn't want to say too much.

The four members of the defense team sat around a table eating their catered lunch from the Blue Dolphin. They had discussed the testimony of that morning and the two lawyers were now considering how to proceed.

"The fingerprint expert we consulted won't be of any help but we figured that beforehand," Chyrise said. "We have not found a psychiatrist who is willing to express an opinion of Keith's state of mind based just on the dying declaration."

"The only other witness we have ready to go is a handwriting expert and she admits that she can't really add anything," Phil said. "Keith's handwriting is sloppy because he was drunk but there is little sign of stress or coercion in his opinion. It is Keith's handwriting, she is certain of that."

"So where's that leave us besides in deep shit?" Howard asked.

"With the two of you," Chyrise said. "You have explained your proposed testimony to us and it gives you a chance. We wish you had been more truthful with us from the start because we would have had more time to prepare a better defense. That bastard judge isn't going to give us much time. He feels that we should have been prepared but, as we all know, we didn't know what to prepare for."

Elise look at Howard and then at Chyrise. "We didn't want our story to get out because we – really me, I admit – was afraid that we could be tried for murder in some other country since it happened on international waters."

"That comes under Maritime Law. I am not that familiar with Maritime Law," interjected Phil. "The Caribbean Isle is registered in Liberia and that probably means they have jurisdiction although it may be something that the cruise line would have a say in. Liberia has the death penalty and, if I remember correctly, they're pretty strict. If you knew that, I understand you keeping quiet."

"We didn't," Howard said. "We were just scared."

"Phil and I have discussed our course of action and we feel that at this point you two need to testify," said Chyrise. "We will put Elise on first since her relationship with Stuart is the basis for your actions."

"Are you prepared for this, Elise?" Phil asked.

Elise sighed deeply. "As much as I can be."

CHAPTER 89

When court reconvened at 1:00, I was surprised to see Elise take the stand. She was wearing a white blouse, black skirt with black pearl or bead necklace and earrings. Today's skirt was just below mid-thigh, so she had noticed Michel Villar's ogling of the first day. Take advantage of everything you can.

After she was sworn in, Phil Dombrey addressed Michel Villar. "Mrs. Andrews would like to tell you the truth of what happened to Stuart. She feels that she can explain things better that way than if you ask her questions." Michel Villar frowned.

"Of course, you can ask questions but ones that come during her statement, if the court permits."

"I find that most satisfactory," Michel Villar said, "Please begin, Mrs. Andrews."

"Stuart and I met over twelve years ago at a charity event, I think it was a disaster relief benefit but I don't remember the disaster."

I did. It was for people in the Naples, Florida, area which was hit by Hurricane Mitch, although at that time was just a big tropical storm. With maximum sustained winds of 180 mph making it one of the most powerful on record, Mitch was the third major hurricane of the 1998 Atlantic season and, at that time, was the most powerful October hurricane.

"I was introduced to him by a mutual friend who at that time was dating him."

It was the end of the relationship anyway, not because I met Elise but because the other woman found someone at the party she felt was better and more fulfilling.

"We talked for quite a while – family, education, the usual party small talk."

That's because Renee, the woman who I brought to the party but didn't take home, was talking to the man who would take her home.

"I gave him my phone number and he said he'd call, but didn't for almost two weeks."

She forgot to mention that I was out of the country. Actually I was setting up the front for what became the very lucrative money laundering business that I, acting as one of my "employees," had to end because of my death.

"Finally he did call and asked me to dinner – I think it was a Saturday night. Of course it had to be because that was the only night that he really had free with no markets and that stuff he does – did."

She acted like she broke down a bit right there. Good acting, but that was always one of her strong points. She was correct in her statement of my business, because she could not have cared less and never really knew more; what she really was interested in was the money. I should have realized by the time we went to bed for the first time (I think it was the third date) that she didn't give a damn about my business as long as the money kept coming in.

"It was a whirlwind courtship, I guess. We were married six months later. It was a private thing because Stuart didn't want a big wedding. Well, I didn't either. My parents were dead, my mother from breast cancer and dad from … a car accident."

No accident. Drove into an interstate bridge abutment at an excess of ninety-five miles per hour. Didn't leave a note but it was a suicide. He was basically lost without his wife. He had a fairly recent insurance policy that wouldn't have paid for suicide. It was for a million, I think and she went through her half fairly quickly.

"We went to Aruba for our honeymoon. One week, that was all he could afford to be gone from his precious business. At that point, I think, he had two wives, or a wife and a mistress with the mistress – his business – getting more attention."

She knew this from the beginning. I had explained how the markets controlled my life. There was the European, Mideastern, and African Markets that I traded with, then of course the NYSE and the South American Markets, and then the Asian Exchanges. In order to trade in them all it was basically an eighteen-hour day, but I didn't do it every day even when they were open.

"I was able to manage at first being newly married and deeply in love…," W*ith my money!* "… and I had things to do and there were always the weekends. For the first few years, things were good. Then he started spending even more hours working."

Okay, the new business that I had set up when we just met had really taken off and was requiring a lot of my time as the investors were really pouring money into it. I had to put a stop to that though because there was only so much that could be laundered at one time. It wasn't easy and required a lot of my time. That was when I set up the account that I had only recently told her about. I fed money into it off and on but mainly into one of my other ten accounts offshore – spread the wealth was my motto.

"I guess it was four or five years into our marriage. One weekend I complained about the time he was spending away. He got very angry telling me that I should be happy that he could earn good money because you never knew when the markets were going to go sour. When I continued to complain, he … he hit me."

Never, never. Well, there were a couple of times where we into a little spanking to try to spice up our sex life, not that it really needed spicing up at least in my opinion. She was a tiger in bed, almost insatiable but again part of that is my fault because I was really only home long enough for good encounters on the weekend. But she didn't complain, at least not to me.

CHAPTER 90

"He hit you?" Michel Villar asked.

"Yes," she was abashed, her eyes were down and she twisted a Kleenex with her hands. She had brought that out when she had realized that I was "dead."

"Hard, with a fist?"

"No, more of a slap. And he told me that he didn't want to hear any more about it and left the house in a huff."

Hmmm, don't ever recall leaving in a huff. I drove a Mercedes. Oh, there were times that she left in a huff after one of our discussions, arguments, tête-à-têtes– whatever you want to call them. But I never struck her in anger re- gardless of what she says.

"Was that the only time he hit you?"

"No, he started drinking more, and he would get angry when I complained about anything. Sometimes he would slap me, sometimes grab my arms and squeeze shaking me. Sometimes he would hit me with a belt, sometimes with a fist. There were bruises and I wouldn't go out if I couldn't cover them with clothes or makeup."

Ah, the battered wife syndrome. She could build a case in words, but of course she couldn't back it up.

"Did you call the police?" Michel Villar asked.

"Oh, no, I was afraid of what he would do. He told me that if I ever called the police he would really hurt me." She was good, tears were flowing. Go girl, get the mascara to run and he might start believing you.

"Did you ever go to a hospital for treatment?"

"Yes, once when he broke a bone in my hand. I was preparing dinner and he took a kitchen mallet for tenderizing meat and hit my hand when it was on the counter. He was sorry immediately and took me to the hospital."

Good one. Change the kitchen mallet to car door that you closed and didn't get your fingers out in time and make it because you were late for dinner with me. She came running into the restaurant in actual agony (well, she can act well) and I rushed her to the emergency room. X-rays revealed two broken proximal phalanges. Splints for a couple of weeks and Motrin as needed (accompanied by enough liquor to ease the pain) and she was fine. Phil Dombrey probably had the X-rays if needed.

"So there was only the one time with hospital care and no police reports?"

"Right but I have pictures of bruises."

Notice she didn't say pictures of her bruises. Maybe there were some bruises now and again but not caused by me. Tripping over an ottoman, slipping on a wet floor, falling after one "tea many martoonis" – those kinds of things that happen to us all.

"I am certain that you do," Villar said as Dombrey stood up with several folders in his hands.

"We would like to enter these into evidence as Defense Exhibits 1-5." He said extending them to Guillaume Martineau who showed them to Huard Jubert who nodded his acceptance. They were then tagged, receipts given to Phil and Guillaume Martineau gave them to the judge for his examination.

"Continue, Mrs. Andrews."

Wiping a crocodile tear away, she did. She was good. "Crocodile tears" were, according to ancient stories, used to lure their prey. She was trying to lure Villar and the judges into believing her story. Judging from Villar's reactions, it wasn't working on his part at least and I caught a couple of the lay judges conversing a bit.

"Things got worse. About fifteen months ago, I had enough. I told him that I wanted a divorce. I wanted out even if I didn't get anything. He got very angry and told me that if I so much as talked to a divorce lawyer and he found out about it, I wouldn't live to see him again."

I almost laughed out loud. She never asked to a divorce, she never even mentioned marriage counseling or anything that. Just the trip to try to get things back on an even keel.

"Then, a miracle happened. I discovered I was pregnant. I had used a home test packet. I was so excited. I had wanted a child to help hold us together."

She had never been pregnant though we had tried repeatedly. I had been through the odious task of being tested and I was fine.

"I was nervous about telling him. So I waited until the end of the weekend when we would have time to talk about it and get used to the idea. He came home drunk. He had begun to drink on the way home."

Never! Hell, I hardly drink at all.

CHAPTER 91

"I had a nice dinner prepared, candles, wine – for him, pregnant women shouldn't drink – and I was wearing a nice evening outfit. He came in and said 'What's the occasion? Hope you got something good to eat for a change.' I smiled and tried to be comforting. I went up to him, and sort of snuggled, as much as he would let me. 'I'm pregnant,' I said. 'What!' he exclaimed. He grabbed me and turned me around. 'Pregnant! I don't want any snotty-nosed diaper rat messing up my life. Get rid of it.' He shoved me roughly away and I fell hard against a chair, the end of the arm pushing hard against my stomach. Three days later I miscarried."

Michel Villar interrupted, "So you never saw a doctor? Don't have any verification of this?"

She shook her head dejectedly.

"Then I didn't know what to do. I was scared. I thought that maybe if I could get him away from work for a while it would help so I came up with the trip. He didn't want to go but I convinced him, even came up with the fishing trip and he reluctantly agreed. I got my brother to come with us just in case something happened.

"The trip started fine, that one day at sea was fantastic. We relaxed and sunned, made love for the first time in a couple of weeks..." – *true* – "... and it was going well.

"Then Monday morning, the news about Merrill-Lynch seemed to shatter his life. He went on the fishing excursion but he wasn't happy. He seemed very upset. Howard told me that all he did was sulk. He was that way back on the ship, he went immediately back to our suite and wouldn't come out. He was like that for two days. Hardly eating but drinking a lot from bottles we had brought with us.

"Then that night after leaving Grenada we had a terrible fight. He had been really drinking and hit me and knocked me down, then kicked me. I screamed and Howard heard me. He had the room next to us. He came and started knocking on the door but Stuart ignored him. Keith was visiting Howard and climbed between the adjoining balconies to get to our room and he tried to stop Stuart. They fought and Stuart knocked him down and then was coming at me again.

"I had gotten up and picked up a bottle and when he came at me I hit him with it. He staggered back onto the balcony and against the rail. I was hitting him with my hands and he was dazed, shaking his head, fending me off when an arm came around the balcony divider and went around his neck. He was pulled away a bit and up and then I was pushed aside and Stuart's legs came up and went over his head and he went over the rail.

"I looked over the side and saw him hit the water but he didn't come up. He never made a sound. I turned and saw Keith standing beside me breathing hard. 'He was going to kill us,' he said. 'He was a mad man. I had to stop him.' "

She paused and smiled.

"What do you find so amusing, Madame Andrews?" Michel Villar asked.

"I just remembered. Keith laughed suddenly. 'What's so funny?' I asked. Keith pointed to a sign on the wall between the two lanais:

> Don't throw anything
> overboard
> Help us keep our
> oceans clean"

Michel Villar was playing "Here's the church" again.

"Why didn't you tell the ship's captain what had happened?" the judge asked.

"We ... we were too scared. We thought they would think we had murdered him. I don't think anyone else had heard anything." Of course, it never happened. "We thought that we could make people believe that he had committed suicide … people do that on ships a lot. And he was despondent, depressed over the financial situation and Martin-Stanley … ."

"Merrill-Lynch," Villar injected, that sardonic smile on his lips, a player in this drama but still not believing her for a minute. Too bad he didn't have a vote.

"Yes, Merrill-Lynch. Anyway that's what we thought. We waited until the next night … ."

"But why not that night when maybe they could have found him?" Michel Villar asked.

Elise was silent for a moment, crocodile tears streaming down her face. How could she do that? Was the Kleenex onion scented? Damn she was good!

Finally she composed herself.

"I was scared. He was … had become … a beast. A brutal beast. He scared me. I didn't want him found. I WANTED HIM DEAD!"

Yes, she did. She did want me dead. Only it hadn't happened that way.

CHAPTER 92

"I can understand that, Mrs. Andrews. I am sorry for your loss, however it happened ..."

"IT HAPPENED THE WAY I TOLD YOU! DID YOU ...."

"Calm down, Mrs. Andrews." Then to Phil Dombrey. "Would you like to take a minute to let your client calm down?"

Phil looked at Elise who stood ramrod straight in the witness box, arms stiff, her knuckles white from gripping the railing so tightly. Damn, she was good.

"Elise?" he questioned.

She relaxed, lowered her chin to her chest, took a deep breath, and looked Villar straight in the eye. "I'm fine."

"Now Mrs. Andrews," Michel Villar continued, "Your story of your husband's demise is quite different from that of Keith Mitchell. Why do you suppose that is?"

"I don't know. I didn't really know Keith. He was a friend of Howard's and came along on the trip with him. Those seven days are the only time I was ever with Keith."

"Okay, then. You didn't mention two things that have been mentioned in earlier testimony: the camera and the money."

"I don't know anything about the camera. It was one of Stuart's toys. I don't think I ever saw it. As for the money, I got it as an early birthday present for Stuart. He hated spending his own money for frivolous things and I wanted him to be spontaneous and buy things or do things on the trip that he wouldn't ordinarily do. I gave it to him the night we sailed. It was wrapped in gift paper. We were on the veranda as we left port, toasting the trip with champagne our tour agent had sent as a present. I gave it to him then. He unwrapped it and saw what it was and looked at me questioningly. 'What's this for?' he asked.

"I told him and said that it was my own money from my inheritance." *Right! She didn't have any of that left,* I thought.

"I told him I wanted him to have fun and use it for things on the trip, no strings attached. He thanked me, said he would. I went in to shower and get ready for dinner and never saw it again. I have no idea how that fisherman got it."

Michel Villar played church. "Mrs. Andrews, if you had nothing to do with causing your husband's death other than what you have told this court, why did you send ... let's see what is the date ... ." He searched through papers or did he pretend to search through papers? ".... Ah, yes, here it is. Why did you wire transfer ten thousand dollars to Fredek Gavrilovich Kondrashin on March 13, 2009?"

"What? Who? I didn't send anyone any money." The question and information it contained had stunned her.

"You didn't?" Michel Villar smiled that sardonic smile. "But someone did from the account that you and your husband shared with the Hinderman Investment Savings Group in Uruguay, South America."

That stunned her again. One more and she would be down for the count.

"I ... we ...," she stammered.

I could see her falter – and so could the judge – and he was ready. *Here comes the judge.*

"And then again on March 22, less than twenty-four hours after the announcement of Quentin Baston's boat blowing up, you or someone ... wired, transferred, whatever the term ... fifty thousand dollars to one of many accounts owned by Fredek Gavrilovich Kondrashin. Oh, maybe not by that name and maybe that is not the name that you knew him by but that is his Christian ... as the saying goes in your country ... his Christian or true name is Fredek Gavrilovich Kondrashin. According to Interpol he has many identities.

They refer to him as many of his clients do, as 'The Facilitator.' "

And she's down on the mat.

Again the sardonic smile just visible over the roof of his church as he waited for her to say something.

"I don't know what you're talking about."

"Oh, but I think you do. You see we ... now I must be precise ... we didn't discover the account. No, our police are not that good. Oh, they're good, but offshore accounts and such are not within their realm of competence. However, the account was discovered in the audit of your husband's company's books by the police."

But only with a little help from a friend, I thought.

CHAPTER 93

"This account is a numbered account and held in Uruguay because, supposedly, that country is reputed to have the strongest bank secrecy law in the world. And, more importantly, bank secrecy supposedly can never be compromised for tax issues. But this wasn't a tax issue, it was a murder issue and we … oh, yes, truthfully, the United States … found that although the security can usually only be pierced when the owner stands convicted of some non-tax crime, the company felt that the information provided by the U.S. Government was sufficient enough to release the information requested."

"But I didn't …"

"Well, their records indicate that you, or someone using your phone, authorized both of these transfers … ."

"My phone? I don't understand."

Maybe it will be a standing eight count. Michel Villar was silent. He just stared at her over the steeple.

"But what does that have to do with Stuart's death?"

"Stuart's death? Nothing directly."

"But then why …"

"Because it implies a conspiracy to cover up murder … excuse me … a death that this court is investigating. You see The Facilitator … don't you love the implications of that? …" Michel Villar glared at a rising Phil Dombrey who resumed his seat tensely.

"The Facilitator was on St. Martin's ready to board a plane for St. Nantes about the time that the announcement of Quentin Baston's boat explosion was made public. He apparently had a change of plans and returned to Moscow. He was in London's Heathrow Airport when he received a text message that the money had been put into his account. The account to which you … or if you insist … someone wired or transferred that $50,000 from your account ...," he raised a hand to stop her objection, " ... to his account. It is in your and Stuart's name and the authorization came from your phone."

"But I don't ..."

"Know the account number? I think you do. You see, your late husband ...," and he crossed himself but I caught that sardonic smile, "...notified the bank that he had told you about the account and he gave them your access code... ."

Yes, I did, the access code that she had made up.

" ... A code that only you and he had known ... and told them that you should have free rein but that he was to be kept informed of your withdrawals. I suspect that he didn't trust you but that is neither here nor there." And to the clerk, "Strike that last remark."

Then further "But of course he couldn't be notified because he is dead, isn't he."

Although it was a statement he gave it the inflection like a question, or so it seemed to me, and for a brief moment was troubling.

"Of course, if he isn't dead, " Michel Villar continued, " ... either from the drowning off St. Nantes or from the drowning off Grenada ... he must be a remarkable man."

"Your honor, I object to this commentary." Both Phil Dombrey and Chyrise Callahan were on their feet in unison."

"You are right," Michel Villar said. "I apologize. Will the jury please disregard that last comment and will the clerk please strike that."

I felt as though had it not been such a public venue Michel would have slapped his hand in mock punishment but he didn't.

"Oh, yes," Michel Villar said, "one more thing, Mrs. Andrews. How are you paying for your defense?"

"What? I don't ... ."

"Objection," Phil Dombrey was on his feet. "Irrelevant."

"Oh, I assure you," responded Michel Villar, "that it is quite relevant. Overruled.

"Mrs. Andrews, what funds are you using to pay your lawyer, Phil Dombrey?"

"I … ."

"You see, Mrs. Andrews, one hundred thousand dollars was transferred from that same offshore account to your Miami checking account and again the phone used was your phone. And then there is the one hundred thousand dollars check written on that account payable to Phil Dombrey with the memo 'Defense deposit'. "

On the screens on the wall behind the judge, there appeared a photograph of the check both front and back, her signature on the front and his on the back.

Elise was deflated. She was down for the count.

CHAPTER 94

After Elise, Howard took the stand wearing khaki slacks, a navy shirt and a red, white and blue striped tie. His testimony, introduced by Chyrise was given in the same manner as Elise's was. I wonder if he is as good an actor.

"I never liked Stuart. I guess you think that is not surprising, because you think I am somewhat – maybe a lot what – of a bigot. I guess I am and, of course Stuart was half-black, what's the politically correct term now – African-American? Stuart is African-Irish. His mother was from Botswana or one of those frig... other African countries. His father was Irish. They were both with their United Nations delegations, I think, when they met.

"I don't know all the details. Don't care to know all the details especially now. What difference does it make? What difference would it have made?

"Elise was happy at first and then the trouble started. He started being demanding. He started drinking and I guess he was an angry drunk. That's when he hit her or at least that's what she said. I never saw him actually hit her."

Maybe the first bit of truth out of his mouth. He was surprising me with his calmness, with his factualness, his "sincerity" but of course his life and Elise's were on the line. This was tag team and he was going to have to win the match.

"I saw pictures of the bruises. That's about as close as I got. She called me the day the pregnancy test was positive. She was happy but apprehensive because of his moodiness. This was back when the economy started to tank, I think. I don't remember for certain. I was going to be an uncle. No big deal for me, I don't like kids.

"Then she called me after he had hit her, knocked her into the chair or something. I was furious with the bastard. If

I had been there I would have killed him, that's how mad I was at the time.

"Then a few weeks later she called and told me that they were going on this cruise and would I come along. She had reserved a single room next to their suite. I said sure, I could use the break. I have been with my firm long enough and have enough seniority that I could get off during tax season. Not all that easy to do, but I wangled it.

"There was this fishing trip at our first stop, St. Nantes, and Stuart – well, Elise really – asked me if I would like to go along. You know, maybe get to know Stuart better, not that I really wanted to, but she's my sister so I said yes. I asked my friend, Keith Mitchell, God rest his soul, ..."

Now that's pushing it, Howard. Michel Villar let the comment pass but received a semi-glare from Huard Jubert, but then his comment hadn't been as a witness.

"... to come along and keep me company. Actually to help keep me in check in case I wanted to deck Stuart. He said he would and it's a good thing, too, considering what happened.

"That day in St. Nantes we went ashore together and even that early in the day he was moody. Something about Merrill-Lynch announcing their biggest loss ever and with the market the way it was, that was huge – especially with Merrill-Lynch's place of leadership in the market. So we tried to cheer him up, started drinking right away. When the first fish hit, we urged him to take it since he was the organizer of the whole thing. And he did. For the five minutes he seemed to be on top of the world, yelling and screaming. I thought things were going to be okay.

"But after the fish was landed and released, he was his old moody self, even more so. He took his beer to the front of the boat and ignored us the rest of the day. When we got back to the ship, and got to the top of the gangplank, he was behind Elise and he pushed her so that he could swipe his card. She fell right in front of him, her purchases spilling all over the place. He didn't even stop but went right to the elevators or stairs; I don't know which he took. Keith and I and the gangplank staff all helped Elise up and gathered her belongings. It was such a tangle of things that Keith forgot to swipe his card and had to go down when we were ready to sail and swipe his card. He was so embarrassed.

"For the next couple of days, Stuart wouldn't leave their suite. He just sat in there and stared at nothing, I thought—I wasn't there—and drank. He wouldn't let the cabin steward in, he wouldn't go out to eat, and he called room service.

"That evening after leaving Grenada, Keith and I were in my cabin having a drink before dinner. We each had brought some booze along – hell, everyone does and you can buy wine ashore and bring it aboard, only you aren't supposed to drink it in public places.

"We were on the veranda, I guess that's what ships call them, and we heard a crash and heard Elise yell. I went outside to their cabin door, it was right next to mine, but I guess I said that. I knocked, hell, pounded, but nobody came. I could hear the fight still going on, I heard something, someone hit the floor. I went back into my room to the veranda and didn't see Keith. I could hear noise on their veranda and looked around the divider. I could see Stuart's head and shoulders above the rail and Elise's hitting him and he trying to fend her off like he was groggy or something.

"I reached around the divider and got hold of his shirt or something I don't remember and was pulling at it try to distract him. "

"What exactly did you grab?" Michel Villar interrupted.

"Honestly, …"

Nothing, I thought, *I wasn't there.*

"… I don't remember. I know Elise said that I had my arm around his neck but I don't remember. This whole thing was pretty much of a blur especially when suddenly his feet came over his head and he fell. His weight jerked my hold free and he fell into the sea. I watched him disappear … I never saw him surface.

"I looked around the divider and saw Elise and Keith at the rail looking down. Keith said something about how he would have killed us all or something. I asked Keith what happened and he said that when we heard the shouting and I went to their doorway, he had climbed around the railing and onto their veranda. He had tried to stop Stuart, but been knocked down. When he got up Elise and Stuart were out on the veranda and he thought that Stuart was trying to throw Elise over. 'I guess I went ballistic,' Keith said, 'and I got out on the balcony and saw you pulling him up, so I grabbed his legs pushing Elise aside and lifted. Then he was gone.'"

CHAPTER 95

"I got Keith to open their cabin door and we all sort of collapsed and tried to figure out what to do. Keith didn't want us to call security because he had been the one to actually push Stuart over the side. He thought it would be difficult to prove self-defense and they might say he murdered him. He was pretty distraught. We agreed to wait until the next morning to decide what to do. It was wrong, I know but we didn't know what to do.

"In the morning we realized that no one had seen or heard what went on or security would have come. So we decided to wait until that night and say that he had disappeared and see what would happen.

"We did and, of course, the rest is public knowledge. I am not sorry for what happened. I only wish that I had been the one to push that black son-of-a-bitch overboard, pardon my French." Howard grinned devilishly at the judge.

Michel Villar smiled that now familiar sardonic smile. "I asked your sister this question and she didn't have an answer so I will ask you. Why does Keith Mitchell's suicide note differ so drastically from what you have told us?"

Howard took a deep breath as though composing himself. "Keith Mitchell was a sick man. He was very upset with what had happened with Stuart. He blamed himself for throwing him overboard. The weight of this burden – killing another human being – weighed heavily upon him. In the last weeks before he killed himself, he was really getting screwy. He'd say things like, 'Maybe we should have thrown him overboard on that fishing boat.' 'We should have offed that bastard on that fishing excursion.'

"He seemed to get worse and worse as weeks went by and withdrew into himself."

"But according to the transcript for the extradition hearing, the psychiatrist didn't mention this," Michel Villar stated.

"Keith was crafty. He could hide things really well. I guess he did with that guy."

"But why blame you and your sister?"

"To get the burden off himself as much as he could I guess. I don't know. I am not a shrink. You would have to ask that Dr. Edwards."

"No, you're not a shrink, as you say, and neither am I. And the camera with that picture?"

"I have no idea how the camera got left on the boat that day. Stuart had given it to Keith and after that I don't know. We never thought about it aboard the Caribbean Isle because it wasn't ours."

"What about the picture?"

Howard frowned. "I can't explain it. Wait! ... ."

Did sudden inspiration strike? Doubtful, the whole thing was planned.

"... When Stuart quit reeling and went for the fish, Keith and I shouted 'Hooray for Stuart' and I went over waving my arms in the air. I had been drinking a beer."

"With the capped bottle upside down in your raised hand?" Villar smiled. "Interesting technique." Then quickly, "What about the money?"

"I have no idea how it got on the boat. Maybe Stuart carried it with him and left it there. I saw it once, that night we sailed. After we left port I came over to their room to go to dinner with them. Stuart answered my knock and offered me a glass of champagne, the bottle was on the balcony, he told me to help myself. I went out to get the bottle, picking up a glass from the bar and saw the money on the table next to the bottle. I picked it up and asked Stuart what it was. He said it was his, a gift from Elise and took it from me. He went into the other room with it, I heard a drawer open and close and then he came back without the money. I never saw it again."

Villar was in church again. "Hmmm. That explains how your fingerprints could have gotten on the money. But why not Stuart's?"

"I don't know. I picked up the paper and the money. He took them both and maybe never touched the money. How it got on the boat without him touching it I have no idea."

I do!

"One other thing, I think," Villar mused. "Quentin said that you told him that Stuart was a womanizer and beat his wife. Did you?"

"Not in those words. When Stuart was in the front of the boat and Keith, Quentin and I were in the rear. We got to talking. Quentin wanted to know why Stuart was acting like he was. I told him that he was upset with the economy. Quentin asked why he came if he wasn't going to have a good time. I said that he came with his wife because they had been having a rough time in their marriage and they were hoping the cruise and the following week in Aruba where they had honeymooned would help. I never mentioned womanizing or beating his wife so he must have made that up."

"Interesting that he hit the nail on the head, so to speak, isn't it?" Michel Villar asked.

Howard just shrugged. "Make that a 'I don't know'," Michel Villar instructed his clerk. He looked at papers on his desk.

"I note here from the log of your cell phone," and he said the number, "that you called Elise 3:15 p.m. the day after word of the destruction of Quentin Baston's boat made CNN."

Howard shrugged. "I may have, we talk a lot."

"Yes, but what I find interesting," and he nodded in the direction of the prosecution's table, "and so does Monsieur Jubert, is that Elise – or someone using her phone – mere minutes later, called the Hinderman Investment Savings Group in Uruguay, South America, and made the transfer of fifty thousand dollars to the account to Fredek Gavrilovich Kondrashin known to most law enforcement people as The Facilitator. Do you find that interesting?"

Howard shrugged again. "Not really. I don't know who that person is."

"Really," said Michel Villar. "That is extremely interesting because a week before you," and there was the sardonic smile, "or someone using your phone (maybe the same person who used Elise's) called The Facilitator's American contact agent. Oh, yes, and two weeks before that also."

He looked at Howard.

"Don't you find that interesting?"

Part IX

Judgment

CHAPTER 96

The end of Howard's testimony was the end of the defense's case and Michel Villar adjourned the court until the next morning when the lawyers would present their closing arguments. I figured that Huard Jubert would present for the prosecution, but for the defense? I figured Chyrise if they were going to share the burden or was Dombrey a sexist? Time only would tell.

In a French court, the defense always has the last say, so in the morning Jubert was up first.

"Ladies and gentlemen of the jury. The evidence that you have been presented with should leave little to your imagination as to a verdict. Let me recap for you.

"First, the suicide note of Keith Mitchell in which he states that he and Howard Blake, the defendant...," and he indicated Howard who just glared at him. I wondered if Howard was going to keep his cool through the procedure. "...drowned Stuart Andrews in the territorial waters of St. Nantes and bribed the only other eyewitness, Quentin Baston.

"They then conspired and perpetrated a hoax that Stuart Andrews had boarded the Caribbean Isle and some two days later mysteriously disappeared from that ship, an apparent suicide. But no note was found!

"Quentin Baston, who ingeniously faked his own death in order to prevent a possible attempt against his life by the defendants ..."

"That's not ...," was all Howard got out before Michel Villar rapped his gavel as Howard was grabbed by Chyrise and Elise with Phil rising out of his seat to help.

"Mr. Blake, I warned you," Michel Villar said and he was about to motion to the guards when, somewhat miraculously, Howard stopped, sort of shook himself and said, "I'm sorry, your honor. It won't happen again. Please let me stay."

He must have looked like a pleading puppy because Villar consented. "There will be no second chance, Mr. Blake."

"I understand, your honor," Howard said as everyone sat down.

"Mr. Baston had in his possession, and meant to protect, two pieces of crucial evidence. One the bundle of money ...," Huard Jubert held it aloft, "... bearing the fingerprints of the two defendants, Elise Blake Andrews and Howard Blake, of Quentin Baston, and of the bank clerk who prepared the stack. However, there were no fingerprints of Stuart Andrews who, according to Mr. Blake, would have been the one to bring the money on board Quentin's boat.

"Second, there is the camera belonging to Stuart Andrews which has an interesting picture ...," which was flashed on the screen, "... showing Mr. Blake moving toward Stuart Andrews with an inverted beer bottle in his hand." He used a laser point to indicate the bottle, first on the screen to the right of Villar and then to the left. "Mr. Mitchell's dying declaration states that Mr. Blake hit Stuart Andrews with a beer bottle and that was confirmed by Quentin Baston.

"Expert testimony has told us that the picture was unaltered. That it had not been ...," and he intentionally looked at Howard, "... Photoshopped ... ." And here he paused, waiting, baiting – but Howard maintained his cool and only glared at Huard Jubert in return. "... and then replaced on the camera's memory chip. In fact, the defense presented us with a demonstration that it is impossible, or at least extremely difficult, to replace a picture on a memory chip so that it is readable by the camera. There is no body, no forensic evidence to verify that Stuart Andrews was hit with the bottle and then drowned in the Caribbean waters of St.

Nantes, but then very few bodies of drowning victims from ships either small or large are ever found. By humans, that is, I am certain that they are found by sharks and barracudas and other denizens of the deep. What happened to the body of Stuart Andrews, only Davy Jones could tell us."

Here he paused and took a sip of water from a glass handed to him by one of his aides.

Michel Villar smiled benevolently.

"What motive did Mr. Blake have? Well, his sister, wife or widow, if you wish, of Stuart Andrews, had the motive. Seventeen million dollars in motive. Two million from an insurance policy for the accidental death of Stuart Andrews and fifteen million in an offshore account shared by herself and her late husband. And from this same account, using her own phone ...," and now he pointed at Elise who cowered back a bit, "... payments were made to a Russian assassin known as the Facilitator to eliminate Quentin Baston, the only eyewitness not a part of the plan. Fortunately, Quentin Baston acted first ... but if he hadn't...," and he turned to confront the defense table, "THEY WOULD HAVE GOTTEN AWAY WITH MURDER!"

He slammed his fist on the podium. The courtroom was utterly still. Huard Jubert stood there glowering and then, composure regained, he turned to each of the judges' enclosures.

"There is not a shadow of a doubt what happened to Stuart Andrews. Not one single atom of evidence that he didn't die in the waters of our beloved St. Nantes. Just as John-Paul LaPre was made to pay the penalty for the deaths of Genivee Lacour and twenty-five other innocents, so Elise Blake Edwards and Howard Blake must be made to pay the penalty for the death of Stuart Andrews."

This final statement was punctuated by Huard Jubert slamming his fist onto the podium five times. Then he looked at Michel Villar, who again smiled benevolently, and sat down.

CHAPTER 97

"Much of what we have heard and seen during this trial is so much fabrication and little fact."

I was right. Chyrise was giving the closing argument for the defense. She was quite stylish in a peach linen suit with a lavender blouse and a string of deep purple beads and matching earrings.

"Whatever possessed Keith Mitchell to write that horrible note and then, we assume, to kill himself we can only guess. He was a clever man and managed to hide his delusions from his psychiatrist. Think about it, ladies and gentlemen of the jury. He admittedly suffered from addiction to gambling and alcohol. With those problems, it is no wonder that he would have other much more deeply-seated psychoses.

"Finally they must have all come to a head and he had to end his life, but at the same time taking aim at his good friend Howard Blake. He must have thought that if he couldn't make it in this life, Howard wouldn't either.

"But what motivated that fisherman Quentin Baston to come up with this absurd accusation? We are told that Howard Blake gave ten thousand dollars to him to keep him silent. More likely, he found that money on his boat left behind by Stuart Andrews, who in a sullen mood, despondent over the financial disasters that were ruining his once lucrative investment business, returned to the Caribbean Isle leaving on the Mahi Mahi the ten thousand dollars given to him by a loving and caring, although battered, wife who wanted for him only the best. Not only the money but also his camera, his new camera purchased especially for this particular trip and that particular fishing excursion. He had to be in a deep depression.

"You might question whether or not he did return, but Jonni Dillon was emphatic. If his cruise card was swiped then Stuart Anderson was aboard the Caribbean Isle. And his cruise card was swiped.

"Two days later, Stuart Andrews brutally attacked his wife and when Keith Mitchell came to her aid, he attacked him also. It was only by Elise Blake breaking the bonds of fear from further repercussions by her domineering husband and striking back at him with a liquor bottle that most likely her life and that of Keith Mitchell were saved. Together and with the help of Howard Blake they were able to subdue Stuart Andrews who was unfortunately tossed overboard as a result of the fight.

"What would you do in such a case? They were in international waters and Maritime Law is unclear. Most likely they would have been subject to the laws of Liberia where the Caribbean Isle is registered. It was better for them to keep the truth quiet and tell the world that he had just disappeared. Let the world decide what had happened to Stuart Andrews.

"But fate takes mysterious turns and Keith Mitchell let his delusions get the better of him and thus the delusional dying declaration which implicated this innocent brother and sister in a fanciful murder story." She indicated Howard and Elise.

"Had they known what lay in front of them, they would have been truthful and admitted what had happened to Stuart Andrews, but they didn't know what that devious Quentin Baston had connived. For some reason he had the money he had found, and was able to get someone to ... um, yes, ... Photoshop the picture and get it expertly back on the camera's memory chip. Carrie Miller showed you that it was possible to Photoshop the picture to make it look like Howard had a bottle he was going to use to hit Stuart Andrews and not to celebrate his catch."

But what about Jesse James? Did you forget about him?

"What was his motivation? We don't know. Fame … someone has said – I think it was American artist Andy Warhol – everyone gets fifteen minutes of fame. Maybe this was the only way that he would get his. Who knows?

"What you do know, what Elise and Howard have told you, is the truth of what happened. Yes, they should have told the truth earlier, but would you have? That is a question you will have to ask yourselves.

"You will be asked to deliberate, to arrive at a conclusion without a shadow of a doubt that will decide the fate of two people, two people innocent of the death of Stuart Andrews. Innocent in the manner you have been told here and that is the decision that you have to make. Do you believe, truly believe, the story told by Keith Mitchell and then seized upon by Quentin Baston to get his fifteen minutes of fame? At the cost of the lives of two people?

"Ladies and gentlemen, honor the memory of Genivee Lacour. But keep that memory pure. Keep that memory as pure as the blue Caribbean waters that surround your beautiful country."

CHAPTER 98

As Chyrise sat down, Michel Villar smiled at her. Not his sardonic smile and not his benevolent smile but a smile that seemed to say *"Good job but ... ."*

"Do you have anything further to present, Mr. Jubert?"

"No, your honor," said Huard Jubert.

"Does the defense have anything further?" Michel Villar asked.

Both Chyrise and Phil shook their heads.

"So be it," Michel Villar said, and then looking at the jurors, "You have heard the evidence presented by both sides. You will have to evaluate each piece presented, consider the testimony, some of it extremely contradictory, and reach a conclusion eliminating any reasonable doubt.

"Did Howard Blake, with the aid of Keith Mitchell and at the request of Elise Andrews, kill Stuart Andrews by drowning him in the waters of St. Nantes? If that is the conclusion that you reach, then you must find both defendants guilty of murder. The crime of murder on St. Nantes is punishable only by hanging. There is no life imprisonment."

Elise's shoulders seemed to sag at this point but only momentarily.

"If you determine that Howard Blake did not kill Stuart Andrews by drowning, then you find both defendants not guilty.

"And," he continued looking at Elise and Howard, "in that case, based upon the testimony that the two defendants have given, they will be turned over to the proper authorities. Which nation will take custody for further trial will have to be determined by someone else, possibly an international court."

Obviously he felt that their testimony raised the question that I was possibly killed aboard the Caribbean Isle. That was an interesting turn of events. However, his statement drew no reaction either from Elise or Howard.

His gavel rapped three times against the sound block and Michel Villar said, "Until such time that the jury has reached a verdict, this court is adjourned."

CHAPTER 99

The jury was out two days, which surprised me as the defense was basically just words with no real evidence other than those pictures purportedly supporting Elise's claim of spousal abuse. I had left my cell phone number with the court's clerk as I was a "reporter" and received notification of the verdict an hour before court would reconvene. I hastened to get ashore, being dropped off at the beach and running up the hill, thank goodness for conditioning.

The spectator section was two-thirds full when I got through security. There was the usual pomp and circumstance entrance parade with all looking suitably somber. Elise looked terrible and was dressed as she had the first day. Howard wore navy slacks, a white shirt with a red tie bearing white stars. Accompanied by two gendarmes who stood directly behind him as they had during the defense's presentation, he glared around.

The judges looked stern, but on Villar's face there was a trace of that sardonic smile as though he knew what the verdict was going to be. When all were in place and duly earbudded, Michel Villar rapped his gavel.

"Has the jury reached a verdict?" he queried of the center judge of the three professional jurists.

"We have," responded the judge, all of whom had remained officially nameless although we knew he was from St. Martin.

"Let us break a little with tradition and I will poll the jury, which I have to do anyway."

Michel Villar then polled the lay judges. During the trial, the news group had determined who the judges were and where they were from, assisted greatly by the reporter from the St. Nantes Weekly. Each judge stood and stated his or her vote. The first lay judge from St. Martin, Alice

Andrepont, a middle-aged woman: Guilty; the second lay judge from St. Barthelémy, Alexandre Forge, a middle-aged white man: Guilty; the third, Luc Savary, a middle-aged black man from St. Martin: Not Guilty. There was a low murmur from the spectators and I noticed a smile on Howard's face; they had managed to convince the black man of their innocence. The fourth, Ines Massar, a thirty-something woman from St. Nantes: Guilty; Yves St. Jacque, the early-thirties lay judge from Martinique was the fifth: Guilty; and the sixth, Jèrôme Giles, a middle-aged white male from St. Nantes: Guilty.

Howard was squirming a little now, and Elise had her hand on his arm.

Then Michel Villar turned to the professional judges, all middle-aged white males. The first from Martinique, Denis Barre: Not Guilty; Sèbastien Grandjean, the middle judge from St. Nantes: Guilty; and the third, Renè Legate, from St. Barthelémy: Guilty.

Michel Villar nodded to the jury's foreman, for want of a better word, to make it official.

"We find the defendants Madam Elise Blake Andrews and Monsieur Howard Blake guilty of the premeditated murder of Stuart Andrews."

As was to be expected, Howard went ape with this official announcement, maybe he hadn't kept count or, more likely, he had forgotten that unlike American courts, only a two-thirds majority is necessary in a French court. Screaming "You friggin' frogs can't judge me – you don't …," as he started climbing onto the table. He didn't get far as one of the gendarmes stuck a stun gun against his back and he went limp.

Everyone in the courtroom had his or her eyes on him except me. I was watching Michel Villar who, although rapping his gavel to restore order, was smiling that sardonic grin of his. I knew that he had suspected, wanted, and maybe even encouraged Howard's outbreak.

It took five minutes to get order in the courtroom. Howard was then sitting dejectedly in his chair, head down apparently seeing nothing. Elise was stoic, head unbowed and staring straight ahead.

During the time it took to get Howard revived and sitting the courtroom had buzzed about the verdict, which was expected. My "colleagues" and I had discussed the evidence and testimony during the hours spent waiting for the jury to reach its decisions. The conclusion was that the defense – while plausible – had nothing in the way of physical evidence to support it.

The vote was seven-to-two and that certainly brought a murmuring among the spectators because a six-to-three split had been suspected based on the time it had taken. There had been some question of how the "imported" judges would vote because of the death penalty implications.

Michel Villar thanked the jury for its work and dismissed them. Guillaume Martineau led them from the courtroom for the last time and then closed the door. He took his position standing beside it at parade rest. I noticed that he also was smiling.

CHAPTER 100

"The defendants will rise," said Michel Villar.

Elise stood slowly accompanied by Phil Dombrey. Howard tried to stand but couldn't by himself so he was helped by Chyrise and the gendarme who had zapped him. He received a glower in return and Howard shook him off when he was up.

"In capital cases such as this, St. Nantes law has only one punishment: execution by hanging. In my opinion a crime this heinous deserves a punishment of more and longer suffering with ultimately the same end. However, Devil's Island is no longer functioning and therefore there is no other option.

"Elise Blake Andrews and Howard Eliot Blake ..." Howard shuddered at the use of his middle name "... you have been found guilty of the murder of Stuart Andrews. In compliance with the laws of St. Nantes, a territory of the republic of France, I sentence you to death by hanging. This sentence is to be carried out within thirty days of this date or the date of any appeal that is forthcoming. May the Almighty have mercy on your souls. This court is dismissed."

Howard started to say something and then stopped, glancing at the gendarme who stood behind him, stun gun ready. Elise shrank into her seat, her composure broken, and started crying, face in her hands, elbows on the table.

In all the fervor of the end of the trial, I beat most of the crowd out of the building and distanced myself from the point at which Howard and Elise would enter their transportation to prison. I was maybe fifty feet away and near the corner of the building. I, and the crowd that had gathered as word of the guilty verdict had spread, waited about fifteen minutes before they were escorted out by about ten gendarmes who easily cleared a path to the van.

The door was slid back and Elise was about to enter when I whistled. A lot of people can whistle but mine is a special trill that I used to use to catch Elise's attention in crowds when we were separated. I watched her pause only slightly and then straighten up and scan the crowd. When her gaze neared where I was, I raised my arms as though I was signaling a touchdown and then turned and quickly left the area.

Behind me the area was in an uproar or at least Elise was. I could hear her yelling.

"That's Stuart. He's not dead. Please get him. That's Stuart."

No, it's not. Stuart Andrews is dead, I thought. *You killed him.*

I ran down the asphalt patch leading to the seaward beach where Joaquin was waiting with the Zàkpa's zodiac. I found that I was smiling broadly for the first time in a long time. ***Payback is a bitch.***

CHAPTER 101

"Ahoy, on the Zàkpa. Permission to come aboard."

I turned around expecting to see the customs officials, but instead only one man in a zodiac drifting up against the stern. He was dressed in a white short-sleeved shirt, dark pants, sunglasses, and a dark blue baseball cap bearing no logo. I was tired and eager to get underway. As required in this port, Joaquin had called the customs officials to get clearance to depart when he had come ashore to pick me up after the completion of the trial, but they had not shown up in the intervening two hours and we knew better than to harass them – we would never get away.

Before I could collect my thoughts to say *"I'd rather you didn't,"* he had tied his painter to one of the davits and climbed up and through the transom, bearing with him a cloth bag about the size of a plastic shopping bag. Once aboard, he removed his sunglasses and I was stunned at whom I saw.

"Judge Villar," I stammered.

He held up the hand holding the sunglasses, palm out. "Please, that is reserved for the courtroom. Call me Michel."

While he was talking he put the cloth bag on the table, then his sunglasses and reaching into the bag ..., "The question is what do I call you?" ...retrieved two Heinekens with pearls of water glistening on them, and a church key. "I find 'Dawoh' difficult to pronounce," ... he opened one bottle.

I started to tell him that he had pronounced it correctly, but he continued as he opened the second bottle and handed it to me.

There was a flash of green ... but there wasn't. No flash of green. I accepted the bottle.

"I am certain," he continued, "that you don't want me to call you 'Stuart' ...," I stared at him dumbfounded, " ... so let's make it 'Josef.' "

He extended his bottle toward me and mechanically I met it with mine. Then he raised his and said, "To justice, or should I say, payback." He took a drink from his bottle and seated himself on one of the chairs and motioned for me to take the other. It was as though he was host and I was a guest. I just stood and stared at him rudely and a bit stupidly.

"Please," Michel said indicating the chair, "I mean you no harm."

I sat.

"First, let me say again that you have nothing to fear from me. I am, to my knowledge, the only one who knows who you are – or were. The trail was difficult to follow, you did a good job, but then I had more knowledge to start with than anyone else.

"Not knowing about 'Dawoh Mbayo' would cause anyone else quite a bit of trouble. When that name turned up in a routine report I happened to see, I was surprised because that person should have been dead but wasn't. Once I had that bit of information, the digging became easy.

"Then during the trial you were one of only five black men in regular attendance and the Zàkpa was in port so it was easy to trace. Interesting name. Bassa, isn't it?"

I just stared at him.

"If you have any concerns about the trial, don't. Everything was perfectly legal. I have been trying cases for over ten years and I know what I am doing. Any appeal will fail. Your wife or should I say 'widow' and her brother will not rot in one of our worst prisons, I will make certain of that. As I said at the conclusion of the trial, I am only sorry that Devil's Island is not still in existence.

"Oh, and your ... Mrs. Andrews's ravings as she entered the van. I am afraid that she has suffered a breakdown. Such ravings are fairly common in these cases.

"But that is not the reason that I am here." He paused and took a long draft from his bottle . "I wanted to tell you that my employers ... hmm, I guess that makes me your employer..."

That sardonic smile.

"... are completely satisfied with circumstances under which their verbal contract with you was terminated. You ... through one of your minions ...," at this he smiled, "... made certain that all their investments were returned. In fact, over the course of the contract you more than fulfilled your obligation despite – how shall I put this – despite acquiring quite a bit of wealth for yourself. Others they have dealt with have 'skimmed' as much but returned less. They are indeed happy with you and that makes them happy with me as I was the one who recommended you."

He finished his beer and put the bottle on the table. "I am certain that you will dispose of this properly and not consign it to the deep. That would make Quentin Baston very unhappy. By the way, did you know that his great-great-grandfather was British and was named Quentin? That name passed down through generations. I don't know why he didn't name his son that. Maybe the secession stops with him. Shame, it is a beautiful name. Although not French at all."

He put on his sunglasses. "Thank you for your hospitality." He turned to go and then turned back, reaching into his pocket. "I almost forgot," he said and pulled out some papers that he put on the table. "Your customs clearance. It wasn't their fault. I asked them to delay as the court had some unfinished business with you. They won't question anything."

He turned to go and then turned back.

"You are the quiet one, aren't you! Not at all what I had expected. Adieu, Josef, have a good second life."

He climbed over the transom, untied the painter, step into the zodiac, seated himself on the stern seat.

"Oh," he said looking up, "I forgot. There is something with the clearance papers that you forgot."

He pulled the starter cord, the Mercury coughed and started with a roar, then settled into a purr as he throttled down. He waved his hand, fed gas, and motored away.

I watched still stunned with the revelations. Then I turn to the table and picked up the clearance papers and something fell out onto the table. It was a photograph, picture side up but upside down as I looked at it. I knew the picture because I had taken it. It was the port of Genivee. I instantly knew that on the other side of the picture was written

Four went out, three came back.
We know what happened!

Epilogue

\

Joaquin and I spent almost a year going around the world. It was a leisurely cruise, stopping at places we liked and seeing the wonders of this beautiful planet. We spent several weeks in the Philippines visiting his family. His mother was very glad to see him, but sad that he would be spending his life away from her. Fortunately his sister and brother were in the area, being more traditional, and that was a comfort to her.

While in the Philippines, Joaquin renewed a relationship with Jovelyn Baqui and, with my permission, she became the third crewmember and within three months, they were married just before we entered the Suez Canal. I really had no choice in the matter because it was either accept her or get a new crew. There was a little excitement as we went through the Gulf of Aden as we were chased by two boats of the Somali pirates. But for that we were prepared. We had picked up an AK47 and ammunition and Jovelyn was a crack shot. After she picked off the helmsman in each boat, the chase was quickly given up, but we doubted they could have caught us anyway.

We were in Auckland, New Zealand when we received word of the execution of Elise and Howard. Howard was gagged to prevent any of his violent outbursts, which we heard had become routine for him. However Elise held her head high and took her punishment like a man. At her request, the hangings were simultaneous. I felt nothing when I heard of the moment. That was over and behind me when we left St. Nantes the afternoon the verdict was handed down. The photograph that Michel Villar had left for me was framed and hanging on the wall in the lounge and that was the only reminder of the entire affair that I kept. I still don't know how in the world I had forgotten to remove it from

Keith's possession and how it had come into Michel Villar's and had not played a part in the investigation by the Los Angeles Police. I suspect that Lt. Juliet Mills had a hand in that and, based upon the amount of information that Michel Villar had obtained, he probably had a part also.

After the trial had started and Quentin had testified, I had his wife and children brought back to St. Nantes. Quentin and I went to the airport to greet them. Quentin had made a sign saying "Celesse" just as he had when they arrived in Bridgetown, but of course it was not needed. His two children raced to him and started chattering excited about their brother.

"Brother?" I asked Quentin who stood there beaming with his arm around Celesse and then I noticed that she did appear to have put on weight in her abdomen. "Oh," I said."Congratulations."

"Thank you," Celesse said. "It's a boy." And she looked at Quentin. "We are going to name him Quentin Josef Baston."

I must have looked as shocked as I felt and she continued, "That is, if you don't mind."

"I would be honored," I said almost wishing that I could tell them that wasn't my name.

As though reading my thoughts, Quentin said, "We know that is not your name. We don't know what it really is and don't want to know. You have a reason to want to be unidentified and we honor that. But it was Josef that saved me and kept my family safe and that is why we have chosen that name."

Again I was stunned. I don't know how people knew so much about me.

We were anchored in Piraeus, Greece when Quentin Josef Baston came into the world weighing seven pounds, four ounces. I printed the picture attached to the email and carried it in my wallet. They had asked me to be a godfather but I had declined. I knew they knew I wouldn't accept, but felt they wanted to ask me anyway.

With my help behind the scenes, Quentin got his new boat two weeks after the trial ended and was once again offering fishing charters. Business was better than before, but that probably had something to do with his notoriety because of the trial. He named his boat *Renaissance* as it marked a new beginning for his life.

When we completed our round-the-world trip, we docked in the East Bay Anchorage and I gave Joaquin title to the Zàkpa. He and Jovelyn were stunned. "We cannot accept this!" they said simultaneously.

"Well, consider it a loan. You use it to take guided cruises around the Caribbean and have it available for me should I need it." Although I never thought I would. "I have had enough of the sailor's life for now. You have been good friends and can make the best of this boat. You can rename it as you wish but it is yours."

I walked away down the quay carrying only the carry-on I had bought in St. Nantes those many months before and my computer bag. Now they were my only possessions in the world. My past was behind me and it was time for me to start my new life, my renaissance.

It was a beautiful sunny day and I was greeted with a burst of heat and humidity as I stepped off the plane. I immediately headed for passport control, as all I had was my small carry-on piece of luggage and my computer bag. Outside, I got into the first taxi and gave the driver the address.

In a few minutes we topped the hill and the magnificence of the Caribbean was spread out in front of me. There was little traffic and within a few minutes we were passing the harbor as I had requested. At the quay, a cruise ship's tender was disgorging the last of its passengers who were spreading out to explore the beauties of the island.

Soon we were ascending the hill at the southeast end of the town that I had walked down so many months – years it seemed – before. Ten minutes later the taxi pulled to a stop in front of the house. The driver said "Are you certain this is the right house, monsieur?"

I nodded and handed him a bill for almost twice the fare. I exited the taxi and stood there looking at the house, waiting as the taxi pulled away. Then I walked to the door and reached up to get the key that I knew would be there in its little niche.

Later in the day the real estate agent would bring the papers and other keys, but the estate had given me permission to enter the house. The door opened and I replaced the key just in case. I entered and closed the door.

I was immediately enveloped in the warm glow of the floor lighting. Somewhere in the distance the air conditioning hummed into activity. I stood there and was once again enclosed in the security cocoon that had helped save my life.

~